BRIDE ISLAND

Laura Brunellier

ALEXANDRA ENDERS has published short stories in *BOMB* magazine, *Hunger Mountain*, and *Critical Quarterly*, and was a finalist for the Rolex Mentor and Protégé Arts Initiative with Toni Morrison. She has an MFA in fiction from Vermont College. She lives in New York and Maine with her husband and daughter. This is her first novel.

Bride
Island

Alexandra Enders

A PLUME BOOK

PLUME
Published by Penguin Group
Penguin Group (USA) Inc., 375 Hudson Street, New York, New York 10014, U.S.A.
Penguin Group (Canada), 90 Eglinton Avenue East, Suite 700, Toronto Ontario,
Canada M4P 2Y3 (a division of Pearson Penguin Canada Inc.)
Penguin Books Ltd., 80 Strand, London WC2R 0RL, England
Penguin Ireland, 25 St. Stephen's Green, Dublin 2, Ireland (a division of Penguin Books Ltd.)
Penguin Group (Australia), 250 Camberwell Road, Camberwell, Victoria 3124, Australia
(a division of Pearson Australia Group Pty. Ltd.)
Penguin Books India Pvt. Ltd., 11 Community Centre, Panchsheel Park,
New Delhi – 110 017, India
Penguin Group (NZ), 67 Apollo Drive, Mairangi Bay, Auckland 1311,
New Zealand (a division of Pearson New Zealand Ltd.)
Penguin Books (South Africa) (Pty.) Ltd., 24 Sturdee Avenue, Rosebank,
Johannesburg 2196, South Africa

Penguin Books Ltd., Registered Offices: 80 Strand, London WC2R 0RL, England

First published by Plume, a member of Penguin Group (USA) Inc.

First Printing, July 2007
10   9   8   7   6   5   4   3   2   1

 REGISTERED TRADEMARK—MARCA REGISTRADA

LIBRARY OF CONGRESS CATALOGING-IN-PUBLICATION DATA
Enders, Alexandra, 1964–
  Bride Island / Alexandra Enders.
    p. cm.
  ISBN 978-0-452-28834-8
  1. Recovering alcoholics—Fiction. 2. Women alcoholics—Fiction. 3. Custody of children—Fiction. 4. Mothers and daughters—Fiction. 5. Real estate development—Fiction.
6. Maine—Fiction. I. Title.

  PS3605.N423B75 2007
  813'.6—dc22   2006031161

Printed in the United States of America
Set in Janson Text
Designed by Lenny Telesca

PUBLISHER'S NOTE
This is a work of fiction. Names, characters, places, and incidents either are the product of
the author's imagination or are used fictitiously, and any resemblance to actual persons, living or dead, business establishments, events, or locales is entirely coincidental.

For Francesca

Acknowledgments

Many thanks to the writers who read and reread my manuscript: David Jauss, Heather Laszlo, Jacob Paul, Cecily Patterson, Mary Domenico, Catherine Barnett, Michelle Brockway, and Susan Karwoska. And thanks to the Writers Room, the Ucross Foundation, and the Rolex Mentor and Protégé Arts Initiative for their generosity; Carole Ione, Rachel Koenig, and Maura Sheehy for support of all kinds; and Deb Levine for the visit that started everything.

I owe two luminous and intelligent women a huge debt of gratitude: Gail Hochman for her encouragement and faith, and Emily Haynes for her unerring editorial eye. Profound thanks also to my parents, my brothers, and my sister, Camilla, fellow sojourner; and to my husband, Peter, and our daughter, Francesca, who help me make sense of the world.

In the life of each of us, I said to myself, there is a place remote and islanded, and given to endless regret or secret happiness.

—Sarah Orne Jewett
The Country of the Pointed Firs

If a man is lucky enough to possess a whole island—even if it's the merest speck of rock and turf, and a few spruce trees and raspberry bushes—but can spend only a few summer weeks on it, spiritually he is an islander all year round. This is particularly true of children who have had island summers. They become islanders for life at an early age.

—Dorothy Simpson
The Maine Islands

Bride
Island

One

∼

A ll right, you have half," my daughter says. She parcels out the remaining grapes one by one. "Six for you, six for me." They are the last on the stalk, the ones we thought too tiny to eat before, some no bigger than raisins, one little pip the size of a pomegranate seed. I want to tell Monroe to keep them all, I'm half heartbroken that she's so judicious, surely in a child greed and self-interest would be more appropriate? But Daniel, her father, has trained her well, and besides, I'm hungry and the rest of the food is in the trunk of the car. So I eat the tiny grapes, each one popping as my teeth pierce the sweet red skin.

Summer.

We are sitting in my old car, a chartreuse Citroën 2CV, on the headland out by Marguerite Cove. Through the windshield we watch the small white-capped waves of the bay. We should see Steven and the boat that will take us out to Bride Island anytime now. Rays of afternoon sun slant through the open sunroof. The air smells of the sea and of cut grass. It is only the third Friday in August but already there are intimations of fall: roadside ditches bristle with goldenrod; corners of the blueberry fields have spread crimson; the nights are extra starry and cold. My last boyfriend, a gardener from California, charmed me by saying this was the most poignant landscape he'd ever seen.

The tape comes to an end and my daughter flips it. Monroe, who will turn seven in September, has discovered James Taylor this visit; this is the third time today we're hearing "You've Got a Friend." These are some of the things I have discovered about her: She weighs fifty pounds and is the third-tallest girl in her class. She wants to pierce her nose when she is ten. She likes the Spice Girls but thinks Pokémon is babyish. She can swing beneath the monkey bars but can't do a cartwheel. Purple is her favorite color and blueberries her favorite food.

"Excited?" I ask, rubbing her hand. Her fingers, tanned brown from earlier vacations at the beach with her father, have white patches between them. I myself have mixed feelings about this weekend, our annual visit to my mother and stepfather's island. Monnie and I have already spent two and a half of our allotted three weeks, and for me the visit marks the culmination of our time together, a shifting from anticipation to relinquishment.

She nods. "I would be more, except after that it's only two days."

"I know," I say. We're both very quiet for a minute, listening to the music.

"I wish I could live with you."

"You do?" This surprises me. She finds my life and tiny house in Rockhaven "weird"—she told me so the first day of her visit. "But wouldn't you miss your dad and Chloe and your brothers?"

She rubs one tanned finger along the dashboard. "Not really." I'm secretly elated by this and allow myself a glow of pride. Take that, Daniel, I think, you and all your piano lessons and horseback riding.

"Well, what about your friends?"

"I'd e-mail them."

I don't remind her I don't have a computer. "But you said my house is a dump."

She thinks a moment. "I know, we could live in the car! We could drive all over and sleep on the seats. That would be so cool."

The funny thing is I can imagine it too—as it is, the Green Hornet is almost as much home as my house—and I feel all hopeful for a minute. But I know it's just a pipe dream, and Monroe doesn't really mean it either. I look over with affection at my daughter in bell-bottoms, her hair covered with plastic butterflies, a big sun smiling on her tie-dyed T-shirt. "What are you anyway, some kind of hippie chick?" I poke her belly. "I can't believe your dad lets you dress like this."

"Ouch," she giggles.

"Ask Dad about his hippie days sometime."

"Dad was a hippie?"

"Are we still listening to this tape? I can't believe it. You've got to put something else on." And speaking of putting something else on, I know my mother won't like the way Monroe is dressed, so under pretext of it being cold on the boat, I get her to change her clothes. Her body is so sturdy and fine. I have to stop myself sometimes from slapping her rump, I find it so cute. I have to remind myself that she is no longer a baby, that I can't tickle and hold her as if I own her. She's adamant about keeping the plastic butterfly clips intact though, and after a halfhearted argument, I let her. I've exercised enough maternal authority for one day.

As if my own mother's presence has invaded the car, I notice how filthy it is: crumbs, coffee cups, glue-hardened scraps of Monroe's projects, the detritus of the last two weeks. We've spent much of Monnie's visit driving, racking up miles along the secondary roads on the Maine peninsula I call home. Monroe sits shotgun, in charge of snacks and safety. "Batten down the hatches," she says when we fasten our seat belts. "Righto," I say. I know I should track down safer, more up-to-date straps, but I feel lucky the Green Hornet has any seat belts at all. And besides, I've always felt safe with Monroe. Even when she was tiny. As a baby buckled in her little seat in the back of the car, it seemed nothing bad could happen, as if a state of grace emanated from her very being, protecting us.

The Maine winters are hard on the Green Hornet and she shows her age. Last April I replaced the brakes. Next I'm angling for a new clutch. I like doing the work myself. It's not so difficult—just parts broken down, gathered up, rearranged to be in better harmony. This summer Monnie and I are interested in celestial harmony and realignment. We've attached glow-in-the-dark stars to the roof of the car, though we rarely see them because the days are so long. Sometimes, after dark when I sneak a smoke, I creep down to the car to look at them. It comforts me to think I'll still have them after Monnie's gone home to her dad.

I'm collecting stained cups and crumpled juice boxes in a bag when Monroe shouts, "I see him." Steven's boat, a midsize fishing boat that delivers mail to all the islands in the summer, rounds the point into the cove. Monroe stands up through the sunroof and hoots and waves and I step out and yell. Steven toots in response. We bungle around, fumbling and laughing, I'm getting our gear together, closing windows and stuffing sweaters, books, water bottles into a backpack. "Quick," I shout, handing Monroe a bag to carry down to the dock, both of us enjoying the sense of urgency. Slamming the doors shut, but not locking them—the Green Hornet has no functioning locks, plus there's nothing to steal—we head toward the water.

Steven's old dog, Skippy, leaps from the boat before it's even properly alongside the dock and starts licking my bare legs. I've forgotten that about him, how much he likes moisturizer. "That Skippy," Steven says in his sexy drawl as he hands me a line, "always licking the girls' legs." He looks exactly the same, and I find his weathered face and self-deprecating manner as appealing as always. I give him a good long hug. We've been friends since I was twelve.

He's just younger than me, and I've had a crush on him forever, before, during, and after the time we slept together.

As we load the boat Steven sees Monnie eyeing the lobster traps and asks if she knows how they work. She shrugs, so he explains how the lobsters crawl in this *ahere* part (I swear he's exaggerating his accent today) where the bait is, and then after they've eaten they go into the next room to digest. "We call that room the parlor." He pronounces it "parl," then corrects himself: *Par-LOR. Par-LOR.* Monnie giggles. He shows her the little slot where the undersize lobsters crawl out and then pretends his hand is one and tickles her. She's still giggling as he sets her up on the high bench in the cockpit behind the steering wheel.

And off we go. Always there's this magical moment as we leave the land; the colors grow clearer, the smells fresher and stronger. I shiver happily in my windbreaker and huddle next to Steven, breathing in the particular odor of gasoline, brine, and cigarette smoke. We touch shoulder to shoulder, just friendly, and I pretend for a minute we're a family. I don't even believe all that myth about family, but for a moment it's nice to pretend.

He wipes a fleck of cigarette ash from my cheek.

"I was telling Monroe about the boat we had as kids," I say.

"That old tub you found?" He turns to Monroe. "Least seaworthy vessel I've ever seen."

"We had fun though."

"We did." He half laughs as if remembering something. "I have stories I can tell you. When you're older."

"What stories?" Monroe asks.

"Good ones. Your ma will be bribing me not to tell. Ouf," he says as I elbow him. He leans over me to flick a lever, the throttle. The walkie-talkie barks and crackles but I don't bother making out what it says. I turn to watch the wake of the boat. On the shore the Green Hornet looks small and vulnerable. I wave a private goodbye to it, wish it free of vandals and other threats.

I wouldn't tell this to Monroe, or anyone in my family, but I lived in a car once for four weeks. That was after I left Dan, before I got sober, before the Green Hornet became mine. It was a low point in my life, I admit, but sometimes I look back at it with nostalgia and wistfulness. Everything was simple and contained.

My mother and stepfather have spent several weeks on Bride Island every August for the last twenty-three years. At this point it's so much a part of me it feels like it belongs to my family, though it doesn't, really. It belongs to my stepfather. Apparently the man Herbert bought it from, Gus Pederson, is in jail for drug trafficking. The story goes that small planes used to swoop in at strange hours of the night to drop off unidentified packages. I'm not sure I buy that, though as teenagers my brothers and I, who spent an inordinate amount of time cooking up schemes for getting more drugs out to the island, were entranced with the idea that one lone plane from Colombia might not know of Gus Pederson's fate, and it would show up in the middle of the night, drop a kilo (five kilos, a hundred, we could never agree how much) of cocaine, and we'd all be rich. Pipe dreams, indeed.

Bride Island is one of my favorite places in the world, but I usually spend only a few days here each summer, often with Monnie. I'm a painful disappointment to my mother and I'm all too aware she thinks I've made the wrong choices: I live in Maine full-time, instead of just summering here; I'm an alcoholic who had to stop drinking, a tiresome breach in my mother's world; I'm an artist, but I make pots, not portraits of dogs or flowers; I support myself by working with my hands; and I'm divorced, without custody of my daughter. All true, and yet the way I see it, I am alive, I am sane, plus I have my sobriety and a gazillion slogans to fit any occasion. Let Go and Let God, I murmur now.

The wind whips my hair away from my face. Out here on the

water, the shadows are less long, and even through the sea breezes I feel the warmth of the late afternoon sun. A gull loops by and I turn to Monroe to point out a gray seal sunbathing on a rock. She is lounging against the lobster pots, pretending to read our book of Greek myths. The pages keep ruffling and she has a hard time holding on to them. But she perseveres, softly talking to herself. Monnie loves the stories, doesn't seem fazed by them, even though the edition we've borrowed from the library is pretty graphic. Near the beginning, there's a picture of Cronus who has eaten his own children—the babies fill up cavities in his chest—and his wife is handing him a stone in place of his sixth son, Zeus. I'm fascinated by this literal depiction of the harm parents can do their children.

Skippy stretches out in a patch of sun. He grunts, twitches his wirehair brows. I scratch his bald little tummy. Steven hands Monroe a life preserver. I make a dopey face and help her put it on.

"How did they seem?"

He knows I mean Herbert and my mother. " 'Bout the same."

"I worry about their health."

He sighs. "Not much you can do. My father-in-law . . ." he begins, but stops.

I realize he almost never talks about his home life. "What?"

"He's got cancer."

"Oh, I'm sorry," I say.

"And no insurance."

"You've got to fix that," I say too quickly. He blinks hard. I try to squeeze his arm but he moves away. The gap is there between us again. Shit. Despite my efforts, despite my current lifestyle, I will always be an outsider, from "away." It comes and goes, but, stupidly, there has always been that between us.

"How's the season been?" I shout after a time.

"Not too bad," he says. We have all the residents of the different islands to catch up on—who's been ill, who's had which problems, who's renting what—so by the time we enter the bay at Bride

Island we've reestablished our harmonious friendship. "Say hi to Debbie and the boys," I say, when the dock is in sight.

He nods. "Okay."

"We should get together sometime." But we both know that won't happen. I tell him we're coming off island Monday morning.

"I'll be seeing you tomorrow," he tells me. "Your ma wanted half a dozen lobsters."

Mother and Herbert plus Monnie and me is four. "A half dozen? Who else is coming?"

"Russ and his lovely bride, Miss Melanie."

I hadn't been sure my brother would come. "Oh ho. The newly-weds."

"Well, it has been two years."

"Yeah, and Russ's third wedding."

"You should try it again yourself," Steven tells me, so quietly I almost can't hear him.

I snort. "Look at me," I say and give him what I think of as my most crazed, self-deprecating and hopefully winsome smile.

"I am."

I honestly can't read his expression. Does he care? I don't flatter myself. And yet. The silence is awkward and with relief I notice we are almost at the island.

The dock grows steadily larger, the shore clearer, until I can distinguish individual leaves and stones. Steven brings the boat in, throwing first the white fenders along the side, then cutting the engine, sidling in, the boat smelling of fish and diesel fuel, the silence after the din of the engine almost hurting my ears. I leap off and hit the solid wood planks at the same time as Skippy. Steven hoists the bags to me. The air is decidedly sharper. Steven will have to hurry now, hurry home for his supper. *Suppa*. "Thanks," I say, looking into his eyes to make sure we're friends again. I kiss his cheek before I hustle Monroe off.

As Steven's boat chugs away I breathe contentedly. I feel a momentary, purely private wash of happiness at being here again, and it's captured in this sky, this crystalline clarity of light and chill and fresh everything. Even as I'm talking to Monroe, I'm absorbing the landscape around me, feeling it almost on my skin. It's so intimately familiar, and yet wonderfully, beautifully strange: the dock just in from the point, the long spit of land, the islands in the distance; and then, up toward the house, through shady trees and rugosa roses, the path grooved in the tall grasses. Monroe burbles and chirps and points out all the things she remembers from past years. I look at my fine daughter, with her perfectly formed limbs and silky hair, her sweet little nose and clear eyes. My heart swells with gratitude. I refuse to think about the winter.

The island sounds quiet, self-contained. Purple shadows darken the grass path as we walk up to the house. Turning a corner, we come upon my mother, half-hidden by the leaves of the lilac bush, taking down sheets from the clothesline, a wicker basket at her feet. I haven't seen her since Christmas and her oldness shocks me. She could almost be my grandmother. Her face tans easily but the wrinkles have multiplied, are pale between the creases. Her eyes remain the same soft gray, now surrounded by blood vessels. When we hug I realize how thin she has become. Her voice is soothing as she welcomes us, reminding me of dark afternoons and nap time, her cool smooth fingers resting on the nape of my neck. But at the same time I harden my heart against her a little. I know too well how she is.

"Oh your hair," she says sadly, as she cups the back of my head.

"It'll grow," I tell her.

She releases me, then grabs Monroe and pulls her close. "Well, let me look at you," she says. "Aren't you fashionable?" She fingers Monnie's butterflies. "You'll sleep well tonight," she tells her. "Everything nice and fresh."

"You didn't have to do the sheets," I say.

"Oh but I wanted to. It's so much nicer."

"It's a lot of work for you."

"I don't mind," my mother says. She could have been a pioneer woman, I think. Here she is brushing seventy, spending a month every summer without running water or electricity. But when she reaches for the basket I see how frail she is, how thin her arms are, and I offer to finish. She looks grateful but doesn't say anything; she merely takes Monroe's hand and leads her to the house. "Let's go in and see if we can wake up your grandfather," I hear her say.

Monnie replies, "Did you know I'm almost seven?" I smile after the two of them. Everything might just be okay. I fold up a large white sheet and then another. My mother's right, they do feel fresh. But then I notice the corner of one is still damp and decide to leave the rest on the line until after I unpack.

Monroe and I are staying in the attic room where I used to sleep as a child, only then, of course, I shared it with my sister, Elena. After I unpack our clothes into the tall dresser with the sticky drawers, I examine the objects along the top: a saucer filled with sea glass, a cut crystal bud vase out of which pokes a dried rose marking who knows what occasion, a carved St. Francis that dates back to my sister's fling with piety, an old tin biscuit box containing clues to an island-wide scavenger hunt we played one summer when cousins were visiting. I blow the dust off them and shake out my grandmother's linen runner before replacing them. The small framed mirror on the wall is crooked, so I straighten it and hang Monroe's jacket over the painted green-blue chair beneath it. The floor is dusty too, especially in the corners under the eaves, and I find the broom we keep in the closet and give a quick sweep. There's no dustpan upstairs, so I shush the pine needles and lint under the nearest bed, then head downstairs.

As always, this house beguiles me. It's a simple frame-and-beam saltbox with additions, really nothing more than a series of odd rooms built by a farming family in the early 1900s. My parents rent the house out in July and September and the other people who come here must love it as we do. Nothing ever seems changed. Along every windowsill lies a collection of some kind or other: bleached, crumbling crab shells, delicate green sea urchins, tiny golden "toenail" shells, smooth black stones.

In the living room I see Herbert's drink before I see him. He is slumped in the rocking chair. Herbert was old even when I first met him. Now his body is a combination of protuberances and knobs: mulberry nose followed by pointy chin, thin stork legs beneath pregnant belly. His thick white hair erupts out of a forehead freckled with age spots. He and I have never exactly been friends and as usual I wonder about my mother's motives for marrying him. Some of them must have been financial. After all, when my dad died she had four children to support.

My father used to fly planes. He was a businessman by profession and a pilot for fun. There was a private airstrip on the edge of town and one weekend his plane crashed. No one's really sure how. What I imagined as a kid was that he caught his sleeve on a handle, like in that scene from *Rebel without a Cause*, and then couldn't jump out. Whatever the reason, his death transformed my mother into a tragic figure—she had four kids between the ages of eight and fifteen—and their marriage into a union of mythic happiness. Notwithstanding that they fought and drank too much and his development business was on the verge of bankruptcy. Russ, my older brother, says he crashed on purpose so we would get the insurance money. (That this money never materialized doesn't deter him from this story.) Elena, my sister, says he had a woman up there in the cockpit with him and they were drinking. Colin and I, the two closest in age, didn't know what to think. Even when my mom married Herbert, my father's lawyer, within a year, she still carried the aura of brave widow.

"Hello, Herbert," I say, bending down to kiss his forehead.

He startles. For a moment he looks blank, then he says, "Hello, Polly. Here for your annual mooch?"

"Ha ha," I say.

Herbert stretches his scrawny legs out in the strip of sun that licks the floor. He says I look fit and I execute a mock curtsy. "You gonna tell me you've got a real job?" His voice still has traces of a Louisville accent.

"I have a real job," I say, wishing I had a cigarette or a drink just about now.

"What are you again, a waitress?" He blinks, lizardlike, then laughs.

"I cook for rich old farts like yourself," I say.

Herbert sits up. I can't tell what's upset him more, the fart bit or the fact that I called him as old as the people at the nursing home where I prepare meals every afternoon.

"You'll not speak to me like that." He shakes his head then checks his hair, caresses it back into place. He still combs it in the style of his youth: sharply parted with a crested wave in front.

"Oh, give it a rest, Herbert," I say, looking out the window. "We're on the island, it's beautiful, we're alive and young. Young at heart anyway." I squint to see what he makes of this but he just grunts. "I'm going outside. You want to come?"

He swirls his drink so the ice cubes clink around. "You go," he says. "Find your daughter before she drowns."

Both of us blanch at his slip, but of course we say nothing. No one ever talks about the death of my brother Colin.

Outside the sky radiates a crisp yellow, with an overlay of thin purple clouds. Black spruce trees appear etched against the sky.

The wind in the trees is noisy enough that I scan the horizon for an airplane. And even though I'm not worried about my daughter, "Monnie," I call. "Monroe."

Coming here, it's as though all of my certainty, my patched-together but existing self, evaporates. I regress. Of fifty-two weeks, I can't help thinking, I am down to three. How did this happen? Monroe's father would say that I don't love her as much, that my love hasn't had to grow in the midnight cracks. But perhaps it could never compete with his at all. The day after she was born, Dan wore a pink bow tie and handed out cigars tied with pink ribbons to his colleagues and pink caramel popcorn to his students. At the beginning of each class he wrote her name on the blackboard in pink chalk: Monroe Olympia Birdswell Lerner. As if any of his students cared. I wasn't there, of course. His graduate assistant Chloe told me.

"Monroe!" I call again, and just when I'm beginning to panic, she bursts from behind the house. She sees me and smiles, breaks into a run. "Mom!" she whoops. I smile back at her flushed face, her wide-set gray eyes, and take her hand. Together we run toward the shore.

In the kitchen my mother prepares dinner, a thick stew made with lumps of meat she's kept in the freezer. I lean against the archway and watch, her gestures old, familiar, comforting, dangerous. And always the glass of gin by her elbow, easily within reach. "You must be tired after your trip," she says. "We're soon ready to eat." From force of habit, she won't let me help her. The funny thing is that I am a much better cook than she is; for the seniors at the home I use only organic vegetables and complex grains. Her food is out of cans and boxes, processed, dried, rich with sodium and sugar. But when I am here I enjoy it.

"Daniel's doing a fine job," she remarks. This stings a little, though I know what she thinks of me is nothing compared to what

I think of myself. She pours flour into the dented aluminum measuring cup. "How is he, anyway?"

"Fine, I guess. I don't know. We don't talk much. I think he keeps hoping I'll just go away for good." I laugh, nervously.

"Herbert and I have been thinking," my mother begins.

"Oh?"

"Well, just how nice it would be if you and Monroe could see each other more often." I wait, wondering if she's going to offer me Herbert's money to get a lawyer. "I wondered whether you, I mean, couldn't you rearrange things . . ."

"Rearrange them how?" Suddenly I'm willing to have an out-and-out confrontation. "You know it's not my choice, Mother. You know my life."

"I just think children need both parents," she says quickly, as if I'm going to cut her off. "A mother and a father."

I think about all the things I could say about our own picture-perfect family growing up. Finally, I say, "Monroe has two parents: Dan and Chloe."

"Polly, I don't think that's funny. I think you need to do some serious thinking about your life. I think it's a shame Daniel hasn't looked after you better. Or maybe you'll meet someone else—"

"Oh, Mother," I say. "That is old-fashioned and ridiculous. I have a life and it's mine. I can look after myself. Maybe it's not your idea. Maybe it's not the country club, but I'm trying, okay?"

"I just want you to be happy." She gazes at me imploringly, with that age-old look mothers give their daughters. I glance into the dining room where Monnie, pleased to be helpful, sets the table. I soften for a minute. Was I not once to my mother what Monroe is now to me? Impossible, I think. And yet, my mother stayed with me, kept me. And I have let Monnie go.

"I know," I say. "I know." And something like peace descends on us. I offer to make a blueberry cobbler with the berries we brought. The flour and butter melding in my hands is silkier and drier than the clay I use to make my ceramics, but there is a similar tactility and I enjoy working it. Monroe wanders in. She wedges herself underneath my chin and swipes a few blueberries. A breeze blows the smell of evening through the screen door. The kitchen has grown dim so my mother pulls the string against the wall and the room leaps with light. Even the buzzing from the propane-powered fridge seems homey to me, and when I've put the cobbler in the oven my mother says there's time for us to take a walk before dinner, she'll stay and do the washing up.

Monnie and I see a rabbit in the dusk. It stares at us, then turns and bolts. After that we step quietly, hoping to see another. When I ask Monnie where she wants to go she says immediately, Indian Cemetery. We walk in shadow until we reach the large meadow, which is suffused with golden light catching the tips of the tall grasses. From here we can see across the bay, across Swallow and Sheep Islands, and over to Great Rock and Little Pine, dark mounds in the distance. All the islands around here are named after animals or distinguishing features. But ours is different: Bride Island. Some people think the name is a botched derivative of the island's original Indian name that the white settlers couldn't properly pronounce. Another theory is that it was initially called Bridge Island, because of the way it links at low tide with Swallow Island, and somehow that mutated into Bride. I prefer the story I've always heard. A newly married couple was spending their first winter here and the young man went to the mainland for supplies, promising to return within the week. But he never did. People speculated he'd abandoned his young bride, but more likely he died at sea.

I shudder, I don't exactly know why. I'm not afraid of old stories, and whatever ghosts are here don't scare me.

The Indian Cemetery is not really Indian, though someone did once find an arrowhead here. But there are several real graves dating from eighty to a hundred and twenty years ago, from the families who lived here full time. These weathered tombstones are thin and frail, with *beloveds* and *dearests* and occasional eroding lines of verse. Stones my family added mark the burial sites of our three old dogs, Vixen, Chet, and Bumpo.

There's also a marker for my brother Colin. He drowned right off the point here the summer he was fifteen and I was sixteen. We scattered half his ashes across the island. The other half rests under an engraved tombstone next to our father's, in the cemetery back home in New Prospect, Massachusetts, where we grew up and Herbert and my mother still live. The one here is just a simple granite square placed into the ground, with the word *bless* carved across it.

Monnie looks around quietly, stands for a minute at my brother's stone; she's heard the story, though it must be only that, a story, for her. She holds my hand briefly, then wanders off, talking to herself. Already she's invented a game with a twig and a feather, is making little leaf clothes for them. Tomorrow I will gather some shells for Colin, arrange them across his stone.

On the way back, I rest my arm on Monnie's shoulders and she puts hers around my waist. We fit surprisingly well like this; as we walk we bump comfortably together. Sometimes, often, she feels more like a kid sister or younger cousin than a daughter.

"Mom? At school? We did a project about women who were brave. We had to ask our mothers and draw it and the teacher read it out loud."

"Did you ask Chloe?"

She nods. "She said I should ask you too."

I think a minute. "Oh God, sweetie, I can't remember a time when I was brave." I laugh, though what comes to mind, in fact, is when I left my marriage—Monroe was fifteen months old—and my memory of that time is of the earth caving in, of falling downward into a pit that left me alone, broke, and drunk on a Greyhound bus traveling northward through the night. Of course, I can't tell her that. But she looks so serious I don't want to disappoint her. I rack my brain trying to think of a time when I rescued a stray dog or rushed into a burning building. Quitting drinking was brave. Could I say that?

"Did you ever go into a forest alone?" she asks in a helpful voice.

"Hmm," I say. "That's the kind of brave you want? Well, let's see. There was one time. I was just a little older than you are now." I tell her that when I was nine I sometimes rode my bike home from school alone. "Normally I went home with one of my brothers, or my sister—"

"Aunt Elena?"

"Right. Anyway, this one day I had to come home by myself. Everything was fine except there was this one house that was really scary—the witch's house." Monnie drops her arm from around my waist so she can look at me more directly. "As I was riding by I saw an apple lying on the ground. Goodie, I thought, a yummy apple." She stops walking and looks at me with wide eyes. "So I pick it up, all ready to take a big bite out of it, only the bottom is bitten into and gross and covered with ants." Monnie mimics my repulsed face. "So I fling it onto the grass and then I hear the witch laugh: ha ha ha!" I cackle loudly. Monnie's hand moves to her mouth. "She was a mean ugly witch," I say, playing it up, "with short red hair and sunglasses."

"What happened?"

In real life, as she would say, I ran away terrified and humiliated. But since this is supposed to be a story about me being brave, I say, "So I yelled, 'Foo on you, ugly witch!' And I shook my fist at her." I demonstrate.

Monroe covers her eyes as if she were at a scary movie. "Then what?"

Too late I realize how frightened she is. "Well, I grabbed a bucket of water and strode up the steps and doused her with it. And guess what? She melted." Monnie peeks at me between blinkers made of fingers. She still looks scared, but dubious too, so I say, "And then a nice family moved into that house with lots of little kids and a jungle gym and a chocolate Lab named Buddy and a parrot named Elliot and everyone lived happily ever after." I smile at her, wondering if she's bought it. We start walking again. Monroe's silent and I kick myself for not remembering how scared she gets. I splice a blade of grass and whistle through it. But when I offer to show her how, she refuses to be distracted.

Polly!" My mother comes out of the kitchen drying her hands on a dishtowel. "Polly, you forgot the sheets. Really! How could you?" Her voice carries in the twilight air.

"Oh God, Mother, I'm sorry." We've just come up the path.

"The dew has come in and now they're damp." She looks at me accusingly.

"It's okay," I say, "I'll start a fire and hang them to dry inside."

She shakes her head. I go round back of the house and gather the heavy sheets. I shiver. The dew has brought out a slightly mildewed odor, a smell that reminds me of cheap, lonely motels.

"Mom," Monnie whispers, not looking at me. "I'm scared of the witch."

"It's just a story," I say, and keep folding the sheets. "About a time when I was brave."

"Mommy, I mean Chloe, told me about the time she made the town put in a new traffic light."

"Did she. Tie your shoelace." Obediently, Monroe ducks down and then we turn toward the house with the basket of folded linens between us.

At dinner my stepfather brandishes a wineglass. "Will you join us?" And when I shake my head, he asks, "Still on the wagon?"

"That's one way of putting it," I say.

"It's been several years," my mother says. "Sur[e] have a little sip? That wouldn't hurt."

"You had a problem, you dealt with it, you moved on," Herbert says. His voice sounds slurred. "Case closed."

"It's not that simple," I say. I'm aware of holding my knife and fork in my hands, aware of how stubby my fingers are, the nails broken or bitten down. "It's not like it just ends." You would think they would know all this by now, but if I want to avoid a fight I have to pick my words carefully. In AA they say to call a friend, but here there are no telephones. "I'm fine," I say. "I'm fine with water. Really."

"Well, okay, dear. But I still think a tiny sip—"

I sigh and put down my fork. Monroe watches my mother and me. When I catch her eye she ducks her head and puts her fork in her stew. What on earth was I thinking by coming here with just Herbert and my mother? Usually there are other people, my brother or sister, cousins, more of a buffer.

"Just forget it," I say.

My mother and Herbert exchange glances. "What?" I say.

"Nothing, dear."

I let out a loud sigh. I'm sorry Monroe has to see this. She picks at her lip with her finger, twisting the dry skin. "Monroe, leave your mouth alone," I say.

She looks at me, startled, then stops. Instead she spins her fork over and over. She doesn't care for my mother's cooking. "Stop it right now," I say, "or you're leaving the table."

"Polly," my mother murmurs.

I breathe deeply, count to ten, search for a slogan. "De Nile is a river in Egypt" is all that comes to mind, but it's enough to calm me for a moment. And all the while I'm thinking about the choices that brought me here and how Monroe lives with Daniel. I'm sure her life is better with him. It has to be better.

After dinner I go upstairs to kiss Monroe good night. She asked my mother to read her a story, and when I mount the thin, steep stairs to our attic room I can hear my mother's wavery voice. I've warmed water on the stove and washed the dishes, dried and put them away. My mother pecks Monroe's forehead and calls her "dear." As she passes she staggers against me, her breath ripe. I wait till she makes it downstairs then turn off the kerosene lamp. Tucked under her blankets, Monroe is almost asleep. The nightlight, a tall candle flickering in a glass, sends shadows to the ceiling. And I remember what it was like to go to bed here, the sky still light at first, the little room at the top of the stairs warm from the day, the chamber pot in the corner, the detritus of my ramblings (pieces of sea glass, shells, pinecones) jumbled on the windowsills and bureau tops, when I was a child and dreaming of all the wonderful things that would happen to me.

I stroke Monnie's face gently and she sighs and turns over, her hands clasped under her chin. I press my lips to her hair, kiss her and inhale. In my daughter's sturdy but graceful body I feel reassurance, salvation. I am greedy for it.

And another memory rises: the summer she was eleven months old and constantly in motion. Dan walked her and I walked her but her desire for movement surpassed her ability and she ended up having her first tantrum. Nothing would appease her—she screamed for hours—and I steadily got drunker and drunker until I tripped coming down the stairs and lay laughing in a heap at the bottom and had to spend the rest of our vacation with my foot up. I continued drinking, at first to dull the pain and then to pass the time. I also fixed things that had been sitting around for years, like the old radio and the wire oven-top toaster, and Dan took care of the baby. Was I a bad mother, or just a not very good one? What if I could stop the clock right there and go back? Would I? I'd thought marriage would be an end, a container. But it wasn't a house I stepped into, it was only a gate I passed through.

In the living room the sheets hang on the furniture like ghosts. I wrap a shawl around my shoulders and sit a few moments in the rocking chair. And that's when I see the half-finished glass of wine on the side table. My mother must have put it there after I came downstairs, when she was playing backgammon with Herbert, the clinking of their pieces wrapping them in a kind of quiet domestic harmony that didn't include me.

I don't move for a while, just look at the wine. Light from the kerosene lamp catches facets of the pressed-glass goblet. I could drink it, less than half a glass. It's dangerous even to think that. Call a friend. My sponsor, Joan, would understand that the temptation to drink never leaves, even after four years of sobriety. But there are no phones here.

Get up, I tell myself. Do something. I do get up. I walk to the side table and pick up the glass. I hold it by the stem and swirl the wine around so that it coats first one side, then the other. I smell it, imagine tasting it. And really, would it be so bad if I did drink it? It's not like it would lead to a drinking binge. I remember wine, how it tasted strong and raw at first and then pleasant. That wasn't my drink of choice though—like my mother, I preferred gin. And all along another voice is saying, leave it alone, put it down.

I'm thirty-four, not so very old. But I feel I've already lived my life, I've already had my chance. I haven't told anyone, but I had my tubes tied. Five weeks after I got sober. I did it out of fear and because I didn't trust myself. And now the inside of my body feels hollowed out, strange to me.

I put the glass down. The firelight wavers on the sheets. On the window seat next to the side table I spy the book of Greek myths and pick it up. I sit and flip through the book, looking at the pictures. So many bad family dynamics: cheating Zeus and jealous Hera, cold Artemis, angry Demeter and lost Persephone. As daughters we crave our mothers, as mothers we crave our daughters. And yet there is no satisfaction, no fulfillment in the equation. We are caught between two states, anticipation and relinquishment. And soon Monroe will leave me.

I shove the book aside, onto the table, and inadvertently topple the glass. Bloodred wine spreads across the table, seeping into the book's pages and splattering onto the sofa below. The glass rolls and smashes on the floor. Of course, I will clean this up. Even so, my mother will ask about the sofa, Monnie will ask about the stains on the book, and I will have to explain.

Monroe must have woken up before me because her bed is empty, a green camp blanket coiled midway down the mattress, another tossed and dangling along the sunlit floor. I stretch and listen to the sounds of the house: the hum of the fridge, the dull buzz of a bee caught in a corner of the window, the gentle thud of a shade knocking against a sill, the particularly soundless quality of an empty house.

I stand up, my head almost bumping the ceiling. The air is used in here, smells of sleep and must. I lean toward the window. On the lawn, two deck chairs are angled awkwardly, as if their occupants had quarreled before leaving them. The bee stumbles against the glass. I grasp the upper half of the window. It doesn't budge. With difficulty I push until the casement moves and the bee flies outside. The sun is already high in the sky. It is later than I thought, perhaps after 9:00. I can smell the sea. Leaving the window open to air out the room, I bound downstairs.

For a moment I am torn between searching for my daughter and examining every inch of the house. Monnie is safe, I am certain, so this morning I do a real inspection, searching the house for leaks and other problems. I spend the good part of an hour repairing things. A shutter that is off-kilter, a clogged gutter. It's my way of becoming connected again. I check the propane tank, making everything ship-shape and ready. I wish I had thought to bring paint—the windowsills could use another coat. In the fall I'll come back. But even as I'm thinking this, I've started hatching a plot. If I radioed Steven and got him to bring over a couple of gallons and some primer, I could sand the windowsills and then paint a coat or two. When I come back in October to close the house, I could add another coat.

My mother has folded the sheets and I take the stack upstairs. First I make up Monnie's bed, then my own, pulling the sheets and wool blankets taut, centering each white chenille bedspread. Then I go back downstairs into the room Russ and Melanie will stay in. Here there is a double bed and as I snap the sheets above it and watch them float down, I wonder if my brother is happy. What fantasy propels him into marriage again and again?

Down by the shore, my mother is cutting sea heather. She and Monnie gather bunches of the delicate purple flowers that my mother will dry and bring home to New Prospect. When I tell her my plan to paint the window frames, she is skeptical. To my mother, the house has always been about decrepitude; she and my stepfather have taken a certain anorexic pleasure in passivity. But I like doing the work; it makes me feel useful.

"Oh, Polly," my mother says, looking up from her clipping. "I just don't know if I can stand another of your projects. You're only here a few days. You'll just get started and then leave it midway through. And Herbert and I are too old for that."

"I'll finish it," I say, more stung than I care to admit.

Her expression looks doubtful, but "we'll see," is all she says.

"For lunch," Monroe says, following me up the path, "Grandma says we can have a picnic and go swimming. And after lunch, after we rest our tummies, she said we can go for a walk and look for fairies." She skips and jumps around the path, then stops to look at me. "This place is magical, you know."

"I do know," I say. "It's what I've always thought."

After radioing Steven, I work in my bikini top and shorts, sanding the windowsills. Sweat runs down my belly. Monnie helps for a while, until she gets bored. She announces she is going to get her bathing suit on. I don't blame her but I'm sad to see her go. A part of me wonders why I have chosen to do this instead of be with her but I don't dwell there. Luckily the paint is old and flaky and I'm able to get up big chunks at a time. I don't care if it looks pristine, I just want it to be watertight.

At lunchtime I join the others on the pebble beach. It's sheltered from the wind here, and warm and pleasant. They have brought out some old orange canvas chairs and a picnic lunch. Monroe splashes in the frigid water, her blue flotation circle brilliant against her red one-piece suit, and I wade in and help her find interesting pebbles. The water's crystal clear and later we dip our carrot sticks for the salt. After we eat, my mother reads to Monroe while Herbert dozes in the shade. I'm tempted to linger with them, but make myself leave. I don't want to disappoint my mother again.

Several hours later, when Steven's boat arrives, I'm just about finished with the sanding. I tidy up quickly, then race to the shore. Ahead of me Herbert shuffles down to the dock, drink in one hand, his trousers hitched below his belly. Walking looks painful, but he doesn't complain or make any comment. His veiny hand catches the rope Steven throws him.

Russ steps off the boat and I am shocked for a minute to think that this paunchy middle-aged, balding man is my brother. But then he smiles his gleaming toothy smile and winks and the handsome Russ of my youth is back. We hug. He's larger than I remember. "Where is she?" I ask. "Your lovely wife?" Now Melanie emerges from the cabin. She has an elegant monogrammed week-end bag, and wears crisp linen pants, a soft black top, and delicate leather sandals. What is wrong with my brother—didn't he tell her what this place is like? Steven helps her onto the dock and she and I peck each other on the cheek. I tell Russ they are starting to be an old married couple, looking more and more alike, which is a joke since Melanie is Asian American.

Monroe is shy and stands near me till Russ takes her and, groaning loudly, tosses her up in the air. He calls her a pipsqueak and, beaming, she tells him she is not a pipsqueak. Herbert claps Russ on the back and kisses Melanie's hand.

While the others are chatting, I help Steven unload the supplies—the paint cans, a box of groceries with champagne bottles tucked inside, a carton squirming with the wet backs of lobsters—into the cart we'll wheel up to the house. He teases me about the size of my biceps and, pretending his fingers aren't big enough, cups one in his hand. His touch floods me with warmth. His face and arms are tanned but I can see underneath his shirt where his tan stops and for a second the old longing comes upon me. I look out at the water, at a cormorant drying its wings on a rock, then back toward land. Herbert is watching us, but when he sees I see him, he turns for the house. Steven pulls out a pack of cigarettes, starts to offer me one, and then stops. He knows I don't smoke in front of Monroe. He gestures at the champagne bottles and says, "Looks like there'll be a party."

"Guess I'll skip that."

He laughs and climbs back on board. "You want to come for a ride?"

"Where to?" I ask.

He shrugs. "Anywhere you like. The bluff?"

Not far from the island, on the windward side, is a flat rock with a few spindly trees on top, some wild roses, and creeping honeysuckle. We've often sat there side by side, smoking and watching the sun set. I haven't been there yet this year.

He smiles at me and I smile back. Skippy sniffs a scrap of dried seaweed on the dock, then jumps on the boat. Steven starts the engine and I know I have to climb on now or let him go. I glance at Monroe who's already heading up the path with Melanie and Russ, then shake my head. "I'd love to, but . . ."

"But . . ." He sighs. "That's okay." He begins to reverse and I untie the line and toss it to him. "Good night, dear," he calls. *Deah*. I look to see if he's smiling and he is.

Back at the house, my mother sits on the sofa with Monroe, the two of them sorting sea glass and shells. Herbert has the paper Russ brought and a drink. Melanie, wrapped in a shawl, has skeins of colored silk on her knee and Russ is reading the label on a bottle of wine. It's only a short while since the others got back, but the cold look my mother and stepfather give me is eerily similar. They disapprove of my friendship with Steven, always have. And because they look at me like that, for a minute I wish Steven and I *were* sleeping together. That was the problem. I was always willing to rise to the challenge, always ready to do the thing they believed me capable of doing. I take a breath and remind myself that things are different now.

"Mom!" Monnie cries and flings herself at me.

"Well hey."

"We're sorting colors and Melanie's going to make me a friendship bracelet."

"Cool," I say. And I hug her until I can feel all the little bones in her spine.

Dinner is festive, fueled by the lobster and bottles of champagne. Afterward, Russ pulls down our grandmother's old Victrola off its high shelf, dusts it off. "Melanie," he says. "Take a look at this. I think I can still get it to work."

She stands at his shoulder. "Wow."

"Oh, Russ!" My mother claps her hands.

Monroe is examining the records, the LPs and old singles. I hear her softly trying to make out the words.

"This is fantastic," Melanie says, looking over Monnie's shoulder. She's smiling, hugging her shawl, the most animated I've ever seen her.

Russ sets the machine on the table. "I think this is how you do it," he says, his big hands getting ready to maul it.

"Oh, let me," I say, edging him aside. The needle is bent just slightly and I straighten it. "Hand me a record," I say, and Russ selects something. I crank the handle, and watch the needle come down. First silence, then a noisy scratching, and then the opening bars of a swing band. The quality is terrible, but romantic and touching.

Russ offers his arm to Melanie, who accepts. Side by side, he seems enormous, she tiny. But I forgot what a good dancer Russ is. And Melanie too. They move gracefully together, twirling and spinning, the way only people who have been to dancing school can. They know all the moves and seem to fit together. The song comes to an end and they stop midswirl, laughing. Everyone claps. I select another record and they begin again. Now my mother and Herbert dance together, and he clasps her about the waist with his gnarled hands and her face goes solemn and youthful. She is not a confident dancer, but she moves neatly, and Herbert, looking magisterial, his eyes closed, pulls her tight. Monroe watches, her eyes wide and her mouth half open. It must seem magical to her, these people dancing in the candlelight.

"Mademoiselle, will you dance?" I offer and, giggling, she takes my hand. I spin her this way and that way and together we're the buffoonish ones bumping into the others, just the way I used to be with Colin.

We play a few other records, all of us waiting for a moment until we recognize the melody or at least get the rhythm. Russ dances the jitterbug with me and Herbert waltzes with Melanie. We all attempt the Charleston, Russ going lower and wilder than all the rest of us, until the song ends and we have to collapse on the sofas and chairs out of breath. I land next to Russ, who's laughing and looks incredibly young and sweaty. I smile at him. The love you feel for a sibling is different from the love you feel for anyone else, I think.

After a bit, Monroe and I go outside. We use the outhouse side by side, then wander down to the shore. The waves come in, half peaceful, half restless. The air is chilly but pure and the sky brims with stars. Monroe shivers and I hug her tight.

"I see the Big Dipper," she says, pointing. "And there's the North Star."

"That's right," I say.

"I love it here," she says, and my heart overflows.

A mosquito bites my leg and another one drones in my ear. "Are you getting bitten?" I ask. For answer she yelps and together we run toward the house, pausing just for a moment to watch the dancers through the windows, then dash inside, laughing.

"I think it's bedtime," my mother says.

"We're on our way," I tell her, pecking her cheek.

"Sleep well dears," she calls.

From the stairs I look down. Melanie is swaying by herself, my mother is sitting on a chair, and Herbert and Russ are conferring over which new bottle to open. "Good night," I call.

The next morning Monroe and I are up early. After last night's champagne consumption, I assume the others will sleep late. Monroe and I eat breakfast outside on the wooden chairs. We watch some of the birds hopping from branch to branch and dip our feet into the wet grass. It is a perfect day for painting, with sun and a dry breeze coming over the southern tip of the island. After rinsing our dishes, I give Monnie a paintbrush and we get to work.

"My dad," she begins, glancing quickly at me.

"A good man." She gives me her "be serious" look. "Sorry, go on."

"He said we can get another dog when Madame Manet dies."

"How old is Madame Manet? She's what, a dachshund?"

"I think she's sixteen. That's like being a hundred in people years."

"Wow. That is old. I bet Chloe will be sad when she dies."

Monnie nods. "She's had Madame Manet since she was a little girl."

Hardly a little girl, I think. She's not that much younger than me. "What do you think of the name Madame Manet? Didn't she have a different name first?"

Monroe shrugs. "Mommy, I mean Chloe—" glancing at me until I nod "—says she used to be called Tiny, but my dad likes to name the pets. He likes to have a theme."

"That's a big word," I say, daubing my brush.

She nods. "He teaches the Impressionists."

"I'm impressed," I say, "your knowing such big words." She looks proud of herself. "How are your guinea pigs?"

"They're good. I bet Claude will try to feed them when I'm gone. He's not very good at feeding them. He makes a big mess." She laughs and then falls silent. After a while she turns to me. "Mom? At school, some of my friends don't have dads. You're the only mom I know of who left." She says it not accusingly but wonderingly.

For a minute I don't breathe. She looks at me out of those gray-blue eyes and nods. I bite hard on my lower lip, then manage a smile. I can't think how to respond.

And a little later, when Russ and Melanie come outside, I call to them in a cheery way. "Hey, you guys want to help?"

"Do we have to?" Russ says. He's wearing a button-down shirt, untucked, long linen shorts, and expensive-looking loafers. "Don't answer that."

"Look, maintenance is entirely optional," I say.

Russ sighs. "I'm not going to make you," he says to Melanie, "but I guess I could."

"Maybe you want to change your fancy duds?" I point to his shirt.

"I'll be okay."

"Mom?" Monroe squinches up her face. Her wrist sags and the brush appears about to fall out of her grasp.

"Go ahead, give your brush to Russ," I tell her.

"Monroe, do you think you could show Mel here around the island?" Russ asks. "Show her all the hot spots?"

Monroe nods.

"See if you can find a rabbit," I say.

"A rabbit?" Melanie says. "I'd like that." She holds out her hand and together they head off down a path, Monroe chattering away. I like Melanie for being kind to my daughter.

"She's good with kids," I tell Russ.

"Oh yeah."

"Does she get along with Susie and Becca?" Russ's twins from his second marriage.

He shrugs. "Fine. Good enough." He slaps some paint on. I wait for him to expand on this but he doesn't. After a while he says, "I can't believe we're doing this. God, this place is a dump."

"Nothing a lick of paint can't help."

"This whole place should be torn down. Started over."

I smile. "But then it wouldn't be Bride Island."

"Yeah, the place we go to pretend we're poor."

I laugh. "Who said that?"

"Susie, when she was about nine."

"Aren't they coming out this year?"

"Are you kidding? No running water? They must take five showers a day. They wouldn't last ten minutes. Actually, I'm not sure Melanie's going to make it. She likes the amenities, you know. And who can blame her? Oh shit." We both look down. A glob of white paint lies on Russ's loafer. I promise I can get it off.

"Oh, it's all right. It's only two-hundred-dollar Italian leather."

I tell him maybe he should take them both off. Grunting, he bends over and tosses the shoes under the apple tree. Side by side we continue to paint. It's a bit strange being with Russ. Growing up, it was always Colin and me together, with Russ, eight years older, a sort of natural satellite. Russ was our merry leader, the king of vice, chief instigator of illegal activities. Now our affection and friendship buoy us along, disguising the fact that we don't really know each other anymore.

When the conversation dwindles, I start whistling. Russ joins me after a while, surprising me. We do Beatles songs—"You're Gonna Lose That Girl," and "Help"—getting the harmony right.

"You really love this place, don't you?" he asks.

"Yeah, I do." Looking around, surveying. "Don't you?"

He waggles his head back and forth. "Yes and no. To a point."

"Which point? Sandy Point?"

"Ha ha." Russ's plump face is reddening, sweat popping over his balding pate.

"I wish I could spend more time here," I say. We let this settle into the atmosphere. "What about you?"

"Yeah. It's like, we were so happy here, you know? It seems like such an innocent time."

I raise an eyebrow.

"Sure shit happened, but we were happy. We were *kids*."

There are so many things I want to say, about Colin, about all of us and our struggles, but all I can manage is, "Yeah, I know."

"Polly?"

"Yes?"

"Why did you leave Monroe?"

What is it about this morning? "Oh my God, Russ. Don't beat around the bush or anything."

"If you don't want to talk about it, that's okay. It's just, Melanie was asking me and I realized I didn't really know."

I clear my throat, try to clear my head. "Well, you have to understand, I was a raging alcoholic, okay, so a lot of my thinking wasn't so great then." I wonder if he's going to see in my drinking any reflection of his own, but of course he doesn't. "I was desperate. I had to get out." This is the part where it usually gets hard, where I feel judged and misunderstood. He nods. "I guess some people have maternal genes and some don't. Believe me, I wish I'd done it differently. I wish I could have done it differently," I amend. For a moment I look off down the path, as if to bring Monroe to me. But the path is just green, empty. I splash more paint on. "Luckily Dan and Chloe are fantastic parents and she's a great kid. She's turning out fine."

"Oh, no doubt of that."

For a minute I'm quiet, remembering. It was January when I left Dan and I spent the spring months drunk and sleeping with anyone I could. I'd thought I'd camp out here on the island, but of course I couldn't. It was far too cold. And then I moved down east, to Rockhaven, got a job canning for a few miserable months at the blueberry factory and then cooking at the home, got sober, got my life together. I want to change the subject, so I ask, "What about you two? You think kids will be in the picture?"

"Well." He lowers his voice and looks around to make sure no one is listening. "Truth is, we're trying and it's not happening. Mel's pretty upset about it."

"I'm sorry to hear that," I say automatically, but actually I'm kind of shocked they're considering parenthood. Russ is not exactly winning father of the year awards as it is and Melanie . . . well, what do I really know of Melanie? "Have you done all the tests?"

"She's done a bunch. I had some stuff done too. Next I'm supposed to go for a sperm penetration assay."

"A what?"

"Yeah, that's where they see if you can impregnate a hamster's
egg."

"What happens if you do? What do they do with the fertilized
egg?"

"I wondered that too. Maybe there'll be a little hamster with my
face running around a lab somewhere."

We both laugh, but after that we're silent until he declares he's
finished, sticks his brush in a can of turpentine and collapses on the
lawn, his beautiful dress shirt now tied about his head.

After lunch, I grab a tin pail and head across the island to Sandy
Point. The beach here is not real sand, but muddy silt. I dig for
clams for what seems like hours, putting their spitting little selves
into the pail of water to let them clean themselves. Then I lug the
pail back across the island, through the wooded paths and over the
meadow. At the crest of the hill I stop for a moment and crane my
neck to see if I can spot the canoes that the others, even Herbert
and my mother, have taken out. I regret letting Monroe dance
away from me again, but at the same time I'm happy she's making
the most of being here. In so many ways she is Dan's daughter, but
I consider my best legacy the love Monroe feels for Bride Island.
That somehow makes her mine in a way straight biology doesn't.

Leaving the pail in the shade of the house, I spend the afternoon
by myself, painting. I don't regret the project—it makes me feel
good to take care of the building—but I wish I had more time. At
last I am done with the base coat and am putting away my brushes
when I turn to see my mother and Herbert come up the path,
Monnie straggling after them. I go to meet them, hug Monnie, and
take her paddle, show her how to rinse it with a scoop of rainwa-

ter. Then, when the others go inside, we sit on the grass and I teach her how to tell the temperature by counting the number of chirps a cricket makes. We have to count for fourteen seconds and then add forty. It doesn't work for temperatures below forty degrees, I explain, because then the cricket is too cold and stupid. She seems to like counting with me, feels proud when we've figured out it's sixty-five degrees outside. "You know so much stuff," Monnie says.

None of it means anything, I want to say, but don't. "Everything I know I'll teach you," I promise her.

Evening approaches the island. To the north, Swallow Island is already in shadow, and dark clouds clump on the horizon. The most beautiful and most melancholy part of the day. Arm in arm, Monroe and I head up to the blueberry barren. It's hard work scrabbling among the low bushes, but we pick a quart and feel pleased with ourselves. On the way back to the house we gather wild greens, dandelions, sorrel, the little mache that grows like a ground cover. The salad will be bitter, but bursting with vitamins and taste.

When we come back in I take over the kitchen. I power up the old stove and begin to cook. I am proud of the dinner I put on the table, proud that it all came from our island. Monnie has set the table and decorated it with leaves and grasses and wildflowers. There is a beautiful, strange quality to her twinings. I am tired from a day of physical activity, from the sun and fresh air. But I relish the fatigue. It feels well earned. At intervals, Monnie and I yawn sleepily.

Gathered together, we sit around the table, and for a moment I look at my family with unconflicted affection. We eat the clams in silence, and except for the fact that my mother has only a few and Melanie none at all, they seem to be satisfactory. Russ helps himself to seconds, then thirds, slurping noisily. When everyone is finished and there is a mountainous bucket of shells in the center of the table, I clear away the soup bowls and bring out the salad and a dish of baking-powder biscuits.

"Your family's been coming to Bride Island how long?" Melanie asks.

My mother rubs her nose with the back of her hand. "Oh, goodness. Twenty years. No, more." She waves at Herbert. "Since we were married. Do you know," she says, leaning toward Melanie, "the funniest thing is that I feel as if I came here as a child. I didn't, of course, my family never went to Maine, we barely had vacations, but I have all these memories of running along the paths here." She laughs. "Peculiar."

"That's so weird," I say, tossing the salad. "I feel the same way. I can see myself playing down by the shore, just the way Monnie does. But I was eleven when we first came here, not six." I smile at Monroe and she murmurs, "Almost seven."

"Russ says this place really gets in your blood," Melanie says.

"It does. Don't you think, Herbert?" I'm teasing him but he doesn't respond. Instead, he waits until I've served myself and passes the bowl to my mother. Then he says, "I've got some news for you all." My mother shoots him a look, but he doesn't see, or chooses not to. "Well, the truth is, it's a bit awkward. Thing is, it's a hard time financially. Everybody's hurting, and not just in New Prospect." He clears his throat, then says, "Uncle Sam's being none too friendly. For instance, a client of mine—poor old man—choked to death on a slice of pizza." Herbert sighs. "I hate to think of it."

"A piece of pizza?" Monnie says.

I nod at her, meaning we'll talk about it later.

"The thing is, his widow was not properly taken care of." He shakes his head and crumples up his napkin. "I haven't said anything to anyone, well, frankly, it's not anyone's goddamn business, but we mentioned it to Elena when she was here last week." He makes a loud sound against his bottom lip. "I wouldn't want to spoil your visit," here he looks at Melanie, "but unpleasant as it is." He's silent.

"What?" I ask. "Did I miss something?"

"You haven't missed anything," he says irritably.

"Herbert's been making some decisions," my mother says, folding her napkin into neat squares.

He waves across her. "I'm putting the island up for sale."

What? Two thoughts flash across my mind: Elena knew and didn't tell me. And, Herbert's doing this to provoke. He's not serious. "You're not serious," I say.

"Oh yes I am."

Russ and I look at each other.

"Sell the island? What about the renters? I thought it paid for itself."

"It's a business decision," Herbert says.

"But the island's ours," I blurt.

"No it's not," Herbert says.

Monnie is looking from one of us to the other.

You bastard, I want to say. And then I think, we so resent him, and yet his money has given us the life we have.

"Mother?" I demand. She looks trapped. It was so much easier when I drank, when I could have screaming fits and "act out." When I wasn't trying to behave myself. "Mother?" I say again. Then I notice her hand tremble as she cuts butter for Monnie's biscuit. "What about us?" I say more softly.

Herbert barks a laugh. "What about you? I'm tired of everyone thinking it's their goddamn right to be king or queen."

My mother stares at him.

"Well, Caitlin," he says, "we've been over this before. Your children have big dreams and no follow-through."

"Oh, come on," I say. "That's not fair." I look to Russ for confirmation, but he's staring at his wineglass. "Maybe we haven't done as well as you want because you haven't supported us."

"You be quiet. You don't know a thing about this."

"About what?"

"Polly." My mother's tone is warning.

"You have to face it, Caitlin. Your kids haven't made it."

"What are you talking about?" I say. "That's crazy, right Russ?"

My brother rubs the stem of his wineglass between his forefinger and thumb. He doesn't answer. All around me I feel the weight of disapproval, though I can't figure out what's going on. It's my youth all over again, except Colin is not here to bolster me.

At last Russ speaks. "I could advise you on a business plan," he says to Herbert. He doesn't look at me. "What if, for instance, you were to develop the island?"

"What's that?"

"Get a backer and then develop the island into rental units. Time share kind of thing."

I remember this from our adolescence, how his allegiance could turn on a dime, from the kids to the adults. "Yuck," I say.

"Don't be rude," my mother says.

Russ ignores me. "Mel and I visited this place out west where they filled all the cabins with art."

"On our honeymoon," Melanie says to my mother. "It was gorgeous. You'd ski all day and then head to the hot springs."

"Five hundred bucks a night."

"They had this fantastic chef who made fresh bread daily. Every room had beautiful linens and a fireplace and fur rugs."

Their vision rings around us. Even though this house looks its best in the lamplight, when the stains and nicks vanish, when the old lace curtains and faded sofa seem fresher, cozier, I can imagine it done up: the floor resanded, stained walnut or honey gold, the sofas reupholstered, the leak fixed in the roof, the noisy refrigerator replaced with a more efficient one. But then I imagine this house gone, and another larger one here, with thermal floors and solar panels and indoor plumbing, state-of-the-art kitchen. Everything clean and fresh-smelling, everything working.

I am not immune. Who wouldn't want that? I try to imagine the island with other people, people who'd spend a lot of money to come here and do—what? "What would they do?" I ask Russ. "The visitors?"

"Sail, kayak, canoe. The same stuff we do."

"Drink," I mutter.

"You know what?" Herbert says. "I don't care for your hare-brained schemes, not on my dime." He pokes at his salad. "What is this crap? I can't digest this."

Nobody can eat the greens glistening on our plates, not even me.

My mother begins clearing the table, and Melanie leaps up to help. And suddenly I feel sorry for her, stuck in the middle of nowhere with this crazy family.

"If I want your help, I'll ask for it." Herbert coughs into his napkin.

My mother brings out crackers and cheese for him. In the kitchen I spoon out some blueberry crumble for Monnie. She's too sleepy to say much, but eats obediently. "Mmm, your cooking is so good."

"These are the berries we picked," I remind her.

I drag her out to the outhouse, get her to scrub her teeth, and then pull her up the stairs to bed. She's too tired even for a book. I lie down beside her and kiss her brow. I should get downstairs, help clean up, but I'm exhausted suddenly. Monroe's breathing has slowed, lengthened. Promising myself that it's just for a minute, I shut my eyes.

I wake to silence. The cover of the paperback next to my bed has arched over completely. At the windows, a white, muffled heaviness. Fog. Next to me Monnie is still asleep. The fog is like pudding. Dressed in yesterday's clothes, I stretch my stiff limbs. It must be early in the morning.

From downstairs come the sounds of Herbert and my mother arguing. I can't hear individual words, but I imagine their argument is the same one it was all my growing-up years. "I took on three—four—children that weren't my own. Not many would have done it." Herbert could always silence my mother with that.

Suddenly I hear his raised voice clearly.

"I've worked hard all my life," he says. "I just want some goddamn peace." A stirrer clinks in his glass, then the porch door claps shut. He has taken his Bloody Mary and gone outside.

How much does the island cost? Can any of us afford it? Could we buy it from Herbert as a family? I do a quick calculation. I have no money, although I also have no debt. Russ is rich, I think, and so are Elena and her husband, Roger, though would they (I really mean he, they have the most old-fashioned marriage I know), would any of them want to spend it on the island?

Downstairs, my mother won't look at me. She stabs at the counter with a sponge. I reach to touch her back but she is stiff and moves away from me.

From the doorway I watch Herbert on the deck roll out a cigarette. His fingernails are long and yellow but always clean. He has his insistent masculine rituals: the cigarette each morning after which he uses the john, the postprandial cigar. He licks his cigarette, but obviously the paper is damp, the matches are damp, the cigarette will not light. At last he throws it down and stomps off to the outhouse.

Of course the island is impractical. At the country club, Herbert and my mother have martinis and play golf. Why would they choose to spend close to a month each summer on an island with no running water or electricity? No doubt their friends think it's a strange choice. But still.

Colin, I want to whisper. He would have understood. But would he? Maybe he wouldn't have wanted to come here either. I remember his brown tanned fingers, cool and dry. The sunny hair he wore to his shoulders. He will always be young, even when we are old.

I try to push thoughts of money and the island to the back of my mind. Monroe and I play cards, slapjack and rummy, games I remember playing with my father. When Monnie tires of cards, she draws page after page of princesses. And all morning I wait anxiously for the mist to clear and the air to dry out. Usually after foggy mornings the sun comes out and the wind comes up around 11:00. But as noon approaches I realize I have to get started painting or I'll never finish in time. So I do, though the moistness means the paint won't dry. Shit, shit, shit.

All afternoon I paint, hasty, slapdash. The fog finally lifts around the house, but too late to really help. While the paint is drying (if it will dry), I take Monnie for a walk. On our way out we pass Melanie and my mother in the kitchen, my mother teaching Melanie how she makes blueberry whatchamacallit. Mel's very observant with my mother, dutiful, almost, but I've noticed how little of her cooking she actually eats. Russ has told me how health conscious she is, that she keeps a stash of nuts and dried fruit in their room. That Melanie sees my mother as someone to impress, to make nice to, amuses and alarms me.

Monroe and I wander down the paths. The fog hovers about two feet above the ground. When you're in it, you can see about an arm's length ahead of you and no more. It's so quiet, each sound muffled, with the occasional flap of a bird shaking off its wings or the plop of some animal in the water. I realize that everything (my life in Rockhaven, for example) has been predicated on the fact that I will . . . what? Move to the island? Inherit the island? No, honestly, I think it has more to do with proximity to a place where I've been happy. More than happy. The thought of losing the island makes me feel as if I've been punched in the gut.

Through the trees the foghorn sounds, distant and mournful. I love the sound, though it gives me chills. Monnie and I are each wearing two sweaters and a windbreaker. The temperature has dropped and it is cold. A damp cold. I recall some story about a lady coming out of the sea, something about her arms and legs. Were her limbs made of seaweed? Pieced together somehow, perhaps from other broken bodies? I shiver.

At the point we hear a voice. "What's that?" Monroe asks and I tell her maybe it's a radio from a boat. But then we come upon Russ. He looks more disheveled today. His wool sweater's got moth holes along the seam and is unraveling at the waist and I'm pretty sure it's one he found in the bedroom, from when we were kids. Over that he's got a beat-up old yellow sou'wester. His hair looks greasy and tufts of it stand up straight. It's as if the island is calling him, claiming him again.

"Hey," he says.

"Hey. What are you doing here?"

"Trying to make phone calls. But I can't get any reception." He pretends to throw his cell phone into the sea. "I only get annoying artificial voices sorry they can't help me."

"Well, you'll be back on the mainland in a couple of days. You'll be able to call then."

"But I don't want to call in a few days. I want to call now." He groans. "This stupid island, so many problems. What we need is a serious overhaul."

"I like it here," Monnie says stoutly and I could kiss her.

"Do you think Herbert is serious about selling?"

"You know Herbert, always saber rattling."

"What's so urgent, anyway?" I nod at his phone.

"Nothing you would understand."

For some reason this wounds me. I think he thinks I am some hippie deadbeat, some ne'er-do-well who just has to be tolerated.

Later, I hear him arguing softly with Melanie in their room and feel a perverse pleasure. I can't tell what the fight's about, though I pause for a few moments and listen. Russ says, "We've been through this." The room goes quiet and then the sound of Russ walking across the floor, his voice soft and consoling now. Melanie must have started to cry and I can't say I blame her. Everyone's in a mood today.

If last night's dinner was explosive, tonight's is anticlimactic. We all play with my mother's worse-than-usual food except Melanie, who has a stomachache and hasn't appeared at the table.

"Mom, I keep thinking about the witch," Monroe says.

"Polly, I wish you wouldn't feed the child these terrible stories," my mother says. Both she and Herbert have large gin and tonics by their sides, and Russ is steadily polishing off a bottle of wine.

Everyone is cold and glum. It feels like we're ignoring a coffin in the other room. The island is alive and well, I want to shout. At the same time I'm thinking, is this to be my last time here? I mean, I know I'll have to come back out in a few weeks, to close up. But is this to be my last summer? And on top of that, it's our last night on the island—our last night together this summer, I think with a pang—and Monroe is clingy and whiny, unlike herself.

"M—mom?" she asks. "What about the witch? I'm scared."

"Oh, Monroe," I say, sharper than I mean to.

"Just cool it," Herbert says loudly. He stands up, holding on to the table to steady himself.

Monroe blinks, close to tears, but as a former drunk, I recognize the signs in him all too well. "Come on, sweetie," I say to her, "let's get you to bed."

Monnie doesn't object and I can't help thinking how good she is. By taking her upstairs I feel like I am bringing her to safety. On the stairs I turn to see Herbert, holding the screen door by the knob, sway backward and forward. I hasten Monnie up and into her pj's. She won't let me leave, insists I hold her hand.

Their voices reach me as Monnie drifts off to sleep. "This goddamn place is so goddamn dark," Herbert says. My mother offers him a flashlight.

"I have to take a piss," he says in a querulous voice. "I assume that's not going to trouble your ladyship." And then, a thud and Herbert's cursing. Either he stumbled or my mother threw something, I can't imagine what. I haven't seen her do that in a long, long time, but it takes me back to my childhood, to the scary house I grew up in. I forget about those days somehow, there's such a veneer of restraint and formality now.

More scuffling, thudding, cursing, a door slamming, and my mother crying out. Then Herbert bellows.

Monroe stirs but doesn't wake and I take myself downstairs.

"Caitlin!" he's calling. "Caitlin!" Herbert's cut his head open, blood is dripping down his hair and ear and into his eye. He looks truly horrific, like some ancient Greek caught in a very bad place. Tiresias?

"Get ice," my mother says. "A towel." Together we lay him down. He rears back up. I wrestle him while she dabs. I'm imagining a desperate call to Steven, a cold boat ride to town, the hospital at midnight. But as if we both have been waiting for this moment all night, we are calm and confident. My mother's sobered right up. I forgot how similar we are that way: we both behave best in crisis. She washes, we examine. Blood flows.

Herbert mutters incoherently.

"A nasty crack," I say.

"Concussion, do you think?"

"He's still conscious. Herbert," I shake him gently. "What day is it?"

He groans, then says, "Sunday. No, Monday by now."

"Who is president?"

"That asshole."

We exchange glances. I bundle ice into the cloth and put it to his head. She checks for a fever.

"Head wounds bleed a lot," she says.

I nod. "He *is* conscious."

She looks at me. "Do you think it helps that he's drunk?"

I almost smile—being drunk was what caused him to hurt himself—but just shrug. "Alcohol makes you bleed more. At least he's probably not in pain. Should I get Russ?"

"No, let's not bother them. Help me carry him in? I'd hate for Monnie to see him here in the morning."

I know this is all part of the alcoholic behavior, but I assist her. We get Herbert semi-upright and half carry, half drag him into their room. He's making nonsensical but clearly lewd comments that he laughs at. We lay him on the bed.

"Oh Polly," my mother says. "I'm sorry."

"It's not your fault," I say.

My mother starts unlacing his shoes. "I used to do this for my da when he came home from the pub." She grunts. "He did the same for his da." I barely remember my grandfather, a second-generation Irish immigrant, and certainly not my great-grandfather.

She looks at me. "Your father was a different sort altogether. Not so simple as a few drinks too many on a Friday night."

"What do you mean?" I say. I can hardly believe it. At last she's going to tell me something about my father.

"Oh, his people were fancier than mine."

"Yes, yes." I know all about the Waspy Birdswells, the way you pronounced the last syllable *well*, not *swell*. How my grandmother gave my mother lace-edged handkerchiefs and taught her how to wash them, how my grandfather corrected my mother's manners at the table. Nasty or not, the Birdswells were part of me. But I still wanted to know about my father, what he was like. He was younger than my mother, I knew that, and crazy for her, if she was to be believed. She once told me she turned him down three times before she gave in. He was handsome. Unreliable. My sister always remembers how he could go from buying us identical English tweed coats with velvet collars and matching bonnets to having no money for school shoes.

"Oh, nothing, I guess. I forgot what I was going to say." She smiles at me suddenly. "Well, but you're luckier than most. You had two fathers."

I stare at her in amazement. "Daddy died when I was nine," I say. I don't tell her that I've never thought of Herbert as a father, but it angers me that she would think that, that she feels justified in this way, that she's done her duty. I think suddenly of Monroe. Lucky her, she has two mothers. She can't possibly miss me the way I missed my dad, can she? For one thing, I'm not dead. For another, I'm damaged goods. But she knows that, doesn't she? Of course she does. "I think Herbert'll be okay. But you should probably see a doctor next week, just to be sure."

She wrinkles her nose. "I'm sure he'll be fine."

"You do realize he drinks too much?"

"Polly, that's enough." She can still silence me with her maternal authority. Between us, the gulf opens again, impossible to bridge. Such secrets, such shame, such unwillingness to speak. Then she touches my arm and smiles at me and, despite myself, I smile back. "Sleep well," I say, and leave her.

Monroe's cry is hoarse at first and, in my half sleep, I hear it several times before I can place it. Then she calls for me as if she's in pain, and I rush to her.

"Momma," she says. She's sitting up, looking wild. "I'm scared."

I get her to lie down and then stretch out beside her. I stroke her back. "Shh, sweetie, you had a bad dream."

She holds my neck, tight, pulling me in. Her warm breath smells milky. "Why can't I live with you?" she whispers.

I know from my lawyer friend Wally that Dan's got an airtight custody agreement. "Your life's with Daddy," I say. "All your friends are there, your half-brothers. Your pretty room, all your toys." I can't bear it and yet somehow I can. I begin telling her a story about her guinea pigs, how they can fly, and soon her eyes close. I, on the other hand, am wide awake now in this room lit by stars and the flickering candle. There is no electric light anywhere for miles and the night seems brighter for that, the strange outside noises almost within the room. Through the window the air comes fresh, chill, and moist. Expectant. Monnie sleeps again, one solid arm splayed out. She tosses a little, murmurs. I stroke her hair up, away from her face, then kiss her salty skin.

It's a gorgeous morning, the wind light and warm, the sun dappling the bay and the islands. As a child I always loved the morning; it seemed to bring promises of renewal. No matter what craziness went on the night before.

With the exception of Herbert, we are all standing on the dock. When I went in to say good-bye, he was holding an ice pack over one eye and looked rakish, handsome even. A swell of affection overcame me. He forced a grin and tried to make a joke, but stumbled over the words. Finally he urged me out with batlike gestures.

Now my mother says, "Your stepfather's not feeling well, he might be coming down with something."

"Mother, he's still drunk, or else extremely hungover. Either way he's got to feel pretty bad."

"Now, now, sweetie," my mother says to me, tilting her head at Monroe. "Small jugs have big ears." I try to catch Russ's eye but he's got his arm around Melanie, whose entire body language bespeaks reluctance, even her pink button-down shirt looks wilted in an immaculate kind of way, and together they're gazing at the horizon.

Eventually Steven chugs around the corner. I hug Russ and kiss Melanie, telling her it was good to see her. She tickles Monnie's chin.

"Mother, Russ," I say quickly, "please tell Steven to call me if there's a problem, I can be back out here in a jiffy." They nod and hug me, my mother especially. She clasps Monroe to her. "I'll see you soon, okay?"

Monnie nods and then we climb on board, all of us waving and waving.

"Well," I say to Steven as we round out by Swallow Island and Bride Island becomes small in the distance. Monroe is up front, wearing her life jacket.

"Well."

We stand close together and I breathe him in. Sometimes I wish I could bottle that smell. I glance at him. The wind blows his sandy brown hair. His cheeks are ruddy, his creased eyes kind. I can imagine what he'll look like in thirty years.

"It's nice to see you, Polly," he says.

"And you."

"It'd be nice to see you more. Why don't we do that?" he says in a mock serious tone.

"Why don't we?" For a minute an image of us making love comes to me and I blush. I have to look away, out over the blue waves and up at the cloudless sky. It's odd having such a history with someone. Back then we weren't really man and woman—we were kids. It would be so different now. I shiver.

"Cold? Want my jacket?"

I shake my head. Our hands are lying near each other on the rail. He picks mine up, squeezes it quickly, and releases it. We're old friends, there doesn't have to be anything compromising about this, but somehow it feels significant. I remind myself that I have to be careful, that I need to protect Steven as much as myself. A moment later he begins switching levers and fiddling about on the boat, and I head down the deck to Monroe and swoop her in my arms and kiss the top of her head with loud kisses until she squirms.

At the dock, I hug Steven good-bye, a big bear hug, and for a moment he buries his head in my neck and I can feel his lips on my skin.

"Thanks," I say, lamely, when we let go. "I'll call soon. Maybe we can go bowling."

"Shoot some pool. Bag some lobsters."

"Yeah, something fun." Monroe and I walk backward for a ways up the hill to the Green Hornet, waving to Skippy and Steven and the boat, and beyond, to our island in the cluster of purple islands out at sea.

Monnie's flight isn't until late afternoon and we have plenty of time to make ourselves look respectable once we get home. First I tackle Monnie, washing her in the tub with shampoo, soap, conditioner. I can get the dirt off, but not the tan, and when I'm done, despite her screeching over the comb, she looks taller, browner, and healthier than when she first arrived. Together we pick out a suitable outfit for traveling, something I'm sure Dan will approve of, and pack up her bag and her backpack with things for her to do on the plane. We make sure to add her collection of pebbles and sea glass from Bride Island. I tell her we'll buy presents for her brothers at the airport gift shop.

Then, with Monnie watching, I scrub the Green Hornet's high, round roof and swab her bug headlights, vacuum her, and, not content with that, take her over to the deluxe, no-brush car wash in Augusta. When we're done, the Hornet smells like a bad beauty salon.

"She doesn't look like herself," says Monroe. "And you don't either."

It's true. At the last minute I changed out of my shorts and put on a khaki skirt and a blouse, clothes I usually wear only to my job. I've put on eye makeup and even styled my hair a bit, tugging at it to make it appear longer. When I look in the mirror, I surprise myself by thinking I look pretty. Monroe stands next to me and I realize we have the same smile.

The service station next door to the car wash has some touristy-type items and we pick out stuffed toys for her brothers, a lobster and a moose. And for Chloe I buy a jar of blueberry syrup wrapped in a blueberry-patterned pot holder. We also pick out sandwiches for lunch and I get coffee to go.

We get back on the road and eat the sandwiches and when Monnie spills on her lap, I tell her not to worry. Then she has to go to the bathroom again. In the next service station washroom, I lean against the wall, waiting for her, remembering Steven's smile and how his lips touched my neck and his fingers brushed my waist, and all of a sudden I notice the time and realize we're not going to be as early as I thought. Construction along the highway means what should have taken half an hour to forty minutes has taken an hour and a half and I'm worried we're going to be late. "Shit, shit, shit," I say. "Shoot, I mean," looking at Monnie as we hurry to the car.

On the highway again we bump along, and as soon as I can I edge out onto the safety lane and floor it. A car's parked there and I have to go back into my lane, but this being Maine, no one will let me until someone thinks I've learned my lesson. Sweat slides down my back and I'm thinking, Polly my girl, you've blown it now (actually what I'm really thinking is, you fucking asshole) but I try to be calm for Monnie's sake and remember to do my deep breathing. "Keep it simple," I hiss to myself.

At the airport exit we tear off the thruway and crank past the parking lot and service roads straight to departures. I pull up in the no-parking zone, start the hazard lights, grab Monnie's bag, and yell, "Run!"

We dash along the corridor and make it, panting, to the gate, where we stand, waiting. Shyly, Monroe scans the disembarking passengers for her father.

"Write me?" I say.

She nods.

"Daddy!" She runs to a man whom I would have said was much older than Dan. My sister, Elena, drove Monroe up to Maine this summer, so it's been a full year since I've seen him. My ex-husband looks prosperous and middle-aged with his trimmed beard, his careful, buttoned shirt, his good dress shoes. I cannot believe we were ever married.

Dan hugs Monnie tight and spins her round. "How'd it go?" he asks, looking at me for the first time.

"Great. She is one cool kid."

"I saw your car racing toward the airport, thought you'd kill someone getting here."

"Ha." So like Dan to be watching me from the air. "Listen, God," I say, "She has a snack for the ride home and her bag is already checked. Have a great flight."

Their departure gate is only a few feet away and we all walk over so they can check in.

"I'll be in touch," Dan says. Clearly he wants me to go, and obligingly, I move several yards away.

At the security gates I hug Monroe again, briefly, tightly. I want to make promises that I can't possibly keep—that I'll see her soon, that we'll always have the island—but instead I brush my lips over her hair and let her go.

From the window I watch them on the tarmac, then climbing the steps to the plane. Monnie and Dan are side by side, speaking intently. She climbs and I fear there will be no last moment. But then she turns and scans the window and I wave frantically. I'm not sure she has seen me and then the next minute the plane swallows her up.

Oh, I would like to have a drink at the airport lounge. Something strong, obliterating. I consider getting coffee, but know that's a subterfuge. Just sitting at that bar is enough to get me into trouble.

I buy a big pack of gum, the kind that squirts flavor into your mouth, and then I buy another. Back in my car I chew up every single piece, one after another, until I've got a wad so enormous it hurts my jaw to chew it and I slurp and suck away and turn the tape deck up high. No James Taylor for me now. It's Janis Joplin and I know it's a cliché—I know I'm a living, breathing yuppie cliché, but I don't care. In moments of great intensity I turn to the comforts of my youth, which were, even then, someone else's nostalgia.

So singing 'bout me and Bobby McGee, the sunroof cranked way back, I head to Augusta and from there it's a straight shot out Route 1 to Rockhaven and all I can think of is Monnie, Monnie, Monnie.

Two

The kitchen counters were clean, the sink sparkling. Even the walls had been scrubbed and I was about to get to work on the floor.

"You're still here?" Stella, my least favorite manager, asked. She was a short woman with short hair and big trunklike legs.

"I'm just going to do the floor," I told her.

"I'm not paying you for overtime," Stella said. "Your shift was over, what, half an hour ago?"

An old lady popped into the kitchen, Mrs. Elliott, one of our seniors. "Oh, Polly, you're still here. I just wanted to say that my mother used to make fish chowder, and yours is even more delicious."

"Why, thank you," I said, leaning on the mop handle. "What did she put in hers?"

"Well, potatoes, of course. And milk. And she said she always used haddock, never cod."

"That's exactly what I do," I said. "Sometimes I have to use flounder. But I'll tell you a little secret. First I sauté the onions in butter and thyme."

"Ah, no wonder," Mrs. Elliott said.

Stella was glowering at me, so I just said, "I'm so glad you like it."

Another senior, an old man in yellow trousers, entered the room. "My compliments to the chef," he said.

"Thank you, Mr. Harper."

"Now, now, everyone, let's not dawdle in the kitchen. Polly here doesn't have time to chat." Stella glared at me as she ushered the old people out into the hall. "Run along, Mrs. Elliott. Mr. Harper, I'm sure there's a nice show on the television."

"All right, Stella. You going to wash my floor?"

She sighed huffily. "I don't know why you had to start this project. Where's Audrey?"

"Out of here if she's smart," I muttered. "Oh, I guess it can wait till tomorrow. Ben cleaned earlier." I put the mop and bucket away, looked around the room, and sighed. "I'll be going, then. See you tomorrow."

Stella's harrumph was world-class. Neither Audrey nor I could quite capture it, though we tried all the time.

Outside I stood for a minute by the kitchen door until I caught a telltale whiff. "Audrey?" I whispered.

"Shh," she said. "Over here."

We were not supposed to smoke here, out by the dumpster, but we always did.

"How you doing?" she asked.

"Okay." I tried to decide whether to elaborate or not. "Okay."

"You hear from her yet?"

I took a drag off Audrey's cigarette, nodded. "Just that she got back safely."

"Monroe's a sweet kid."

I exhaled. "Yeah." I was average height, but next to Audrey I felt small. She wasn't enormous, just kind of lean and treelike. Weathered, yet stylish in her way, with soft wavy auburn hair. She was my closest friend in Rockhaven. We'd been working together for three years. We were pretty different—she was eight years older than me, had spent all her life here, had grown kids of her own—but I never felt she judged me. Then I said, "I had some bad news. My stepfather wants to sell the island."

"I heard he's got a Realtor looking at it."

"Shit," I said, "I didn't know that. How'd you hear?"

"Oh, Bill's cousin." Bill was her husband.

"God, Bill is better connected than anyone I know." Trust the locals to know everything first. Between Audrey and Bill they were related to half the town.

Stella called, "Audrey, you coming back to work or not?"

"Just a minute," Audrey called back. "Yeah, and I heard of a good lawyer. My sister-in-law's cousin needed some help and hired this lady lawyer from Camden and she fixed her right up."

"Why would I need a lawyer?" I said.

Audrey shrugged, stamped out her cigarette. "I dunno. Why would you?"

"I hope you're not thinking custody battle, Miss Audrey. I mean, I'm not ready for that."

Audrey shrugged again, then smiled at me. We both watched Stella pacing back and forth in the kitchen in front of the screen door, occasionally harrumphing. "I gotta go," Audrey said. "The fire-breathing dragon'll have my head."

"Okay."

"Look, it's Bill's night out. Why don't we go out for pizza later?"

"Oh Audrey, great. I'd love to." Then I added, "Are you sure you don't have to go over to your sister's?"

"I think for one night she can manage. I mean, she's the one had all those kids."

Audrey had a huge extended family and someone always needed something from her. But she was my friend, and she knew I was in a hard spot. We waved good-bye and I got in the Green Hornet. I welcomed all the double shifts I'd had to work to make up for the weeks I took off in August, but at some point the second shift always came to an end and I had to face going home.

Monroe had been gone just over a week. For the first few days after she left, I was stunned. Mornings I walked through my little house and touched the things she'd touched. I'd hear her, I was about to hear her—footsteps, the toilet flushing, the paper towel flapping, even though I always told her not to use so much. I didn't pick up the living room, afraid I might find one of her toys or the parts to one of her games. I avoided my pottery studio because the last time I'd been in there was to teach her to make pinch pots.

I drove slowly, delaying the moment when I would get there. Since she left, my stomach had felt alternately hollow and full, queasy and empty and yet lumpish. What was in there? An old anxiety about having my tubes tied had surfaced. Had I done the right thing?

I made a left turn and then a right one and then there I was. Home. My house was a small rectangle on a triangular piece of property at the intersection of two streets. All the neighbors were in neat rows, except me. My house had been various things over the years: a vegetable stand, a mom and pop store, most recently a crafts shop. When I discovered it, the building was run down and abandoned. I hunted out the owner and negotiated the deal of the century. Now patched up and transformed, it had become a little fairy-tale cottage. A little too much of a fairy-tale cottage.

Standing in the corner of the yard I tried to glimpse the house as if I didn't live here, as if I were just walking by the blue door and windows, the pink stucco walls, the climbing vines. I loved the house but sometimes, catching sight of it anew, it embarrassed me. That I was the person who had created this vision scared me.

I walked down the path, up the steps, and across the small front porch; all my flowering plants needed watering. I unlocked the door and braced myself. The outside might be cute, but the inside was crazy. I had so much relentless creativity in the winter months, and it showed in the linoleum floor I cut through, designing a pattern of swirling leaves from the layers below (good, hard work that required precision and patience and time—lots of it), the beaded curtain separating the living room from the hall, the cupboards I'd painted, the cushions I'd sewn, the shells I'd stuck to a wall of the bathroom. I hadn't had money to refurbish, nor the inclination. I transformed and then added my collections: tiny circular saws painted with landscapes, postcards of old cars, vintage pocketbooks, and, of course, shelves of my own vases and bowls.

The need to make things leaked out of my fingers: baked goods I sold at the farmer's market, crochet bags and scarves I gave as gifts, bead necklaces and earrings. But what I liked best was to sit in my small studio at the back of the house and throw pots. I'd learned how several years ago and had a deal with a potter friend who fired pieces for me. I had worked hard, mastered various forms and glazes, and had made some money producing objects for local shops. But now that bored me. To make endless blueberries and puckered cranberries, tiny pinch leaves, whales and seals to decorate the same bowls and dishes, season after season. What I wanted was to craft something big, sculptural, funky and yet useful.

Monroe's birthday was coming up. She probably wanted a Barbie, but I always sent something I'd made. One year I painted a stone from Bride Island to resemble a turtle and attached green felt for feet. Last year I molded a school of dolphins out of clay. This year I was trying to make the kind of seal sculptures I'd seen in gift shops: a cute little seal fashioned out of periwinkle shells and glued to a rock.

On the mat inside the door was an envelope. I recognized Monnie's large, uneven handwriting and opened it at once. "Dear Mom," it said at the top. "I miss you Mom. This is us on the island." A picture of two princesses by a tree. They were standing on what looked like a green doughnut, with water surrounding it.

"Dear Monroe," I wrote on an index card at the kitchen table,

"I love your drawing. I can't wait to be back on the island." I drew a seal. Then, not caring about the waste of gas, I got back in the Green Hornet and drove straight to the post office so my letter would be in the 6:00 A.M. mail.

When I got back, I still had an hour till Audrey would meet me for pizza. I stayed outside. Golden afternoon light spread across the overgrown garden. I hadn't weeded or deadheaded in weeks. I tackled the lilies first, scratching around the bulbs and pulling out dried leaves. As I plucked the engorged seed pods, which made a satisfying snap, from the dying stalks, my sorrow began to recede. Life was becoming ordinary again.

"I'm glad to see you're doing something about your garden." My neighbor Mrs. Kerrey peered over my fence. She'd snuck up on me. Normally I avoided her if I saw her coming. All the residents on this street were tyrannized by her. Like deer, my neighbors came out only at dawn and sunset when she was least likely to be around.

"Yes," I said. "I finally had a moment."

"Your impatiens are probably already dead."

"Oh, I think they'll be all right."

"I suppose you won't have any new projects for your house this winter." She sniffed. She had let it be known, directly and indirectly, that she disapproved of my renovations, and the increased traffic they brought to our quiet little street, with people coming to see the pink house.

"I don't have any planned right now."

"You should mow your lawn."

I told her I was just about to, and reached to get some oil from one of my jugs to put in my ancient hand mower. My pots and jugs were everywhere, especially the failures I couldn't sell, old lumpy top-heavy things. They made the yard look peopled by tiny misshapen beings.

Mrs. Kerrey sniffed again. "I saw the child left. What kind of mother doesn't keep her own child?"

I stared at her.

She squinted back. "You should spend more time making a decent home." Then she added, "Your phlox has mildew," and disappeared behind her hydrangea bush.

I had begun to wonder if Mrs. Kerrey was mentally imbalanced. Nobody actually said things like that, even if they thought them. For a moment I indulged in a pure fantasy about living on Bride Island, the peacefulness that comes when you don't have to deal with anyone else. I could have chickens for eggs, several goats for milk and cheese. Sheep for wool. A garden, some fruit trees. The house would be winterized, preferably with solar panels. And I would live alone there, self-sufficient. And then the Stellas and Mrs. Kerreys of the world wouldn't be able to bother me.

Audrey and I stood outside the pizza parlor. BOILER BUST, read a sign taped to the front door. And as an afterthought, CLOSED FOR DINNER. Audrey clucked. Our choices this time of year were pretty limited. There was the clam shack, the scary Chinese place, or the fancy inn on the outskirts of town. And then, across the street from the pizza place was the bar where we could get a hamburger. Audrey glanced at me. After a moment I nodded. I felt safe with her, plus it was only late afternoon.

When I still drank, I'd gone to the Hornblower often. I'd always liked the beadboard walls painted white, the crumbling lobster buoys, the occasional boat license plate or net nailed to the wall—it seemed so much what you'd expect in a coastal town. Still, it was strange to be entering now. The door closed behind us and just about the first person I saw was a guy I'd slept with, Eddie, standing at the counter with his friend Mack. Both of them looked like they'd had a few. Easy does it, I told myself, taking a deep breath.

"Hey Polly, Polly," Eddie said. He jabbed his friend's elbow. "Polly want a cracker?"

Eddie had a weakness for dumb jokes. It was hard to feel proud of sleeping with a guy across whose T-shirt was written, I GOT UP. I GOT DRESSED. WHAT MORE DO YOU WANT?

I waved and headed for a booth.

"Oh, come on, Polly," Eddie said, craning his neck so he could see me, "you know I do it 'cause I love you."

The friend snorted.

"Love ya too, Eddie," I called.

"Small town purgatory," I said to Audrey as she sat down. "Your past crimes will always haunt you."

"He doesn't mean any harm," Audrey said. "Just a pain in my butt."

"*My* butt," I said.

"You didn't?"

"*No!*" I said.

She sighed with relief. "Sometimes you city folks are pretty advanced."

"Oh come on," I said, "that stuff goes on everywhere. Even in Rockhaven."

"I know it," she sighed again and lit up. "I hate to think what Maggie gets up to." Maggie was one of her daughters. We talked about Maggie and her boyfriend, which led to Audrey's other daughter Jen, and Jen's boyfriend, and then to Audrey's sister, the one with all the children who was getting divorced.

"I can't imagine my sister getting divorced," I said, after the waitress had taken our orders. "Elena has a huge loyalty to the institution of marriage." Elena was five years older than me, and sometimes that felt like a generation. She'd always been serious about the business of life, the business of acquisition. There was one boyfriend I'd quite liked, but clearly he was not ambitious enough for her. She'd dumped him when she met Roger, to whom she'd now been married fifteen years. Roger was a developer in Pennsylvania, and even though he was handsome and could be funny, I thought he was a cold fish.

"You don't see her much, do you?" Audrey asked. "Do you ever get lonely away from all your family?"

"God, no. Well, okay, a little. But my family is so messed up. I mean, it's not normal like yours. People aren't kind, the way they are in your family." Even as I said it, I knew that wasn't it. The truth was, I did miss my sister, and wished we were closer. But there had always been something prickly between us, some competition or lack of trust. "Elena's such a Super Mom," I told Audrey. "You know the type—not one of her children's needs go unmet, or even unanticipated. Of course, she has no life. You can imagine what she thinks about the situation with Monroe."

Then I remembered what my sister told me years ago, when I first left Dan: "Nobody is perfect, but you still have to try," she'd said. "You want to just give up. You think if you can't do it perfectly, it's better not to do it." How could she talk to me about perfectionism? But I'd also been hurt by her misunderstanding of my predicament and choices. "I don't believe in inflicting more damage just for the sake of togetherness," I'd answered.

A little later when I got up to go to the restrooms—labeled GULLS and BUOYS—Eddie followed me. "Hey Pollywog. I hope you don't mind me ribbing you," he said. "You know I'm just joking. I mean, 'cept it's true. We had some good times." He leaned up against the wall and fixed a moist eye on me. "And I still feel it." He thumped his heart.

I patted his arm. "I know you do." Then I ducked into the bathroom. It mortified me that I'd been desperate enough to hook up with Eddie.

Back at the table, our food had arrived. Audrey dipped a fry into ketchup and said, "So what's going on with your daughter?"

I opened my bag and showed her Monnie's letter. "And look," I said. I held up my wrist with the friendship bracelet she had knotted for me.

Audrey admired it, took a bite of her burger, then set her laser beam gaze on me. "So, Polly," she said, her mouth full. "Do you want Monroe or not?"

"Oh Audrey, I don't know. She's a great kid." I sighed. "I don't want to mess her up."

"Fair enough."

"But I miss her, you know?"

"Sure." Audrey nodded, flipped off her top bun and poured on more ketchup.

"But I don't think I'd ever get custody. I mean, Dan's got it sewed up tight."

Audrey covered the burger again. "You never know till you try." We chewed in silence for a bit, then Audrey said, "I could use some coffee."

I signaled the waitress over and ordered us both coffees.

"Make 'em Irish coffees," Eddie called from the bar. *Haw haw*.

"Now, Eddie," said Audrey in her cigarette voice, "Polly here doesn't drink the hard stuff." She balled up her soiled napkin and dropped it on her plate.

"And what could I offer her. This?" I shrugged to indicate the bar, the gritty street, the windswept town.

"Well, if that's what you think of us." Audrey pretended to be hurt.

"You know it's not," I said. I pushed my plate away. "But it's a serious thing. I don't know if I'm ready for it."

Audrey looked philosophical. "Well," she began. "You can always—"

Our coffees arrived. Audrey liked hers with two packets of sugar and four creamers. I took mine black. "Don't look now," she said, "but Handsome's coming."

Bowlegged Eddie in his ridiculous T-shirt approached our booth. "So yer stepdad wants to sell the island?"

"Word gets around," I said. I was glad I'd never taken Eddie there.

"Why doesn't he just give it to you kids? 'Course you might get awful snooty. You've got to watch out for these summer folk."

"You mind your own business," Audrey said. "Polly here works double shifts as it is."

"Yeah," I added, "and some people don't even work one."

"I work," he said with mock hurt.

"Sure you do, Eddie," Audrey said. "We know how hard you work."

He looked as if he might like to install himself in our booth, so we began getting up, counting out bills, and gathering car keys and purses. "You have a good day," Audrey told Eddie earnestly as we left.

Outside I walked Audrey to her car. "The thing is," I said, continuing the train of thought Eddie had started, "it's a total fantasy, but I do wish Herbert would just give the island to us. I don't know what to do."

"What can you do?"

"Well, try to buy it. Try to get my siblings to act." I shook my head. "I feel like it would be cutting my heart out if I had to part with the island. Do you think I'm crazy?"

"No," she said, her curls flapping in the breeze. "I don't."

"I can't explain it." But I felt compelled to try anyway. "I've made so many mistakes but I just feel like I know what to do there, *how* to be. It's the only place that makes sense to me. Oh, I hate talking about it, I sound so stupid. But," unable to stop, "I just feel this ability, this *responsibility* to look after the land. Plus, Monroe loves it too. I've already hurt her so much, I can't let the island go." I was leaning into Audrey, preventing her from getting into her car. Hectoring her. "Jesus," I said. "Sorry to rant."

"I don't think it's an island she needs," she said, hugging me. "Oh honey, I have to run. Don't worry. It'll work out."

After Audrey drove off, I walked through town and out onto the beach. The waves splashed high but I didn't mind. Though I had to drive almost fifty miles by land to get to Bride Island, from this point it was only twelve miles by water. I stood on the shore and looked out, longingly. I couldn't see our island, but I could see some of the others, some of the archipelago.

Audrey, Steven, Eddie, none of the locals would ever own an island. In fact, more and more fishermen were selling their waterfront property because they couldn't afford not to, property values—and taxes—were so high. People whose families had for generations been fishing these waters were losing their proximity to the sea, moving to trailers in the scrublands or woods. Yes, but, I couldn't help thinking, how would it change any of that if I had to give the island up? Instead, I could preserve the island, become its steward. That would be something to be proud of.

The suddenness of the sun setting left an empty place inside. I thought of what I should have told Audrey when we were talking about how much Monroe loved the island. I should have told her that I half hoped Monnie would demand to leave Dan and come spend summers on the island with me.

When I was growing up, my father was rarely at home, hardly interested in us. And yet I remembered his hands, his warmth, the smell of his aftershave. I remembered thinking he was the handsomest man in the world. I was nine when he died. If I died tomorrow, would Monnie really remember me? Or would she think I was just some kooky lady she once knew?

Three

One evening toward the end of September, a few days after Monroe's seventh birthday, Chloe called. I was at the kitchen table piecing together a collage from some of the photographs I'd taken of Monnie on our visit to Bride Island.

"Polly? I'm just going to leap in here. I know you don't mean to, but the letters are upsetting Monnie. She's having trouble doing her schoolwork."

"What? What are you talking about?" I tried to think. It's true I'd answered each of her letters (there'd been two since the first) promptly and had sent her a few postcards, plus a couple of cards and a present right before her birthday, but that wasn't excessive, was it?

"Here, let me put Dan on the line. Dan, pick up in the living room." A moment and then Dan was on too.

"Look, Polly, these letters have got to stop."

"Dan," Chloe said, "let me. Not stop, exactly. But here's the thing—"

"We think she's depressed."

Maybe she misses *me*, I wanted to say. Maybe that's why she's depressed. When I looked down at the photos, my daughter smiled up at me. "I think she likes being in touch," I said. There was silence on the other end. I could tell by Dan's breathing that he was trying to check his irritation. When we were married, I used to long for him to get mad, rather than always be in control. "I think she likes hearing from me. She never said she didn't." Taped to my refrigerator were all of Monnie's drawings, the messages spelled in large handwriting. "I *am* her mother," I said softly.

"It's not that we want to forbid it," Dan said, ignoring me.

"We want you to be part of her life," Chloe said.

"Could you forbid it?"

"Polly, I'm trying to work with you," Dan said. "Look, it's a distraction. She's in first grade this year and she needs to really focus. This is the big reading year."

I looked down again at the collage I was trying to assemble, the pieces of Monroe. What did I want? I had left her voluntarily, willingly, and should be grateful for whatever I got. I sighed, reminding myself to think of her welfare, to be egoless. "All right," I said. "I guess I could stop writing so much."

"I knew you would understand," Dan said.

So I cut back. But then something unexpected happened. Monnie called.

She called to tell me long involved stories about school, about friends and princesses, stories that meandered and that I couldn't follow. Her phone voice was so high and insubstantial there was barely anything to hold on to. But I did, even though my neck had a crick in it, even though it meant letting the dinner burn, or not putting groceries away, or sitting in my overcoat and wet boots just to hear her talk.

Dan called me again. "I got the phone bill," he said. "This can't go on."

"Dan, Monroe was calling *me*." I took a deep breath. "She wants to talk. I think she misses me."

"She's discovered the phone, it's her new toy."

I was silenced because I suspected there was some truth in this. I'd asked Monnie where she was when she talked to me, and more than once she said, "In front of the mirror." And I wasn't sure how much listening she did.

So we set up a new system. I was to call at a certain time, on a certain night, twice a week. And I did. I called her on our appointed nights. Both of us felt the strain of these calls, the forced conversation—what had happened at school, how her brothers were, some anecdote I squeezed out of my day—the horrible sadness that inevitably arrived halfway through. I took to going out afterward, walking along the streets of my town. I couldn't see any way to change my situation, and didn't even know what I wanted. The bars looked so inviting then. What did people *do* when they didn't drink? I thought of the familiar comforting smells, the booze, the dim lights, the jokes. The atmosphere was too close, too dangerous. I drank coffee and diet soda. I bought a pack of cigarettes and smoked. And I walked and dreamed of the time we could be together on the island.

On that front, meanwhile, there had been no progress whatsoever. I'd been trying to reach Elena for a while, and when she finally picked up the phone one Sunday, I told her it was about the island.

"I figured. But listen, I bet if we just ignore it, the problem will go away. I mean, Herbert's not really going to sell it, is he?"

"I don't know. I thought I'd ask Mother directly."

"That's brave of you."

I laughed. "Isn't it? Have you and Roger talked about it?"

"Not really. It's not exactly his favorite place. The last time he was there he had a total fit over something I forgot to bring. I can't remember now what it was. Not tonic water, not toothpaste, no! It was those wheat-free crackers."

"Elena, you really are a saint. I don't know how you put up with it."

"Oh, it's not so bad. Bark worse than his bite and all that."

It made me sad to hear her say that because I couldn't imagine how she could be happy with him. And yet she always put a good face on it.

"I don't know why it's so hard for me to think about the island," she continued. In the background I heard the clicking of her knitting needles. "It's not that I don't love the island—sometimes I think it's the most beautiful place on earth." She lowered her voice and it felt unexpectedly intimate in my ear. "I guess I feel scarred by all that happened there. The wildness, you know?" She laughed. "I didn't want to be wild. I wanted to be safe."

I knew what Elena meant, but it was more complicated than that. "I guess we were a bit wild at times," I said. "But let's not be overly puritanical. I mean, we were free too." I drew a breath. "Anyway, as far as I can tell, Herbert seems pretty determined to sell it. What I want to know is, are you interested in trying to buy it with me?"

"Buy the island?"

"Buy the island."

Elena laughed. "Can you afford it? I didn't think you had any money."

"Well, there are banks, there are loans, there are mortgages."

"Yes, of course, I didn't mean to imply . . ."

"What? That I'm immature?"

"Don't be prickly, Polly. Well," she continued, but she sounded doubtful, "I could ask Roger. But I don't think . . . I mean, it's not as if he ever goes there . . . and business has been bad. Roger's worried, and you know how he never worries. Or never admits it. He even said we might not go skiing this year."

I sucked my breath in. "Not go skiing?"

"I know, can you believe it?"

"Horrors."

Elena realized I was being sarcastic. "For us, it *is* horrible," she said coldly. "I don't expect you to understand. You don't want to live nicely."

"Oh come on Elena, don't be uptight—sorry—please!" Too late I remembered being called uptight always made Elena more so. This conversation had taken a wrong turn, as so many of our conversations did.

"Do us all a favor, Polly. Stop trying to get everyone all stirred up."

"Is that really how you feel?"

"Yes, I'm afraid it is."

"Elena, couldn't we—"

"You know what? I can't talk about this now. Missy's practice is just about to start, Marielle's got a friend over, and we've got people coming for dinner tonight. I'll call you later."

"Okay, fine." I hung up the phone in frustration. Why did there have to be so much animosity and conflict between us? You'd have thought being sisters, we would have been close.

A cold spell came. It was only early October but already winter was in the air. One morning when I was digging clay out of a pug, I heard a knock on the studio door. I wasn't expecting anyone and figured it was one of my neighbors. I yelled, "Come in."

"So do you let in any Tom, Dick, or Harry off the street?"

I looked up, my fingers slick with red clay. "Only Stevens." He stood just inside the door. "This is a surprise. What are you doing here?"

He shook his head but looked pleased with himself. "Had some errands in town." He looked around. "Never been in the inner sanctum before."

"This is where it all happens," I said. "Give me a minute." I began putting the clay back in its bag, happy to see him but also a shade wistful I wouldn't be able to work. "Can I get you something? Coffee?"

He shrugged. "I wouldn't want to disturb." Then, after I told him not to worry about it, he said, "Coffee would be good."

In the kitchen we smiled at each other. I didn't know whether to hug or kiss him or not do anything. In the end we pecked each other's cheeks and then laughed. "Sit, sit." We both pulled out chairs. "I was thinking about how you were," he said.

"Were you?"

"I'm always thinking about you." He blushed. I jumped up and put the coffee on. "Can't remember the last time I was here," he said. He was looking through the archway at the living room behind us—the turquoise walls, the painted circular saws, the nubbly orange and brown couch I'd found at the thrift store. "You've done some work on it."

I grimaced.

"It looks good. Has personality."

"Oh come on, it's the crazy house. The witch's house."

"Now Polly," he said. I poured coffee into a mug I'd made and he added two spoonfuls of sugar and a good dose of cream that I was amazed to find unspoiled in my fridge. He got up to examine the pictures Monroe had drawn, and the collage I'd made, and watching him look at the photos of the island, I felt for an instant I had my whole world about me, as if we were all together, safe.

"How is she?" he asked.

"Fine." I smiled at him.

"You're lucky to have a girl."

I nodded.

"We talked about having a third, to try for a girl, but Deb—we decided two's enough."

"How are the boys?"

"Good. They're good boys."

"It'd be fun to get the three of them together, maybe next summer. Maybe you can all come to the island," I suggested.

"That 'ud be nice," he said. He said it softly, without his usual wryness.

I imagined the two of us and our kids, camping out, weenies and marshmallows toasting over the fire. It wasn't until later, after he'd gone, that I remembered there might be no island next summer.

We sat without speaking. There was nobody I knew who was as comfortable to sit with in silence, but I did wonder why he had come. I became increasingly aware of my open bedroom door, through which my unmade bed seemed to gape.

He was playing with a placemat on the table, rolling it up and then smoothing it out. I mentioned some gossip that had been floating around the home, and he told me a story he'd heard about a local businessman. I watched his hands stroking the fibers of the mat, his fingers curling it up and then straightening it.

"It's nice to see you," I said. "We should do it more often."

He half smiled, as if he'd been waiting for me to say something like that.

"You have to go back out to the island to close up, don't you? I'll take you then."

"We'll have the whole day?"

"Well, I don't know about the whole day, but I'll do the best I can."

On the porch we hugged, close and tight. Too late I remembered that Mrs. Kerrey was probably watching. Screw her, I told myself. I felt too warm and goopy to care. Ever since Steven's wet lips had brushed my neck on the boat that day, I'd longed for him. It wasn't that I wanted him to be unfaithful or cheat on his wife, nothing like that. It was more that what was between us went back years and seemed preemptive. It was a mistake, just stupid untidiness on our parts that we'd gotten entangled with other people and weren't together.

I sighed, stepped out of his embrace, and waved good-bye.

That afternoon I called my mother. When she picked up, she sounded far away. "Hello, Mother," I said.

"I'm not going to talk about the island."

"Who's bothering you about the island?"

"Oh, Russ is."

"Really? What's he saying?"

"It's boring and tiresome. He wants me to intercede with Herbert. But I can't, you know. And especially not now."

"Why, what's going on?"

"Herbert's got pneumonia. He's in the hospital."

"Oh no. I'm sorry. What do the doctors say?"

"Well, he's obviously not in the best of health. Elena tells me he's got years left. But of all you children, she's the one who always got along best with him. She made an effort. She never challenged him the way you did." This was bait, but I didn't rise to it. "I'm not going to worry," she said. But she sounded worried.

"He'll be fine, Mother, I'm sure he will."

"Thanks for calling. It means a lot."

"Actually I did have a couple of questions about the island. Well, Herbert's plans, really." My palms were sweating and I rubbed them against my jeans. "I'd like to try and keep it in the family. I thought maybe you could talk to him."

"Haven't you been listening? I learned long ago I can't be involved. Herbert has made up his mind and I'm afraid he's quite determined."

"But why? I'm not asking him to give it to us. I'm just saying that if we took over management of it, we could probably keep it afloat, without any bother to him. Or perhaps we could work out some kind of long-term payment plan. I mean, does he really need the money from the sale?"

"Don't be impertinent."

"I'm not."

"That's enough. Polly, I will not discuss this with you." My mother had a way of shutting down, going kind of cold and hard. She was such a mix of "do the right thing" and "do without."

"But think how much it means to us."

"I said, that's enough. How's my granddaughter?"

"She's fine. I talked with her yesterday. They're studying the Arctic in school and she made an igloo out of sugar cubes."

"It just breaks my heart," my mother said. "Your siblings can't understand it, nor can I. You had everything, a wonderful husband, a darling baby, and you gave it away. For what?"

I clenched my fingers into a fist. There was so much she didn't see. This had been true all through our years growing up. "Mother, you don't get it," I said. Suddenly a surge of anger coursed through me. "I was a drunk. That is not the perfect life. You should know that better than anyone."

"How dare you?"

"Please, just tell me what Herbert says in his will, so we know how to plan—"

"I most certainly will not. Your ingratitude stuns me."

"Mother, I didn't mean it that way."

"I have to go. Good-bye." And she hung up.

I sighed. It was so complicated dealing with her. She twisted everything up. After all, other families seemed to manage to talk about these things. I dialed Russ's number. I had tried him a couple of times in the last few days, but kept getting his machine.

He picked up on the second ring. "Hi Polly, how's my girl?"

"Sucky."

"Sucky? What kind of word is that?"

"A perfectly good, descriptive word. I just talked with mother and got the run through."

He laughed. "Obviously you don't know how to manage her."

"And obviously you do."

"Well . . ." he trailed off modestly. "Anyway, I've been wanting to talk to you about the island."

"What about the island? Do you want to buy it?" I couldn't help being excited.

"As a matter of fact I do. But I want to run it as a business."

"Nobody's made an offer yet," I told him before I focused on what he'd just said. "What?"

"Let's face it, none of us can afford the island on our own. But if you come on board, I'm sure Elena and Roger will, I've already talked to them—"

"I don't understand. What are you saying?"

"I've got an idea that would keep the island in the family, but bring in some cash. You know there are all those guys who've just made a fortune and they want to enjoy the good life, but they don't want the hassle or responsibility of looking after a place? Well, I'm saying, what if we sell time-shares and set the place up as a resort?"

"You're talking about developing the island."

"Well, development's not a nice word, is it?" Russ's voice grew low, conspiratorial. "But I guess, if you want to call it developing, sure. Only we run it, keep the profits. I'm talking about maximizing it as a resource. Like renting it, only on a grander scale. Making a classy joint, a little jewel of a place. A bijou." He said the word carefully, as if he'd been practicing. "Where nice people could go to relax, do a little sailing, a little hunting in season—"

"That sounds awful," I interrupted. "I'd rather be dead."

"Don't be so dramatic."

"Herbert's not going to go along with it."

"Herbert wants to sell the island. He doesn't care what happens to it. You know he doesn't care about our family; he's never cared."

Russ's hardness surprised me, almost made me want to defend Herbert. But Russ and I had always been allies, plus I agreed with him. "My plan keeps the island in the family," he said.

"In the family," I repeated. I thought of a dozen objections, then said, "But you're not a developer. You have no experience doing this."

"I've got contacts. I've got ideas. And for your information, I've had a lot of experience putting deals together." He exhaled. "Polly, I don't expect you to understand the details. But I do expect you to be realistic. I'm not the enemy, you know."

"Russ, of course not. No one's talking enemies." I laughed. "I know you care about Bride Island—"

"Care? I *love* that place. I was *king*."

I remembered summers there, Russ, Colin, and me. Everything was possible. We'd sailed around the island in an old rowboat with a homemade sail. (Colin claimed he could navigate by the stars, though he was probably just lucky.) We'd caught lobsters and crabs, dug for clams, and picked mussels from their beds by the shore. We'd built a tree house out of driftwood and a birch bark canoe (never finished); we'd made cider with an ancient apple press. Russ had to remember those things too. Over time, our interests changed, became less boy scout, more juvenile delinquent. One summer we collected potato peelings and tried to make vodka. We grew poppies for opium—a vaguely sleep-inducing tea was as close as we got—and smoked pot and played tricks on each other and discussed all kinds of improved worlds. "Do you ever think about Colin?" I asked in a small voice.

He hesitated. "Sure I do. Sometimes."

"Me too." We were silent. Neither of us said anything, but the quiet held us.

I tried Elena again a few days later. "Has Russ told you his idea about developing the island?"

"Yeah, he called, wanting Roger's advice." Her knitting needles clicked in the background.

"Did Roger talk to him?"

"I'm not sure. I don't think so. Maybe."

"It's important, Elena. Can you find out?"

She said she would, but she sounded vague. "Anyway, I don't know about developing. The best thing the island's got going for it is its purity. It's the one place I can get the kids away from video games."

"I totally agree. I think he's nuts."

"I don't know why he wants to develop. Roger's always buying these rural places and then building new stuff on them. It's too much. Sometimes I just want everything to be quiet. Why does he always need more? But they do, don't they?" She answered herself. "It's like inertia, or entropy, or whatever that principle is called."

"Capitalism," I said.

"Still, I can't complain. It's our bread and butter. Though why we still have this massive debt . . ." She trailed off. I hoped she would go on. Any glimpse into their life was interesting to me. But she said, "What's Monnie going to be for Halloween?"

"A princess."

"So is Missy! I should really take her to see Monroe. They're only a year apart and Daniel doesn't live more than an hour and a half away. But somehow our weekends are always so busy."

"I know," I said. "Don't worry about it." I could also imagine it would be awkward for her hanging around with Dan and Chloe the whole time. "I wish Russ wasn't plotting something."

"Oh, Russ," Elena said. "When is he not plotting? But if it's anything like his other schemes, I'm sure nothing will come of it." Her knitting stopped. "Oh my God, I can't believe I forgot—did you hear? Russ lost his job."

"Not again. He didn't say anything to me."

"I think it just happened. Mother told me. Apparently it

brought Herbert back from his deathbed. He's been cackling all day."

"Poor Russ," I said.

"Poor Melanie. She's the one I feel bad for. Anyway, let's talk soon. I've got to run."

The news surprised me. Then again, Russ's news often did. Big things were always happening to him: marriage, divorce, job loss. Yet he seemed to weather it all with surprising equanimity. On the other hand, this latest development made me uneasy. I didn't like the thought of Russ with too much time on his hands.

Four

On a mild and sunny Saturday morning in late October, I drive up to Marguerite Cove. As Steven promised, he's taking me out to the island. He's already at the dock when I arrive, not in the mail boat he uses in summer, but the smaller lobster boat. The wind ruffles his hair and he looks young and fit. Indian summer has arrived and the day could not be more perfect.

Skippy leaps off the boat to lick my hand, then noses my jeans. My legs are smooth underneath them, shaved for the first time in weeks.

We chug out. My heart is beating with anticipation. I'm excited to be with Steven, to be on the island. We stand together, our jackets touching, our hair mingling. When we reach the cove, I turn and ask if he'll stay. He shakes his head no, says he'll come get me in four or five hours. I'm disappointed but it's okay. I have enough to keep me occupied.

And then, there, impaled in the grass right next to the dock, is a stupid ugly FOR SALE sign. It looks absurd, the kind of sign you'd see in the yard outside someone's small house.

"Who are they trying to attract?" I ask. "A seal?"

"Maybe some poor lobster fisherman," he says.

I jump off the boat and onto the dock. Steven shouts good-bye and I wave back, but I'm focused on that sign. By the time I've yanked it out of the ground and tossed it behind a rock, he's on his way again.

First I check the house. I sweep out the dead wasps, put down mouse poison and traps, make sure the furniture is covered, and the windows taped with plastic. I stow the rain barrels and put cedar chips in the outhouses. These acts of caretaking are satisfying, but soon done. Then I apply one last coat of paint to the windows. I don't have enough time to do them properly, so I decide to paint them shut. I know this is sloppy work, but it seems the best alternative. Early next summer I will have to chip them free. If indeed I am allowed to return next summer.

After lunch I paint for another hour or so and then, suddenly, I am done. I wash the brushes and pack up the paint cans and other dry garbage left from the summer. I lock the doors of the house, walk my bags down to the dock, ready to be hauled onto Steven's boat, then wander up to Indian Cemetery. From here I look away across the field, over the tall grass, golden now and waving in the wind, down to the pine trees ringing the shore, and out across the purplish blue bay. A bird darts through the grass and for a second I believe it's Monroe running as she had in the summer. She was so happy those days in August. I wish she were here now, smelling the sweet fruity air, listening to the rustling of the yellow leaves in the trees. We'd look for wild apples and make a pie from them. And in the evenings we'd play cards and I'd braid her hair and tell her fairy tales.

As I tidy up the graves, clearing the dried leaves away and reading the inscriptions, the sun warms the back of my shoulders. It will be warm for another day, possibly two, and then it will be winter. And winter is so long here. I think about my brother and sister, my mother and Herbert. I wonder if he will make it until the holidays. For a second, I wish we could all be here together, harmonious. Bride Island, more than New Prospect, is where we came together.

And yet, in a family, it seems, there are only a certain number of roles. Russ takes after my father, and Elena after my mother. And I take after Colin.

Before he died, Colin was wild. We were both wild—drinking, doing drugs, carrying on—and Russ, of course, paving the way before us. Herbert used to check the liquor daily, not only to keep an eye on it, but also with a sort of pride, to see how much had been consumed and to make sure there was enough. He begrudged us so much, and certainly complained about our excesses, but I know he took a perverse pleasure in our debauchery.

Wind rushes through the leaves, the island's music. As teenagers we listened to our grandmother's Victrola, scratchy records wound up and released, the dashing, stilted rhythms stirring us, transforming us temporarily into more courteous creatures. And underneath, the unspoken language of sex. Four of us, and sometimes our friends. So much physical intimacy. So much annoyance and affection. So much alcohol. On the island, we felt free. We could run. There were no dangers. But of course it *was* dangerous. What was good about the island was also what was bad. It was only us. We were supposed to need only ourselves and no one else. We were conditioned to be self-sufficient.

The night Colin died I roamed the island. The deputy, arriving from the mainland at dawn, eyed us: unslept, hungover. Russ and I sobbed, both of us still half drunk. Elena was superhelpful; she took the cops around everywhere, showed them everything. Herbert was in his shirtsleeves, his belly smaller than it is now. I wonder if he thought, There's one fewer now. And my mother was enigmatic as always. Part of me hated her for surviving it.

I flop down in the tall grasses. I want to grab the grass like a lover's hair. At my brother's grave I brush my cheek along the granite. I want to sob or shout, but I don't. Like Colin's stone, I'm dry.

Steven joins me on the rock overlooking the bluff. "I've been walking all over this here island," he says.

I smile at him, then call to Skippy, who licks my hand and bounds off. Steven sits down beside me, grunting softly. Sex is so simple when you're young. I can remember his body, the smell behind his neck. Why is he not free? As much as I desire him, I cannot willfully be involved in the breakup of his family. I sit on my hands. On the horizon, the white trails of a jet trace across the sky.

Steven bends forward, takes a strand of my hair, and tries to brush it behind my ear. I close my eyes. Without intending to, I lean toward him. Just the gentlest of sways. He comes closer, his finger touches my cheek, then my lip. My mouth opens, my breath slows. I want him so badly it is agony to sit still. I have tried to resist and he has too and maybe the truth is it makes no sense to resist, maybe—

He pulls away. "I can't."

My eyes open. I want to say, Why do you tease me, lead me on, and make me hopeful? I want to tell him I'm in love with him, in lust with him, that I want to feel his body against mine, inside mine. But "I know" is all I say. Then I turn over on my belly and yowl into the grass. "Sorry," I say when I'm done.

"The marriage thing," he says, apologetically.

"Don't."

He takes out a cigarette, offers me one, and rubs a speck of tobacco off his lower lip. For a while we smoke in silence.

"Why didn't we get married?" I ask the sky. I turn to him. "Didn't you want to?"

He laughs. "How do I know? We were kids, we weren't thinking about those things." Silence, in which a motorboat buzzes by and the jet's trails merge into cloud. "You went off to that fancy college." A gull swoops. Then, "You married someone else."

I glance at him to see how I should take this.

"Did you mind?"

He shrugs. "It was a long time ago."

I put my hand on his wrist. "Tell me."

"Of course I minded. But I knew that was the way." He smiles to himself.

"I'm sorry," I say.

He shrugs again. "And then I met Debbie."

I nod. And we sit there, together, quietly, her name between us.

Overhead, clouds pass. Leaves shimmy and flutter on the trees. If denied long enough, desire of any kind will evaporate. Mine seeps into the ground beneath me.

"This is peace," I say, at last. Both of us on our backs, our shoulders just barely touching, staring up at the sky. "And where are you supposed to be today?"

"Boat show," he says. We laugh.

"I'm so afraid this is the last time I'll be able to come here," I say. "I can't believe Herbert wants to sell the island. He won't, will he?"

"I don't know, Polly."

At the shore I say, "Hey, let's go swimming." I give Steven a naughty look. "Skinny-dipping. Take off your pants." Reluctantly he does. He is wearing black briefs, rather more stylish than I would have expected, the kind you see advertised on male models in the Sunday papers. Though he looks fine, he seems deflated somehow. He half cups his hands over his crotch as if he's embarrassed and his shoulders cave in a little.

"To spare your modesty," I inform him, unzipping my jeans, "I'm going to keep my unders on." Then I remember my own new and uncharacteristically sexy lingerie.

"I don't mind a show," he says, but he glances up and down the shore and slouches farther.

"Ha." I strip down to the lace push-up bra and boy-cut panties I bought two days ago but am suddenly confused and humiliated by the messages they might convey—I'm desperate, I'm trying to be sexy, I bought these especially (of course, he might think I wore them all the time)—but mostly wearied by all this *thinking*, at the last minute I decide not to keep them on and scramble them off. I dash into the water, aware of all my jiggling parts, and shrieking, the water is so cold.

"Aren't you coming?" I yell.

He shakes his head, looks remorseful. He is pulling his pants back on. "Not brave enough."

Steven as a young man is somehow merged with my brother Colin as a young man. Our best selves, lost there. Despite the sun I'm shivering on the way home. Steven has to lend me the stinky sou'wester he keeps underneath the hatch. I try not to be melancholy, but I feel absurd and ashamed, and to cover it up I sing songs. Steven smiles indulgently, but he's not there. I could be anyone.

At the cove I hug him tightly, whisper sorry, and turn to go.

He pulls me back. "Don't be sorry," he says, looking me in the eyes.

And really that's all I can ask for.

Five

~

A month later, Herbert was dead. When my mother called, I couldn't tell if she'd been crying. She sounded calm, distant. For an instant, I regretted not having come down to see my stepfather one last time. My mother had told me it wasn't necessary, but now I realized I'd done the wrong thing.

I managed to get time off from the home without difficulty. Audrey was always willing to switch shifts with me; people there understood about family. Even Stella agreed to give me a few days off without sighing too heavily. I called Dan and told him I didn't expect Monnie to come to the funeral, but that I wanted to tell her about Herbert's death myself. He agreed, and said that I should call when she got home from school—after she'd finished her homework, of course.

The next morning, I packed a small bag, checked that all the windows were locked, and took out the trash. Then, right before I left, I decided to call the Realtor, to tell her that until further notice my family was taking Bride Island off the market. I would tell my mother what I'd done later, when we had a quiet moment. My heart beat quickly as I dialed. I felt funny doing this without discussing it with anyone. "Hi, this is Polly Birdswell? I just wanted to let you know that my stepfather? Herbert Robbins? Recently passed away?" In my nervousness, my voice kept asking questions.

"Yes, thank you, Mr. Harris phoned yesterday. We're so sorry for your loss."

Roger? I thought. "Did he say anything about the island?"

"Oh yes, that we were to take it off the market. Of course, we'll do whatever your family thinks best. Either way," the woman added, "it won't make much difference. This is not our busy season. Don't have much call to look at islands now." She giggled slightly.

I told her we'd be in touch if we needed her services. Then, for four and a half hours, as the Green Hornet puttered down the interstate, I wondered why Roger had called the Realtor.

My mother still lived in the house I'd grown up in. It was an old Victorian, taller than it was wide, with small fish-scale shingles and mansard railings on the roof. We'd nicknamed it the Mansard Monstrosity because of those fencelike railings and because it was both ugly and forbidding. The house, which could have been comfortable, had not been well maintained. The foundation sagged and the roof leaked. Enormous arborvitaes crowded over many of the downstairs windows so that the rooms inside were dim and airless, and as always when I saw it, I felt cramped and slightly desperate.

I entered through the back door, into the small, pea green kitchen. It probably hadn't been painted since I was a teenager. One drunken evening Russ and I had tried to figure out what it smelled like: I said old sponges mixed with rules and oppression; he said boiled cabbage and failure.

The room was empty and so was the pantry and small back parlor that my mother and Herbert used as a TV room and also the more formal living room. "Hello?" I called. No one answered.

The dining room had been converted to a sickroom; Herbert

had died in there. I knocked gently on the closed door. When no answer came, I turned the knob and peered in. The shades were drawn and the room was murky, the light coming in a sort of waxy yellow. The mahogany table, broken into parts, had been placed against the wall. A basket of wrinkled apples and pears and dusty, gelatinous grapes rested on its upended surface. I could imagine Herbert, his skin pallid, coughing continuously and croaking out orders from the hospital bed that had been raised to prop him up.

At first I didn't see my mother sitting in a wingback armchair by the empty fireplace. "November," she said. "My least favorite month."

I switched on a lamp. "Mother?"

"There's more dead than living here now."

"What are you doing alone in the dark?"

"Who's there?" She focused. "Polly, is that you?"

I walked to her, touched her papery cheek with my lips. "I'm so sorry."

"We're over all that unpleasantness now." She gestured around the room.

I didn't know if she meant the sickroom, or Herbert's illness, or even her life with Herbert. I squeezed her hand. "Where is everyone?" I asked.

She sighed. "Coming." She held on to my hand, looked at me. "Anyway, you're here now." She tried to smile and ended up biting her lip. "Come have something. A glass of sherry? What time is it?"

"It's only two o'clock."

"Well, I'm having a little something." She stood up shakily. I wondered how long she'd been sitting there. I knew we should try to clean up the room for the funeral the next day. When Elena comes, I decided.

In the kitchen my mother poured out two glasses of whiskey with hands that trembled slightly. I didn't want to remind her I didn't drink so I said nothing, just let the glass rest on the old

Formica table in front of me. We sat in silence. She held her glass
with both hands and sipped from it. I felt completely unequal to
the task. I reached for her hand. Not letting go of her glass, she
gave me her little finger to squeeze.

Her eyes watered. "I hate a house that smells of death."

I wanted to ask if she and Herbert had been happy.

"It'll be me next."

"Oh no, you've got years more." I tried to smile at her. At the
same time, remembering all the old ways—the priests coming to
visit, the dark rooms, and dingy brown furniture—made me a bit
frantic. I feared getting sucked into it all again. It was with enormous relief that I heard the sound of someone stomping up the
back steps and then the door opened and Russ strode in.

I jumped up. "Russ," I said. I embraced his wet overcoat, helped
him take it off.

"Mother," he said, kissing the top of her white head. He seemed
enormous, alive. Next to him, our mother looked tiny.

She smiled at last. "Russ, dear. I poured you a drink."

He sat beside her, his big knees directed away from the table, and
now the kitchen seemed full, vibrant. He held up his glass. "To Herbert," he said and sipped. "Everything's all set at the funeral parlor.
I talked to the priest. The service will be at eleven." His stomach
rumbled. "God, I'm hungry. Do you have anything to eat?"

My mother waved at the cupboard. Russ stood and pulled open
the doors. "Hmm. The usual fine fare." He rolled his eyes at me. I
looked too: boxes of minute rice, mashed potato mix, tapioca; cans
of soup; an old packet of lentils. On the bottom shelf were some
bags of potato chips already opened and bound with rubber bands,
a box of chocolates I knew would be white along the tops, and a
half eaten package of mint-chocolate Girl Scout cookies. He selected a bag of chips. I tasted one and made a face at how soggy it
was.

"Which church?" I asked.

"St. Mary's, natch."

"Oh Russ, thank you." My mother pressed his hand.

"Herbert wasn't Catholic," I said.

Russ said, "No, but with a few friends in the right places . . ."
He upended the bag and shook the chip crumbs into his mouth.

"Your brother has been most helpful."

"Not a bit of it," he said in a big voice. He slapped his palms on
his knees and said, "Thanks for the nibbles."

My mother stood up. "I'm going to lie down."

"Do you want me to stay with you?" I asked.

She shook her head. "I'll be fine."

"She'll be fine." Russ balled up the empty chip bag and tossed
it at the garbage. It missed. "Why don't you come with me to pick
up Melanie? Her car's in the shop."

Russ still drove the low-lying orange Alfa Romeo convertible
I'd helped him pick out a few years ago, after his second divorce.

"How's she holding up?" I asked, getting in.

"Oh, terrible. Melanie refuses to drive her, says she's not safe. In
fact, I had to buy Mel a Volvo." He made a face. "A *sedan*. Melanie's
pretty conservative, actually." He looked over his shoulder as he re-
versed, then straightened the car out. "To tell the truth, it's been
hard lately—"

"I heard about your job."

"Oh, that's not the problem," he said, pulling into the street.
"That's turned out to be a great thing. I mean, technically they
fired me, but basically I quit. And hey, it's working out pretty well.
For one thing, I finally have time to exercise, not that I've really
started yet. But I bought a whole new set of dumbbells. I can stay
up late, get up late, my natural circadian rhythm. What else?" He
drummed his fingers on the steering wheel. "I got out my guitar
and tuned it up. I'm thinking about writing some songs. I'm teaching myself to cook. No, no, that's all fine."

"Good," I said.

"There *was* a woman at work, my new assistant, stupid girl, it was nothing. Anyway, Melanie got all upset about it, took it completely the wrong way."

"You were having an affair?"

"No! I was just trying to be friends. But God forbid you touch anybody these days. I explained everything to Mel but she got bent out of shape anyway."

"Is that why you got fired?"

"Of course not," he said impatiently. "Haven't you been listening?"

"Russ, now that Herbert's dead, what's going to happen to the island?"

His hands on the steering wheel tightened for a moment, then he shrugged. "We shall see what we shall see."

"We should probably talk to Mother, but I don't want to bother her."

"Yeah, I think we should just let things breathe a little for now."

We'd driven out of our old neighborhood and were heading downtown. Like so many New England towns, New Prospect was always on the verge of an economic upturn, a flowering that never quite materialized. To reach Melanie's office, we had to drive through the sparse business district with its two skyscrapers, past the new civic center and parking garage, past the hospital with the Birdswell wing, and the old bank where our forefathers had made and lost fortunes. The Birdswells were—had been—an integral part of New Prospect. Russ liked to tell people our family hadn't done particularly much, except be there first and longest. Then he always added, well, there was a bit more to it than that—they'd run the bank, started an insurance company, owned and developed real estate. Of course, their heyday had been a century earlier, and our father's branch of the Birdswell family had never been the grand one. But there it was, at the bank, the library, the academy—the name recognition.

"I always forget," I said, "what a big deal the Birdswells were."

"Do you realize I'm the last one? The line dies out with me."

"What about those cousins—Grandpop's second cousins? They must have some boys."

"They're not our branch."

I thought a moment. "I guess that's so." I looked at him. It surprised me that it mattered to him. When he was younger, in his rocker days, any obligation to live up to anything would have been seen as anachronistic bullshit. He'd had his music, his unconventional lifestyle. But maybe now he was feeling it was time to take his place in the world. "Does that stuff matter to you?"

"Well, it is a legacy. And since Colin shirked his duty . . ."

"Shirked his duty? Is that how you see it?"

"I was *joking*, what do you think?"

I didn't know how to reply so I said nothing. The silence continued for some time, and then I said, in a different tone, "Are you feeling the pressure?"

He snorted. "Only from Melanie."

"How's that going?"

"I'm doing my part. It's her body that doesn't want a baby. My little guys are fine."

"I hope you don't talk to Melanie like that."

"Of course not."

Russ followed the winding streets into the old seaport and parked outside the converted industrial warehouse where Melanie worked as a graphic designer. We got out of the car and Russ rang the buzzer outside the building. When the door clicked open, we went inside and took the elevator upstairs.

The office was one large open space. Huge windows looked out over the river. The floor was raw concrete covered with layers of polyurethane. Glossy posters advertising restaurants and hotels had been tacked over the brick walls.

I spotted my sister-in-law at a cubicle midway down the floor, her shiny hair falling perfectly over her soft beige sweater. When she looked up, she greeted Russ with a small wave, but when she saw me, she stood up and beckoned us over. She wore white corduroys cut in the latest fashion, which she, being thin, could pull off. We walked toward her and she kissed me hello.

"What about me?" Russ said. "Don't I get a kiss?"

She pecked him on the cheek and said to me, "Give me a few more minutes," and returned to her computer. Russ took me over to show me some of the cards and posters displayed on the walls. "Mel did that," he said, pointing at a menu for a restaurant.

"She's very talented."

"She's talking with her boss about becoming a partner." He nodded. "Actually, she's been working on something for me."

Back at her desk, I peered over her shoulder. She was designing a baby announcement, selecting the perfect little dingbat—a sky blue stork and bundle. She circled the computer's mouse around and around, getting the placement exactly right.

"It looks great," I said.

She sighed. "These projects are so hard for me. But I keep thinking, if it were mine, how would I want it to look?"

Russ squeezed her shoulder and shook his head. I couldn't help thinking he looked like a parody of a man who was being sympathetic. "Almost ready?" he asked, lightly drumming his fingers on her shoulders.

She flinched ever so slightly, then nodded. "Let me just shut down."

Downstairs a station wagon had parked in front of Russ's car and a blonde woman in a shearling coat was locking the door. "Russ?" she said. "Russ Birdswell? I'm Judy Williams." She shot out her hand. "Your girls and mine were on the same soccer team."

"That's right," Russ said, shaking her hand, "You're—"

"Samantha's mom."

"Yes, of course." I could tell he had no idea who Samantha was.

He clapped Judy on the back. "Samantha was the one with the amazing kick."

Judy beamed. "Well, I don't know about that. Actually it's Becca who—"

Melanie cleared her throat.

"Oh, Judy, meet my wife, Melanie, and my sister." Judy shook our hands but smiled at Russ.

"So, how are you? You still with old what's-his-name?"

She shook her head. "Divorced. And could not be happier. I'm a Realtor now too, got my license and everything."

"Did you? Congratulations!" Russ squeezed her arm and she blushed. "I'm in development myself. We should have lunch as they say."

"I'd love to."

Melanie coughed.

"Oh, but I'm keeping you. Here's my card. So nice to meet you," Judy said to Melanie and nodded at me.

Humming, Russ opened the passenger door for Melanie, then walked around to the driver's side. I slid into the backseat. "Judy Williams, what a riot. She looked good, didn't she? She held this party for the soccer coach one time and her husband got plastered. What a dick."

Neither Melanie nor I replied. Russ drove through the icy streets, away from the waterfront. It was dark now, the streetlights a dull orange. Then Melanie said, "So friendly all the time."

One of the things she did to avoid confrontation, I'd noticed, was to make an observation about Russ without specifying it was about him.

"What's wrong with being friendly?"

She didn't answer.

Russ said, "So what if I'm fucking friendly?"

"Russ," I said automatically.

He ignored me. Melanie ignored him. I minded my own business. We drove on in silence over pitted cobbled streets and up the hill to the oldest residential area of town.

"I'm sorry," Russ said. "That was out of line."

Melanie shook her head, though whether with forgiveness or anger or indifference, I couldn't tell. Russ started whistling. He glanced over at Mel and patted her hand. Almost immediately he pulled up in front of a large old Federal house. The house might have been grand once, but now it just looked decrepit. Ancient rhododendrons grew around the foundation, and on this chilly evening, their leaves had wrinkled into dark cigars. A window was blocked, another taped. But still it carried an imposing air.

"Why are we stopping here?" Melanie asked.

"I want Polly to see the old Birdswell mansion."

"Oh my. I haven't been here since I was a little girl." I peered out of the window. "What a wreck."

"Nothing a couple hundred thousand wouldn't solve. Our grandparents were the last Birdswells to live here," Russ said to Melanie.

"I know. You've told me before."

"Such a shame Dad had to sell it when they died. It's got one of the best views in New Prospect. Can't you just see this place painted and spruced up, the garden replanted?" he said to me.

"Russ?" Melanie said. "My car?"

"Righto, my lady." He headed back down the hill. "But don't you think it's got great potential?"

"Potential should be your middle name," I said from the backseat.

He laughed.

"All potential, no delivery," Melanie said underneath her breath.

"What?" he said.

Without looking at him she said, "It's strange to worship decrepitude."

"I don't worship decrepitude. Why do you think I want to redo the island?"

"That's not what I'm talking about."

"You haven't seen Polly's house; that is funky, right Polly?"

"Hey, everything works there," I said.

Melanie said, "Actually I meant our house."

Russ and Melanie lived in Westmundton, a suburban enclave about twenty minutes away from New Prospect. Their glass house with its open plan was an anomaly in that area of subdivisions and colonials. Though Russ would be the first to say—had, in fact, said proudly on numerous occasions—it was not an architectural marvel, merely in the style of one. "Modernist Splendor?" He sounded hurt.

The hostility in her voice was like a live thing. "I wish you wouldn't call it that."

"Does the house still leak?" I asked, hoping to divert them.

"What are a few leaks?"

Despite myself I laughed. It was hard not to love Russ's world-view, I thought, as he turned onto the strip of car dealerships and gas stations. Though no doubt I'd feel differently if I lived with it.

Melanie drove me back to my mother's house. As soon as we were in her car, and Russ, saluting, had driven off, Melanie began to talk. "I don't know what to do. It's been six weeks since he lost his job. I mean, what did he do today? Did he even try to find a new one?"

I told her gently I thought he'd been helping out my mother, making arrangements for Herbert's funeral.

"I just know he's going to use that as an excuse not to find a real job."

"He seems happy."

She clucked. "Yeah, right." She began imitating him, speaking in a deep, buffoonish voice. "Russ admires the passionate impulse, he loathes carefulness. Carefulness is what's hindered him till now. If everyone would just spend, not sit bound and tightwadded, there would be more opportunities and success for all. Everyone is so *puny*, so afraid of expansion. Russ *is* expansion."

I laughed. "You do him very well."

"I've heard him enough times." She broke off. "You know, I was top of my class at RISD." She seemed bewildered. "I didn't exactly expect my life would be like this." We sat in silence for a few minutes. "He has all these fantasies. I've told him my salary can't keep us afloat and he said, 'Don't you want me to get ahead? Don't you want me to be successful? I think you could be a little more supportive.'" Her tiny frame quivered, grew tinier. She had a way of retreating, like a turtle into its shell. "I said he was not the man I married, and he said," she started choking up, "he said, 'Look doll, I'm the man you're married to.'"

"That's not very nice." I really wanted to ask why she had married him. Instead, I said, "Well, you know, Russ is like that. I'm not making excuses for him but he does tend to dream big. I guess I'd thought things were better, since he married you and seemed settled in his job. I really do think he means well." I added, "Russ loves you, I know he does."

"I thought he was so together. Have you seen the brochure I designed for him? It's there, in my briefcase." I reached into her bag, which was at my feet, and pulled out a flier. On the front page it read: *Bride Island: A honeymoon getaway!* Inside were computer-generated pictures of lacy white four-poster beds and bouquets of fresh flowers. Underneath, in antique script, it said:

A *bijou* of a retreat, an old-timer's hunting lodge, classy and comfortable, a place where he hunts ducks while she has beauty treatments, and at the end of the day couples gather for the latest, most fashionable cocktails. Swim, sail, luxuriate!

"Oh my God," I said. "Is he insane?"

"My parents didn't want me to marry him. They wanted me to

marry some nice Japanese boy, a friend of friends. I can't tell them what's going on." Melanie had reached my mother's house and pulled up in front. "I keep thinking, if I can get pregnant, that might steady him down some."

I wanted to comfort Melanie, but I was feeling a little freaked out. I'd also remembered about Roger calling the Realtor in Maine. I forced myself to nod sympathetically. Then, tapping the flier, I said, "I'm sure nothing will come of it and Russ will get another job. At least, that's what I'm hoping." I squeezed her arm. "I'll see you tomorrow."

"Thanks for talking, Polly."

I got out of the car and waved as she drove off. It was just past 5:00 yet it felt as dark as midnight. I walked around to the back of the house and entered the kitchen. My sister, wearing an old apron of my mother's, stood at the sink. She was cleaning out juice boxes and wrappers from a tote bag.

"I talked to the Realtor in Maine—"

" 'Hello' would be nice. That's usually the way people greet each other."

"Hello. She said Roger had called her."

"What? Polly, we just arrived. The traffic was terrible and the kids haven't had dinner." She turned the tote bag upside down and shook it. A cascade of crumbs fell into the sink.

"Why would *Roger* call?"

"I don't know. Mother probably asked him to."

"But that's weird. And," I said, remembering, "Russ said you and Roger supported his plan to develop the island. Do you know he's made up a brochure describing the island as a honeymoon getaway?"

"He's delusional. Anyway, I haven't heard a word about this. I'm sure if Roger were involved, I would know. I mean, I think he gave Russ some general advice, but that's it. And Roger may be many things, but he's not delusional." She folded up the tote and took off the apron. "Anyway, he'll be here tomorrow morning, you can ask him then."

"Yeah, I guess you're right." I smiled at her.

"Look, Mother's resting, I have to feed the kids—of course there's nothing in the house, what was I thinking? Come with us, we can talk in the car."

Half an hour later, Elena said, "I should never have done it. I should have been strict. Not strict, *firm*."

The car inched forward. We were at the second of the three fast-food restaurants to which Elena had agreed to take her kids—one for each child—and we were waiting for french fries, the only food Marielle, the youngest, would eat (and only from Chicken Shack). Roge, pronounced *Raj* (and he was a bit too like a maharajah, I privately thought), was already eating, which meant Missy would be last. Again, Elena whispered. She tried to be fair, to rotate the order of restaurants, God knows she tried to be fair. That was how she got into this mess. She should have been firm, insisted that they choose only one restaurant. "Just a few minutes more, baby," she called to Marielle.

"Mom, I'm hungry." Missy said.

"I know, dear. Ask Roge for a bite."

"Mo-o-om." (Roge seemed to have perfected the three-syllable cry of injustice.) "I'm *starving*."

Even though she would never admit it, I knew Elena had fed him first because he was a growing boy. "Just a bite, Roge, won't kill you," I said.

"Gross. Cooties," Melissa said.

"If at all possible, I'd like to stop by the yarn shop—they have the prettiest colors." Absentmindedly she patted her yarn bag, which I was holding in my lap.

"What are you working on?" I asked.

"A sweater for Roger."

"Doesn't he have like twenty of your sweaters by now?"

"Actually, only eight. No, ten. Maybe twelve." Elena sighed, moved the car forward until we were at the open window.

"How y'all doing?" said the girl behind the counter. "What can I get you?"

Elena ordered the fries and a cup of coffee, black with two sugars. "I'm not supposed to drink caffeine anymore," she told me. "My doctor warned me when I started getting regular migraines, but I just crave it." She paid and thanked the girl.

"Do you do this every day?" I asked.

"No! Not every day. Maybe twice a week. Roger wants me to get a full-time nanny, but how can I explain—"

"Mommy, please, I'm hungry." Missy again.

"—that I like doing it myself. I know, darling." Amazingly, Elena's voice was soft. She never seemed impatient. "Just a minute more."

"Mom, can we go back now?" Roge said.

"Sweetheart, we're just getting Missy's dinner."

"What's the use? She never eats anyway."

"I do too."

"Yeah, right. Mom?" Roge asked after a minute. "Do you think ten dollars to a billionaire is like one dollar to Dad?"

"Mmm. Maybe." Elena was turning now. "It's odd to be back here," she said. "I wonder sometimes, what if we'd never left?"

"We went by the old Birdswell house this afternoon," I told her.

"That old place on the hill? It's a dump, isn't it?"

"That would mean a hundred is like a ten, a thousand is like a hundred, right Mom?"

"That doesn't stop Russ from fantasizing."

"Poor Melanie," Elena said.

We arrived at the drive-through of Missy's favorite health-food chain. While we waited to order, Elena drank some of her coffee.

"Two sips, that's all." She gulped, then opened the car door and poured the rest on the ground. She saw me looking at her and blushed. The car ahead moved and Elena pulled up so that Missy, who was sitting on the left-hand side, could order from the speakerphone. She lowered Missy's window and said, "Go ahead."

"A hummus wrap, no onions and extra cucumbers, and a seltzer with lemon."

"She always orders the same thing, and she usually eats some of it, at least a few bites," she said to me in a low voice.

Elena paid for Missy's wrap and passed it back to her.

"Was Daddy really in debt when he died?" I said. "I've always heard he was."

"Mother told me there are things you just deal with. You don't dwell on them. Though God, when I think about our debt . . ." she trailed off. "Roger says I worry too much."

"So, ten thousand would be like one thousand to us, and a million would be like a hundred thousand. Right?" Roge continued.

Elena focused on her son. "Roge," she said gently, "it's not nice to talk about money."

"Why not? Dad does."

I hiccuped.

"I'm a bit ambivalent about Roge's money lust," she said to me in a low voice.

"What?" Roge said. "What are you saying?"

"I'm just telling Polly how thrifty you are, and you've got this great focus and ambition and mathematical ability."

Roge nodded.

"And yet," she said to me softly, "Is it quite nice in a child? Roger of course eggs him on. One time I took him to the bank—"

"Are you still talking about me?"

"I'm telling Polly about the time I took you to the bank—"

"I was seven years old, and I'd saved a butt-load, like two hundred bucks, I mean it seemed a lot then because I was really little.

The bank lady said, 'And what are you going to do with all that money, young man?' And I said, 'Start a CD!' " He laughed.

"I was so embarrassed," Elena whispered.

"Well, isn't saving better than spending?" I said.

Roge burped loudly.

"Gross," Missy said.

"After all," I continued, "Roge isn't greedy for things, right? Just money."

Elena frowned at me. "Are you eating, Melissa?" she called back. "You said you were hungry."

"I had a few bites."

"Rogie made a bu-urp," Marielle sang. She threw a french fry at him.

Elena looked at me apologetically and shook her head, but fondly. I knew she was proud of her three, their blond heads in a row, the backseat filled with the life she had created.

"Roge looks a lot like Colin," I said.

"Do you think? No. God, I hope not. I mean—"

"Don't worry," I said. "He's nothing like him. Look." I pointed at a woman crossing the street in front of us. She was pale and blonde going gray. She had three rambunctious light-haired children hanging off her, and one in the stroller in front. What was striking was how vibrant the children were, and how pale and faded, how husklike the woman.

Elena thought I meant the children. "They're cute, aren't they?"

I nodded. My head ached. I felt like I'd been around too many people.

Nobody really ate dinner. I heated up a can of soup and tried to make my mother eat. She said she wasn't hungry. Elena claimed to have finished the kids' meals, so I ate a few spoonfuls of soup and poured the rest in the trash. I left my mother in the wingback chair while Elena dealt with the kids, and went up to my room. Later I was sprawled across the bed, rereading one of my favorite children's books, when Elena knocked at the door. "Can I come in?"

"Sure," I said.

"Oh, I remember that book. I used to love it. So cozy the way the children decorated their cabin in the woods."

I rolled my eyes. "I liked it better when they were exploring. The kids all asleep?"

She nodded. "Finally."

"I heard you singing the old songs." They were these mournful Irish ballads our mother would sing us when she was in her cups, though we didn't know it then. "I can't believe you do that—to me it's like spoon-feeding children drama and melancholy."

She sat on the bed and pulled out her knitting. "Oh really? I love them." She began humming, then sang:

> I walk adown the meadow,
> Where none can see me.
> The silver moon is shining
> Beyond the branches breaking,
> My heart would ease its aching
> If thou were near me.

She did have a pretty voice and it reminded me of being a child in this house, in this old bed. "It's so cute, Marielle asks me to sing 'Heart Breaking.' That's what she calls the song." She knit a few rows, then glanced up at me. "Can you keep a secret? I think I might be pregnant again."

I stared at her.

"I'm not absolutely sure but I'm a week late."

"What does Roger say?"

"He doesn't know yet. I'm actually a little nervous to tell him. He'll be fine, I'm sure," she added quickly.

"Wow," I said. "Congratulations." I didn't know how I felt. I wasn't jealous exactly, and yet part of me was stunned. "How very life-affirming of you," I said.

She laughed. "Nuts, you mean." We sat in silence for a bit and she kept knitting. She looked both pretty and tired. Little frown lines appeared when she had to concentrate on a tricky stitch. Then she said, "Do you remember that conversation we had years ago, when I tried to reassure you that you could be a good mother? 'You don't have to be perfect,' I said. 'You just have to do it. You just have to be there.' "

I nodded.

"Well, I guess I truly believe that."

"But you are a good mother," I said.

"You're nice to say so." She shook her head. "I don't know. Each pregnancy is a new chance. With each child there's the possibility that this time I'll get it right. Often with Marielle I still feel it." She grimaced. "But with Roge and Melissa, I have to admit, I worry it's a bit late. The most I can hope for now, I sometimes think, is damage control."

"Elena, don't be so hard on yourself. That's crazy. I mean, look at me."

"If you put it that way. How you could give up your only child I'll never know."

Too late I saw the trap she'd laid for me. We'd been getting along so well too. "I hope you won't ever have to know," I said as lightly as I could, and picked up my book.

There was an awkward pause. She should have apologized, but she didn't. She knit a few more rows. "I don't know when Mother had the time to make up the beds with the good Irish linen."

I didn't answer.

She counted stitches, then said, "It's going to be really hectic tomorrow."

"I'm pretty tired," I said. "I think I'll try to sleep."

"Okay." She hesitated. "It was nice to spend time with you today, Polly." She patted my feet. "The kids enjoyed it too. You seem more," she wrinkled her nose, searching for the word, "stable."

After she left I lay awake for a long time. I was exhausted but I couldn't sleep. Tomorrow would be hard. It was already hard. A whole cupboard of drinks sat in the room directly downstairs and because I could visualize them perfectly, I made myself think of Maine, of my island and my daughter.

The next morning the kids watched TV in their pajamas while Elena and I tidied up the house. We vacuumed and swept and made sure the front door wasn't stuck. Russ and Melanie arrived, both looking scrubbed and sober in their good dark clothes. Despite the strained atmosphere, the sadness of the occasion, there was something festive and exciting in all of us being together.

"How's your mother holding up?" Melanie asked.

"She's being very brave," Elena said. "I told her to go lie down for a few minutes."

"Where are the kids? I'll go say hi."

"In the TV room. Actually, can you tell them to get dressed, that would be a huge help."

"You know what's weird?" Russ said, as the three of us walked into the kitchen. "I keep thinking about Daddy. Do you realize he was forty-two when he died?"

"Only forty-two," I said.

"My age, for Chrissakes." Russ shook his head.

"I think about him too," I said.

"A man in his prime." He seemed mystified.

"Russ," Elena said gently, "We've got to get organized." She looked at her watch. "We don't have that much time."

Stacked on the counter were plates of sandwiches my mother

must have made early that morning, deviled ham and egg salad and fish paste, the edges curled, the contents dry and brownish. I was scared to offer them to the guests, not sure whether they were safe to eat. I felt guilty then, because I hadn't even thought about the food. I'd assumed we'd have it catered.

"What are we going to serve everyone?" Elena asked. "You don't mean Mother made everything?"

"Who was in charge?" I asked, knowing the answer. "Why didn't we get it catered?"

"How bad can it be?" Russ asked.

"Pretty bad," I sad, automatically lowering my voice, even though my mother was upstairs.

"Don't worry, we'll pull it together." He jabbed my upper arm with his fist, just the way he used to do twenty years ago, and I couldn't help it, I grinned at him.

Elena rolled her eyes. "Must you regress?" she asked.

"Come on, Sis, we've got a crisis on hand. Or not," Russ said as he held open the door to the pantry where stacks of cardboard boxes from the liquor store stood. "We've got booze, nuts, and finger sandwiches. I think we'll be okay."

Elena and I exchanged glances. Then she seemed to come to a decision because she shrugged. "I'm going to get ready."

"I guess I will too," I said, though for me that only meant putting on a little lipstick.

"Missy?" my mother called, coming into the kitchen some time later. She moved slowly, and I was struck by how old she seemed. And yet she was beautiful, with her silver hair combed and tucked under a small black veil. "Have you seen Missy? I have her hair ribbon."

"I'll find her," I said, taking the ribbon.

Melanie had rounded up the kids, now dressed in their church clothes and standing in the foyer. I secured Missy's ribbon. Marielle's sweater sleeves were askew, so while Melanie fixed

Roge's tie, I helped Marielle straighten them out. Russ and my mother made their way from the kitchen and we all put our coats on. The front doorbell rang and there was Roger, looking thin and elegant in a long black coat. He chuffed his children, who clustered round him saying, "Daddy, Daddy," and pecked first my mother, then Melanie, then me on the cheek. He shook Russ's hand and down the stairs Elena was coming in her high heels, clipping on an earring as she did so, a gesture I'd seen my mother make a hundred times. "Perfect timing," she said to Roger.

Just as he was about to kiss her, his cell phone rang. He frowned at the caller ID but did not answer. "You'll turn that off in the church, won't you?" Elena said.

"Uppie," Marielle said, holding her arms out to her father.

"You're too old for that," he said, but picked her up nonetheless, her dress spreading out across his suit. Russ offered my mother his arm and she took it and slowly we progressed outside. Looking at the two of them on the path ahead of me, I thought about Colin, how he should have been on my mother's other side.

The church was large and drafty, constructed from chunks of brown, rough-hewn stone, the stained-glass windows too dark to pass much colored light. Of all of us, only my mother was still Catholic, and her church had always seemed alien.

The priest droned. I wanted to feel something, but I couldn't. I focused on the bouquets of lilies and roses. Why did we come into this world? Elena was wiping an eye. Could she really be crying for Herbert? She had told me once that for her it was a relief when Mother married Herbert—there at last was security. Roge and Missy stood dutifully still, though Roge's eyes roamed the ceiling and Missy stared at a fingernail. Only Marielle squirmed. Roger tapped her and she stopped. The five of them looked the picture of the perfect family: handsome, affluent, contained.

Melanie stood beside Russ, her hair pulled into a bun, her face unreadable. Russ had bowed his head. His posture suggested a man of importance, a man who was somber and thoughtful, but I could see his hand in his pocket stroking his cell phone. I remembered the way he'd looked at Colin's memorial service. He'd come back from college, driving up in the babe-mobile, as we'd called his red car, his long hair curling over the lapel of his jacket. He had read something at the service—a poem, or maybe a passage from a book. I couldn't remember. We'd been stoned, of course. We'd had to share a bottle of eyedrops to disguise the redness. Though we'd been weeping too.

My mother stared straight ahead with pursed lips. She looked more resigned than old now. Girded for battle. She was such a mystery to me. I could not believe she loved Herbert, really loved him, and yet she had lived with him for over twenty years.

There were a number of other mourners, men who had worked for Herbert, couples they'd known at the country club, a few family retainers, some of my mother's family—respectable, but not a large crowd by any means. When we stepped outside the church, a very young photographer snapped our pictures. Elena slipped her arm in mine. "My God, it's like *Bonfire of the Vanities*."

"He must have come to the wrong funeral." I whispered. "I mean, don't you think?"

Elena nudged me and suppressed a giggle. Roger asked the kid for ID and he identified himself as being with the *New Prospect Courier*. Russ, in his long, navy coat belted at the waist and looking as if he were used to giving speeches on the steps of city hall, pressed his hand. "Thank you for coming. Please let my mother and my family grieve for my stepfather in peace and privacy."

He then supervised the bearing of the coffin, herded us into the cars he had hired, and led us to the cemetery, all of us in dark coats and somber clothes, dark glasses on our faces, all of us stony as we stood around the grave as the priest read the last few words, as we threw flowers that landed hard in the open-mouthed grave.

Back at the house, Elena and I pulled damp paper towels off the sandwiches and set out bowls of nuts. Russ was everywhere. He had grown larger, become imposing. I saw him with the guests, patting their shoulders, filling their drinks. At one point I saw him chatting with the priests, who were laughing, and then later charming our tiny great aunt. I tried to mingle, chat with my mother and Herbert's old friends, some of whom had known me since I was a child, but I felt overwhelmed. There was too much booze, too little air. I felt claustrophobic, displaced. Seeing Elena's children darting under the arms of the grown-ups to get more ginger ale gave me a pang for Monroe. I missed her fiercely.

Upstairs, by the hall phone, I thought about calling her, but what was the point? She was my daughter, not my confidante. In my mother's room I examined the photos on the desk: Herbert in a lounge chair; Russ, looking young and gorgeous, leaning on the prow of a ship; the four of us as children, goofing on the beach; another of Colin and me with Steven.

How I wished Steven was here. He'd been here only once, for Colin's memorial service. He'd worn a jacket and tie and looked ill at ease. Afterward I'd taken him up to my mother and Herbert's room, which seemed the only room off-limits from the invasion of friends and cousins, to have sex with me. He'd been reluctant but we'd ended up on the floor alongside one of the twin beds, next to the wall. We kept our clothes on, his bare buttocks pumping underneath his tweed jacket until finally he'd pulled out. After we were done, we lay tight against each other and he kissed my hair over and over.

We were still on the floor when my mother entered the room. She stood at the door awhile, not seeing us, and I thought she was going to throw herself on her bed and weep. Instead, she crossed the room. We heard her sit at the small spinning stool, her legs shushing under the filmy dressing of the boudoir table. She picked up her hairbrush and put it down. She popped off the top to her lipstick. I don't know whether she applied it to her lips before she let it fall to the table.

One of us must have made a noise, because she started. I tried to keep Steven beside me, but he stood up and so I rose to stand next to him.

"Colin?" she said, with a look of hope and wonderment and even of tolerant scolding at his mischievousness that I would never forget.

Almost at once she realized. "Oh, Steven. Polly." And her face returned to its mask. "You'd better go back downstairs," she said. She picked up the lipstick, which had been bent, and dabbed it on. "Oh, and Polly? Tuck in your blouse."

Did she know what we had done? She must have, but she never said anything.

After Colin's death I was so full of rage, I hated everybody. Russ, my sister, my mother, Herbert (him most of all), all the boys I slept with in college. For one thing, they were all alive and Colin wasn't. But I also hoped they could save me, and none of them could. Colin had been the one person I felt safe with. In him, I saw a reflection of myself. We contained each other. Even before he died I had started drinking pretty heavily—we all did, except Elena—but afterward there seemed to be no reason to stop. It was the same with the boys. I was not a virgin before that summer, but afterward men were fuel. Fuel and distraction both. But with Steven it was different.

He should have come, I thought now. I needed him. Calling him suddenly seemed the most logical thing to do. In the hallway I picked up the phone and dialed.

Debbie answered.

"Hello, it's Polly. Is Steven there?"

"No he's not."

"Do you know when he'll be back?"

" 'Fraid I don't. Care to leave a message?"

"No, no, it's okay."

Stupid, I told myself after I hung up the phone. In the bathroom I refolded all the towels so that the monograms hung straight. I wiped off the sink with a piece of wet toilet paper and then I sat on the rim of the tub and held my head in my hands. Why hadn't we stayed together when we had the chance? Everything would have been different.

On my way downstairs I glimpsed Russ and Roger conversing in a corner of the living room. Russ leaned forward and was speaking intently. Roger stood back on his heels, his hands behind him. He seemed to be concentrating hard, had bent his head down to listen, and was nodding. I was determined to talk to them, to find out what was going on, but at the bottom of the stairs I got stuck between two neighbors and a cousin of Herbert's, all of them wanting to see and touch me. By the time I'd disentangled myself, Russ and Roger had gone.

I checked the dining room, where my mother was sitting with some of her brothers, the TV room, but only Elena's kids were there, looking bored, and then the kitchen, without spotting them. I knocked on the downstairs bathroom door and bumped into Elena coming out. She'd been crying. "Oh, honey." I hugged her. "I guess you were really close to Herbert."

She shook her head, looked sheepish. "No, it's not that. I'm an awful person."

"What? Why?"

She shook her head, tears still leaking from her eyes, and pressed a tissue to her blotchy and red nose. I steered her back into the bathroom and shut the door behind us. "Roger will hate that I've been crying."

"What's happened?"

"Oh, I'm just so stupid. I told him I thought I was pregnant. I thought he would be excited."

"And he wasn't."

She started to sob. "He said he needed another child like he needed a hole in his head."

"Oh Elena," I said, rubbing her back. "Maybe he just needs to get used to the idea."

"I know. I'm sure that's it. But he said, 'Did we even have sex then?'" Her face wrinkled up. "I told him I didn't have sex with anyone else." She laughed a little and then she sobbed. "I don't understand why he wouldn't want another baby. They're the best part of us."

Someone knocked on the door. "Just a minute," I called. "Look, it's a stressful day. Wash your face, you'll feel better. It's going to be fine."

"People always say that, but what if it's not going to be fine?"

I had no answer for her. We came out of the bathroom.

"I'm sorry for being maudlin," she said.

"I hate to bring it up, but I don't suppose you had a chance to ask Roger about calling the Realtor?"

She shook her head. "I'm sorry, I forgot. Let's go find him. He's going to head off with the kids pretty soon." Suddenly she looked young and hopeful again.

I followed her through the rooms. We kept getting stopped and having to exchange banalities. One uncle had heard I lived on the island, and I had to explain it was just Rockhaven. Someone else wanted to be sure our mother would be okay. The mood had shifted. Jackets and coats were coming off, serious drinking beginning. Finally we pushed through and found Roger, alone, in the kitchen.

"It's the sisters," he said. "The Witches of East Prospect. Have you turned the taps off?" he asked Elena.

She blushed. "Polly wants to ask you some questions."

He pretended to be frightened, then winked at me.

"Polly says Russ wants to develop Bride Island. Have you heard anything about that?"

"Yeah, he asked my advice."

She glanced at me. "What did you tell him?"

"I told him it might make sense from a financial perspective and that I could give him some pointers, set him up with some contacts if he wanted." His cell phone rang again. "Goddamn it."

"Who keeps calling you?" Elena asked.

"Business."

"It's Herbert's funeral."

"It's still a working day. But okay, okay." He pushed some buttons and put the phone away.

"Why did you call the Realtor in Maine?" I said.

"What is this, twenty questions?"

I stared at him, at his handsome, regular, too-perfect features.

He spoke as if to a very slow child. "I called because one of my contacts is potentially interested in backing a venture. Most likely nothing will come of it, but—"

"You didn't tell me *that*," Elena said.

"There's nothing to tell. That's all there is, truly. Anyway, the person you want to talk with is Russ." He glanced at his watch, then back at Elena. "I'm thinking it's time to get the kids out of here."

"Okay. All their stuff is packed, but Marielle needs to get her doll from upstairs." Elena started going over the minutia of their baggage so I said good-bye and left them. Russ was still nowhere to be found and now my mother and some of the Irish uncles had begun singing the old ballads, their arms around each other, their thin, high voices wafting tremulously.

I was smoking furtively in a corner of the terrace behind the house, the piazza Herbert had always called it, when Russ came outside.

"There you are," he said. "Give it." He held out his hand for my cigarette.

"I thought you quit?"

"I did," he said as he exhaled. "Oh, that's good."

"Russ," I said, "can we talk about the island?"

"You know what? You don't need to worry. I've got it all sewed up. Nobody needs to worry about a thing."

"You've been drinking."

"Just a few. I didn't quit drinking, remember?"

"Oh yeah, it was just cocaine."

"Cool it."

"What do you mean you've got it all sewed up? Just what is your plan?"

"When the time is ripe, my young friend, I'll tell you."

A wave of irritation washed over me. "What are you talking about?"

"Look, let's just say I'm in charge. You know Daddy never wanted to be some little person doing little things. He always wanted the big break, the big deal. He'd understand me, don't you think? He'd approve." He took another drag, exhaled noisily. "It's just as well I quit my job. Someone needs to look after this family."

"Russ," Elena called, "people are leaving and want their coats. What are you two doing, anyway?" She came outside. "Are you *smoking*?"

"Come on, have a puff," I said.

She took it and coughed. "Jesus, I can't believe I did that."

"Sin," I said.

"The uncles have been breathing in my face and one of them just pinched me."

"He's still got it," Russ said.

"Russ has had a bit too much," I told Elena.

"I want to get lai-aid," he sang.

"Russ, snap out of it," I said. "Where's Melanie?"

"She went home. Come on, don't you want some?" He began jiggling about and then broke into a chorus of "Don't you want me baby?"

"Don't be weird," Elena said. "Go lie down, okay Russ? Sleep it off." She glanced at me. "I'm going back inside."

"Russ," I said as gently as I could. "You've had too much to drink. I'm going to take you home."

He belched and staggered against me. I wondered if he would puke on me. The thought of that made me want to puke, and suddenly the fatigue of the day set in. I maneuvered him back through the living room and the front hall, around the visitors, and then outdoors again and into my car. We drove through the winding suburban streets of Westmundton, streets leading nowhere except more streets and cul-de-sacs, those terraces and lanes, Russ directing me, occasionally drumming his fingers on the dashboard, and then we pulled up outside his house. From the street you could not tell that the walls of Modernist Splendor were made entirely of glass; in fact, it was impossible to see anything other than the nine-foot-high black barricade surrounding the property. It looked like a prison, even though Melanie had tried to soften the effect by hanging a Japanese lantern next to the doorway.

Inside the black wall was a kind of covered walkway. Russ motioned me to be quiet and stand beside him. Together we stared through the wall of window. There was the large bare living room, furnished only with black leather couches, an orange shag rug, and designer lamps. Farther back, in the kitchen area, Melanie sat at the lacquered table. Her long dark hair was pinned in a bun and she wore a simple black kimono.

Russ groaned. "She's got her period. She wears that the day it starts. Well, at least she's not pregnant."

I clucked.

"I can't go in there. Take me somewhere."

"Where, Russ? I can't do that. This is your home."

"You don't understand. She's so conscientious—she doesn't drink or smoke, she only eats healthy foods, takes all her vitamins. We have one whole cupboard of nothing but vitamins." As we watched, she shifted her posture slightly, pushed a wisp of hair behind her ear. Her face was pale and looked scrubbed. He sighed. "She hates being touched when she's bleeding."

Somehow the boundaries I usually erected so carefully between me and my family had become porous. I said, "Russ, I don't need to know this."

"Okay." He took a breath. "Time to turn on the charm."

I watched him let himself in, saw Melanie look up and look away. He weaved, misjudged the distance, started to stumble. He said something. She said something back. He blundered over to her. She flinched, then started to cry. I wanted to cry, looking at the two of them. Why couldn't they just hug each other? Why was it all so complicated?

Later that night, when everyone had gone except two uncles who dozed in armchairs around the TV, I walked down the hall past my mother's room. The door was shut but she was arguing with someone—the words were indistinct, but the other voice was male. It sounded like Russ. I was surprised. I hadn't expected to see him again today. After a moment I knocked and pushed the door open. "Hi," I said. "What's going on?"

My mother ignored me. "I'm sorry, that was Herbert's wish."

"Herbert was a fool," Russ said. "If he'd listened to me from the beginning—"

"Russell Birdswell, you take that back. How can you, speaking ill of the dead and him only newly buried, his grave still fresh and him not cold in it."

"I'm sorry, Mother."

"When your father died we had nothing. We would have starved."

"Well, let's not exaggerate," Russ said.

"Polly, where is your sister? We owe everything to Herbert, and don't you ever forget it."

"Of course not," Russ said. He shot me a grimace, and again I was reminded of how many times we'd been allies growing up.

"When did you come back?" I asked him.

He waved at me like it wasn't important. He seemed remarkably sober.

"Everyone is maligning Herbert," my mother said. She put her hands to her ears as if to cover them. "I can't stand it." This was starting to feel like one of the tirades of my youth, the dressing-downs we'd occasionally receive.

"I wasn't maligning Herbert," Russ said.

"This family. Frames and frames of photos and they all tell the lie, every one of them, laughing, children, smiling, tipping back and forth." She was rambling. But then, surprisingly, she focused. "And you, Polly, what have you done with your life?" Her eyes teared up. Suddenly I realized that my mother was very drunk. She'd been drinking steadily all afternoon and it had crossed over from being manageable to being too much. "You shouldn't have to live the way you do."

Easy does it, I told myself. "My life is fine. I'm not complaining."

"It makes me sad. It just seems so pitiful." She paused. "I wish you didn't have to work that terrible job."

"What terrible job?"

"You know, cooking for those old people. It's really beneath you. Herbert and I used to feel so embarrassed."

"I'm sorry you feel that way. It's only my *life*."

"Mother," Russ asked. "Have you given any thought to what you want to do with the island? Because I have a plan I'd like to share."

"Not this again," I said.

"Well, first off, we turn the old house into a lodge, and build a series of guest cottages, each with running water—"

"I won't go there anymore," my mother said, "not without Herbert. What you children don't understand is that no one is happy. You expect so much."

"—then, to the north, a swimming pool, nothing fancy—"

I said, "Of course you'll go again."

My mother held up her hands. "And another thing. I've decided to give Polly the island. Elena will have my jewelry, and Polly the island." She held out her hand to cup my chin. "Then maybe you won't have to work the way you do."

"Oh Mother, that's fantastic." I laughed. "Though if you give me the island, I'll probably have to work double shifts till I die to be able to afford it."

"Oh," my mother said, "I didn't realize—"

"You can't do that. You can't just give one piece of Herbert's estate to only one of your children." Russ cleared his throat, stroked his cell phone. "Mother, you're upset. Don't do anything rash."

"I'm joking," I said quickly.

There was a half knock at the door and Elena came in. "Here you are. I finished the dishes." She looked around. "What's going on?"

"Mom is talking about divvying up her estate," I said in a whisper, suddenly reminded of other times she had promised me things. "She wants to give me the island and you the jewelry."

"Wait, Mother wants to give you the island?" Elena said.

I shrugged.

"Mother, you can't do that! Can she, Russ?"

"Please children, don't quarrel. I'll make it as even as I can. There is enough. There are some things of your father's, a rifle, a watch. We have all the paintings—some of those are quite valuable." She began undoing the pearls at her neck. "There is enough, more than enough. I am selling this house, all these things." She gestured around her. "I am moving to a condo in Florida. Don't scrunch your nose at me. Those of you who wish it will come visit me there."

"Florida?" Elena said. "But that's so far away."

"But Mother," I said, "is that really what you want?"

"Yes," she said simply. "I want to be alone."

I had to act now or the whole thing might evaporate. "Actually, I meant about the island."

"Yes," she said again. "Take it."

"You can't do that," Russ said again. "Not without talking about it. That's crazy. Polly, don't listen to her."

Elena said, "We all appreciate how much Polly loves the island—"

My mother said, "It's hers."

"But this is a significant legal thing," Russ said. "There are important financial issues to consider."

"The island," my mother said dreamily. "We had so many happy times there."

"Too bad Colin drowned there," Elena said. Everyone turned to look at her. She flushed. "Well, nobody talks about it, do they? We all tiptoe around."

I stood up. "I don't want to talk about it."

"You don't own the past," Elena said.

"Oh, please," Russ said, "this is hardly the time."

"You were always jealous of our closeness," I said to Elena.

"I was not."

"It's fine for you," I snapped at her. "You didn't even care."

"Of course I cared. Do you think I liked seeing my younger brother ruined?"

"*Girls*," my mother said.

"Look, this has been a trying day, let's not get stirred up." Russ again.

"Whose fault was it?" Elena said, looking at him. "That's what I want to know."

"What the hell do you mean by that?" he said.

"I'm giving the island to Polly," my mother said, standing up. "We'll figure the rest out. I'll make it equitable. Now please, all of you, I'm exhausted."

"But it's not decided?" said Elena.

Russ shook his head. "I just think with my idea we can solve a lot of issues. I've drawn up a few plans, just very sketchy and speculative at this point—"

"Oh, can't you all stop talking. I'm getting such a headache. Just go away all of you, and leave me alone. Go, go now." My mother held open the door and we obeyed and walked out into the hallway. She shut the door behind us. The three of us looked at each other. I was too stunned to speak.

"This doesn't mean anything, of course. You do know that?" Russ asked.

No one answered. Then I said, "You both heard her."

"Oh Polly," Elena said, "don't be so childish."

"Don't you be such a queen bitch." We stared at each other in dislike. Somehow the tentacles of our childhood had wound themselves around all of us again.

"Look, at this moment our priority is Mother and her well-being." Russ was head of the family again.

"I'm here," Elena said, tucking in her blouse. "I can take care of her."

"So can I," I said.

Russ shrugged, then straightened. "She's had too much to drink," he warned me. "She'll change her mind."

The island. I went to sleep thinking of the island. And Herbert. He hadn't meant for me to have it, but now it was mine. I felt sorry for him, and a deep gratitude to my mother. She understood me. She knew me. After all, after everything, she loved me.

I slept on her stiff linen sheets and woke sometime in the night, worrying. Of course they were not going to let me keep it. And if, by some miracle, I could get the whole thing, could I even afford it? How could I manage? What if my mother changed her mind?

I got up, got a drink of water.

I had to have the island, I told myself. I owed it to Colin. He was mine, no matter what Elena said. The island was my spiritual home. I didn't care what I had to do to keep it, didn't care what happened to my family relationships. I would gladly sacrifice them. None of those relationships meant that much to me, after all. None of them gratified me the way the island did.

Not even Monroe? a small voice whispered.

That was different, I thought. I didn't *have* Monroe. You can't sacrifice something you don't have.

I took a sip of water. It's late, I told myself. This is crazy middle-of-the-night thinking.

For a few minutes I let myself think about Monroe as a baby. How small and wrinkled she was, how her tiny hands gripped my shirt when I carried her. Dan had let me name her and I'd named her after a racehorse I'd admired, a magnificent horse, strong and fast and spirited. My heart bounded with the loss I'd endured. Stop it, I told myself. I thought of Colin, too, of how we were so close it seemed sometimes we were the same person, that we moved around in separate bodies only because it was more convenient.

I had only myself to blame for these losses. Everything I'd loved, I'd harmed. But that would change now.

Six

After the funeral, I didn't speak to anyone in my family for some time. Even though I wanted to pin my mother down about her promise, I was afraid if I pressed her she would change her mind. I had to tread lightly. All the same, I felt different. I got through the holidays at the home, which were usually a time of stress and aggravation, by clutching my secret to me. I felt benign, buoyed up and important: I owned an island.

Normally Dan and Chloe took Monroe and the boys to see Chloe's parents at Christmas, but this year, on account of their ancient dachshund who was too old to travel, they invited me to come stay with Monnie and babysit the dog while they visited the grandparents with just the boys. The roads were bad, snowy and salty, messy. I didn't trust the Green Hornet on them. So, two days after Christmas I rented a car and drove down to Philadelphia. There had been a lot of snow for the area and, as I drove through Dan's suburban neighborhood, I saw rooftops and phone poles draped with white, tree branches clotted, yards banked up, and lawns marked by crusty angels and snowmen.

The snow muffled my arrival and when I got out of the car, nobody seemed to notice. I walked up to the door but, before knocking, some instinct made me creep to the window. In the living room, Monroe stood by herself, sucking a piece of hair. At first all I could see was my daughter alone, and then I noticed everyone else gathered merrily around a large Christmas tree across the room. Monnie stared at Chloe and Dan and the little boys and I felt for her, the outsider.

Then Dan walked across the room to change the CD. Monnie gestured at him, carry me, hold me. And he, good-humoredly, indulgently, picked her up. The toddler, Claude, began to cry. And Chloe, laughing a little, picked him up, jigging him. And then Dan and Chloe did a complicated maneuver of switching children, until Chloe held Monroe, rocking her back and forth, kissed her and put her down with a groan, and turned to the baby, Edouard. Monroe played with his feet and waggled them and then kissed him squarely in the middle of his forehead.

I went back to my rental car, opened the door and slammed it hard. Then I opened the trunk, grabbed my weekend case, and slammed that door hard too, walked up to the front of the house, and rang the bell twice.

Monnie opened the door and stared. She stood shyly back, letting Dan and Chloe greet me with hearty, false camaraderie. Dusk was just falling, turning the streets violet blue. "Hey," I said, before I even took my coat off, "let's have a snowball fight. The snow is perfect."

Monroe hopped up and down, catching her hands underneath her chin. "Can we? Can we?" She had lost a front tooth. Dan, frowning, checked his watch.

"Oh, come on Dan, it'll be fun. How 'bout it, Monroe?" I said, holding out what I hoped was my daughter's hat.

"Not for me," Chloe said, smiling. "I'll be in the kitchen."

Dan came out reluctantly, zipping up his coat. In his snowsuit, Claude eyed me suspiciously, but Monnie was in the middle of the lawn, laughing, tossing up handfuls of snow. We ran around whooping and throwing snowballs. The glow of the streetlamps cutting into the violet light, the bluish snow on the ground, made it seem magical. I grabbed a fistful of snow and lobbed it at Monnie, who shrieked as it fell softly before her.

"You missed!" she said. "Nah nah ne boo boo." I remembered the taunt from my own youth.

"If I'd wanted to hit you I would've," I said, throwing another snowball that exploded on her shoulder.

"Hey," she said. She grabbed her own snowball and went after me.

"Now, I don't think—" began Dan, but whatever he didn't think was lost when the snowball I sent flying smacked his hat.

And then we were in it, snowballs whirling, all of us laughing, but competitive too. I found a good spot and suggested we make teams. "Come on, Claude my man, let's make a fort over here. You mound the balls up like so, I'll let 'em rip." Of course Claude was hopeless, basically sitting down to eat snow, but I worked hard enough for both of us, cheering him on with a combination of baby and street talk. "This will be a fight to remember," I called to the others.

Dan was not above pelting me in the midriff and soon we were in a silent and not very friendly snow battle. Monnie must have picked up some of the tension because she said, "Mom, what about me? Throw over here."

And I did. Ignoring Dan and Claude, I pretended to charge her; I chased her around the yard, throwing snowballs. Suddenly she tripped and landed on her back in a drift. She looked so comical that I threw a snowball at her, and then another, and then one that smashed right into her face.

"Mom," she said. She was crying. And I stopped, a snowball still in my upraised hand.

"I—I'm sorry," I said. "I didn't mean to throw so hard."

Dan helped her get up, dusting her off, picking out bits of snow from the back of her neck.

"I guess I was a bit rough," I said. I wanted to tell them that in my family growing up it was a free-for-all, that I learned to be tough and ruthless from being one of four, that it was hit or be hit, a dog-eat-dog world. But I wondered at myself—how could I have kept throwing at a child who was down—and at her face, too? I didn't think that Monnie was hurt, I knew she wasn't, not really, but that was not the point.

Dan wiped Monnie's nose. Claude hopped up and down. "Throw more? Throw more?"

"No, Claude," Dan said. "That's enough." Claude looked surprised for a moment, then sucked in a deep breath of air and began to scream. Dan gave me an irritated look and swung the furious Claude up in his arms.

I followed Dan and the children back inside, into the warm house where Chloe, appraising the situation instantly, took Monnie and pressed her face against her waist, her maternal instincts effortless and upswelling. I would have taken it as a reproach, except that I knew she was oblivious to my presence. And when Monnie emerged, red-eyed, blinking, but also smiling a bit, I saw that she had been comforted.

Dan and Chloe's house exuded warmth. This was not the house I had lived in and left; Dan had sold that two years ago to buy this one. Decorations were everywhere, the kind of things I'd seen advertised in catalogs: swags of evergreens over doorframes and Christmas cards arranged on a mini metal tree. Under the big tree in the living room, a red flannel "tree skirt" sported appliquéd reindeer and elves. Even the dog's crate was decorated with red bows. Chloe mulled cider on the stove, the baby on her hip, Monroe beside her.

I slapped my knees. "Come sit," I said. And Monnie came to me, a little reluctantly, a little shyly, but still she came and perched on my knees. "I'm sorry," I said.

"S'okay."

And then I won her favor back by playing "Trot Trot to Boston" and "This is the Way the Farmer Rides," even though we both knew she was probably too old for these games.

It was odd to be here, in Dan's domain again. It was odd that we'd ever thought we could be happy together, and yet I remembered how he'd pursued me. Dan had been my professor in college; he had just finished his PhD and it was his first job. We were only six years apart and in the beginning I found him immensely sexy. He had a kind of desperate hunger for me. But sex was not enough, he wanted to marry me. He begged me: at dinner, at the movies, at seven in the morning. Resolutely I said no, no, no, until once, in his office, he held my legs open and tipped me back as he entered and, giving myself up to powerlessness and pleasure, I said yes.

Everything changed after we married. I remembered standing at the kitchen sink, sticking my hands into a raw chicken to pull out the bag of guts to start supper for Dan, and thinking, I hate this. I had been married three months. But for a while the sex was still good, and we had fun on weekends, drinking and dancing, and driving different places. Almost immediately, Dan began pressuring me to have a baby. I held off as long as I could—I didn't want to, I wasn't ready, I was still a baby myself. I didn't know what I wanted to do with my life, except drink. Which I did, more and more. You're supposed to remember how awful it was, how unmanageable your life became, and I did, but I also remembered how much fun we had. Christ we had fun, I wanted to say sometimes to Dan, Don't you remember? But I knew he wouldn't remember. When I got pregnant, we stopped drinking, which turned out to not be a problem for him, just for me. I stayed sober throughout the pregnancy, but began again in earnest once Monnie was six months old, as if making up for lost time. I had to find a new drinking buddy, which I did, the husband of one of my friends. Of course we became more than drinking buddies and I left Dan soon after. Remembering this didn't make me proud.

"Come see the pets," Monroe said, pulling me to my feet.

After describing my dog-sitting duties, Chloe showed me around the house, Edouard attached to her hip, his fist full of her hair. "I have to put you in our room," she said. "I hope you don't mind. Oh shoot, I forgot to change the sheets." I told her I would do it, but she said it was no problem. The bed was already stripped and she groaned softly under the effort of putting on the new sheets.

"I hear Maine is beautiful," Chloe said on our way back to the kitchen to prepare dinner. I had been forgiven. Chloe used to be my friend too, after all, sort of.

"It can be; it's great in summer and fall. Winter's okay, but spring's the worst. Mud season."

"I'm sorry about your stepfather passing," she said.

I thanked her. And then, even though I felt superstitious talking about it, I couldn't resist telling her I'd inherited the island. "It's the most beautiful place. Monroe loves it there."

"Yes, it sounds very special. She always talks about it."

I smiled at her and she smiled back. She put Edouard down in his bouncy seat and started opening cupboards and getting out bowls. I waited a few moments before asking if she had ever finished her PhD. I didn't mean to put her on the spot, but I was genuinely curious.

Chloe looked up nervously to see if Dan was near. "No," she whispered, "and it's a bit of a sore subject."

"Oh?" I assumed a blank look and fastidiously swiped the counter so that she would say more.

"Well, I'm ABD. All but dissertation. I mean, a lot of my dissertation was, is, done. But then I got pregnant with Claude and then Edouard came along and . . ." She shrugged.

"And you're really busy."

She nodded. "Not that I'm complaining. I wouldn't change my life for anything. But sometimes Dan gets impatient with me, expects me to do it all." She made an airy gesture and then picked up her knife and chopped an onion. "But the fact is, there aren't even any jobs. Around here, that is. I could probably find something in center city or on the other side, but that means a commute. And you know how Dan is."

I did know. "Better you than me," I muttered.

Her eyes were running now and she wiped them with the hem of her sleeve. Edouard began to fuss in his bouncy seat. When I offered to hold him, she said, "Oh, could you? That would be great." I unhooked him, fumbling with the child safety locks, and pulled him out of the seat. I was surprised by his weight, such a dense little creature with very fat thighs. So old-fashioned-looking too, in white tights and navy blue shorts. He was a fine enough little fellow but I felt no maternal rush. I'd never been one of those ovulating females. Despite my attempts to pacify him, Edouard continued to fuss.

"I'm sorry," I said. "I'm not doing a very good job."

"He probably wants to nurse," Chloe said.

"What are you going to do with those?" I nodded at the onions.

"Oh, I sauté them and add them to the stew."

"Here," I said, "let's switch." She washed her hands and I handed her the baby and took up my place at the stove.

Gratefully she sat down to nurse. Chloe was quiet, calm, maternal. She was not fat by any means, but rather what once might have been called comfortable. She wore childlike clothes: today a denim pinafore dress and a flannel shirt. She baked bread and made stews. Of course I could cook too. But somehow her doing it was different. And here she was, married to Dan. His beard had grown and was now quite curly; it gave him even more of a paterfamilias air than ever. I could imagine him in summer, sporting a large straw hat. Was he happy? He appeared very keen to show that he was, which might be as close as I would get to the truth.

Chloe drank milk at dinner. She apologized, but said her doctor told her she needed the calcium. I joined her, leaving Dan alone to breathe his wine, to uncork and decant. Chloe had prepared a pork stew with prunes, a loaf of warm crusty bread, a spinach salad. Dan's face puckered.

"Is everything okay?" I asked, suddenly playing the role of anxious wife.

Chloe, the real wife, fetched. Salt and pepper, a dish of butter, an extra plate for Claude. Dan's face relaxed. He dished out the stew and began to speak, holding forth on the highpoints of nineteenth-century art.

Why did I feel so insubstantial? I had to remind myself that I was a cook, that I made bread and pottery. That I could serve a dinner for eight entirely from objects that I had made, if people didn't mind drinking out of mugs. I thought of my house, the eccentric, bright colors of my bungalow, and then the softness, the quiet, muffled carpeting of theirs, the foot-thick stone walls and heavy old doors. Snow flopped softly against the windows.

Monroe watched us all. I knew I was not "Mother" as Chloe was. If I was "Mom," it was as an unpredictable, erratic figure. Perhaps in Monnie's world, stepmother was not scary but secure. Monnie called her Chloe in front of me, but I knew she called her Mommy when I wasn't there.

The dishes done, Edouard began to fuss again. "Oh," Chloe said, looking at me apologetically, "do you mind?" I shook my head and picked him up. Freer now, she made fast work of filling thermoses with coffee, hot cider, and pea soup for their trip. The rubber spatula she used to scrape out the soup pot was dingy and cracked, the tip melted off, and I was obscurely grateful for this.

They were leaving at bedtime so the little boys would sleep during the car ride. Dan gave me instructions about the heat and the list of phone numbers on the fridge, as if I were the babysitter. Chloe told me about the dog and thanked me again. "I really appreciate it," she said. "It breaks my heart to leave her, but I can't take her. The cold alone would do her in, let alone the journey."

I reassured them both, stood by the door with my arm around Monroe's shoulders while they loaded up the car, making repeated trips for the baby's hat, Dan's reading glasses, special oyster crackers for the soup, Claude's favorite nature video. Very naturally, Chloe kissed me good-bye, then colored. Dan was less easy but he managed something between a handshake and a hug.

After they left, there was a bit of awkward silence between Monnie and me. She seemed shy again so I suggested we check on the guinea pigs, which lived in a hutch in the kitchen. Together we poked our fingers through the wires and they squeaked from inside their wooden hut. Then we patted the dog, stroked her wizened muzzle and threadbare ears. Mme. Manet's snowy eyes did not blink. She couldn't walk straight, see or hear well, but still she could smell. She sniffed my hand.

In the night, I woke up between the flannel sheets Chloe had prepared for me, so horny I could scream. I imagined rubbing myself along doorjambs, the rim of the tub. I fantasized about bananas, cucumbers. (I knew from experience these were more distracting than effective.) Of course I was not going out to a bar—even if I could find a babysitter for Monnie at this hour—of course I wouldn't bring anyone home with me, but I suddenly felt tired of being good.

I had an idea that Dan might have a stash of something. Briefly I tried to imagine Chloe and Dan in bed together, but I couldn't get past the pinafore. I was sure Chloe was sweet, and never withholding, never too tired to say no, but I couldn't imagine her having real desire. Nevertheless I snooped around their bedroom, but her drawers were so wholesome that I quickly turned to Dan's. His rather extensive collection of grooming utensils, his color-coded socks, his English tailored shirts and silk bow ties, his several brushes and aftershaves, all reminded me how vain he was. And as I looked at them I realized that I could not afford to see Dan as a viable male; I needed to reduce him to the role of buffoon. Why? Because it would be too painful? I would want him back? Surely not. And suddenly I realized that while I didn't exactly want him back, not literally, I was longing for some kind of intactness, some vision of harmony and promise. That's why it's good we divorced and he married Chloe, I told myself: so that a version exists. Okay, I wasn't in a starring role, but still.

Downstairs I heard Mme. Manet scuffling around. I turned away from Dan's bureau and headed to his study. My lust had become more focused now, hard and small like a walnut. A little bit mean. In Daniel's study the books, all those glossy art history books, were arranged by subject, and there, under *E* for *erotica*, was Dan's stockpile. How like him to get off on coy Victorian smut. So much more highbrow, I could see him justifying to himself. Then I remembered how I used to visit his office at the college, and he'd set me on top of whatever art history tome happened to be there and fuck me.

Oh, Daniel.

While I was here I decided to check into his desk, no doubt he had all of Monroe's report cards. Of course his files were alphabetized and so logically organized that right behind "School Reports" came "Specialists." And then I discovered the folders of drawings, the quotes from specialists, the careful notes. Dan had always had a side interest in art interpretation, but I hadn't known that all of Monnie's beautiful, sweet, funny drawings were being dissected and analyzed, each one dated after a visit or phone call with me.

"Feet not on the ground," he'd scrawled. Or "Crooked path leading up to the house." Or, "No smoke from the chimney." I didn't know what these things meant, but I knew enough to know they indicated something negative.

The idea that Dan was trying to document my evil influence on Monroe infuriated me. What was he doing to our daughter? Maybe Monnie really did belong with me. I imagined getting up every morning to take her to the school bus, packing her a lunch, meeting the bus in the afternoon. I'd have to change my work schedule but that wasn't impossible, we could do projects after school, I'd help her with her homework, she'd make friends in Maine.

Almost immediately I felt deflated. Here was stability, material comfort (mullioned windows!), the vision of contented family. With me she'd only know incompleteness. We'd be half a family. What terrified me most was the emotional responsibility. How could I pretend to be a guide of any kind for her, when I was so confused and uncertain myself?

But surely (sinking onto the floor beneath the mullioned windows) it was a luxury to think this way. So many people, mothers, just had kids and had to manage however. Well, a) their kids were not necessarily fine; and b) it was precisely because Dan and Chloe offered a better alternative that I had to justify whether I could take her away. But what kind of sick mind would interpret a child's drawings?

Sitting on Dan's thick plum carpet, I told myself he did it because he cared. And if he thought that I might taint her, was that any different from what I myself thought?

When I came downstairs the next morning, Monroe was sitting outside Mme. Manet's pen, talking softly to her. As I expected, the dog had crapped and then walked, sat, and probably slept in it. Her legs were collapsed beneath her, but still she attempted to stagger up when she heard me. Revulsion and pity mingled in me.

First I washed her off with the wipes Chloe had left. Then I asked Monnie to watch her while I removed the fouled newspaper and dog bed. I put Mme. Manet back in the pen with the fresh newspaper and lugged the soiled bed to the washing machine. It stank and, even though I wanted to puke, I felt tremendous compassion for Chloe and for this old dog, and a kind of respect at being privileged enough to see her in her last days, because surely she must die soon. At the same time, I couldn't imagine how Chloe could stand it, on top of looking after the baby and Claude. Not to mention stewing pork with prunes on a nightly basis.

Afterward, when the dog had eaten and was resting and Monnie and I had had some cereal and were lying together on the couch, I had a cozy feeling of accomplishment and good deeds. I played with Monnie's hair, stroking it back and pulling it into sections, pretending to make braids and pigtails.

We brought out the two guinea pigs and held them, squeaking on our chests. They were shrill, anxious creatures, but sweet despite the claws on their feet.

We talked, Monnie and I, about this and that, and the guinea pigs settled down and snuggled. I told her a story about the queen guinea pig and after a while we got drowsy. Three whole days together. It seemed a lifetime. All the same, I was trying to make every moment count, to remember each part of it. It was so quiet, there in Dan's house, the snow deep outside. Let's just close our eyes for a minute, I said, and to my surprise, Monnie agreed. It was cold out but warm inside, and she lay on me like a blanket. It did occur to me that the guinea pigs should maybe go into their cages, but we were all so comfortable that I couldn't bear to disrupt anything.

Dan had suggested we go to story hour at the library, or down-

town to some art classes at the museum. He'd suggested other te-
dious things for us too—cleaning Monroe's room, sorting out her
old toys, taking her stuff to Goodwill. Maybe later, I decided. We
lay together on the sofa, our own little island of comfort, and slept.

When I woke up Mme. Manet had peed and crapped again and
the guinea pigs had vanished. There was an erratic trail of pellets
and hairs and a few cedar shavings leading nowhere. Monroe was
on her hands and knees, peering under the sofa. Not only was the
room quite large, it was also open to the hall on one side and the
kitchen and dining room on the other.

I was mad at Monnie and madder at myself. Why didn't I ever
learn? Of course the guinea pigs were bound to wander off. I took
a deep breath. I pretended to be Chloe. "Don't worry," I said,
"we'll find the little wretches."

Now Monroe told me, unhelpfully, "Mo—Chloe usually shuts
the door to the den when they're out of their cages."

"You can call her Mommy," I told her.

"That's okay." She seemed embarrassed, so I quickly laid out a
plan for finding them.

"Squeak," I said. And she did.

We checked the area by their cages. Nothing. But in the kitchen
our squeaking occasioned a panicked response from under the
stove. "Aha," I said. "I know how to get them out, never fear." I
hunted in Chloe's drawers until I found a prong on a long wooden
handle, the kind of thing used for grilling. I got a little piece of
cheese from the fridge.

"Mom," Monroe said, "guinea pigs don't eat cheese."

"Oh, don't they?" I squatted down. "Now, I will lure them out
and your job will be to catch them." I got the stick in there and
poked away at the shadowy forms at the back. "Squeak," I reminded her. Together we squeaked loudly, and then one of them,
Berthe Morisot, made a run for it. Dashing about, Monnie grabbed
her and together we clamped her safely in her cage. Mary Cassatt

took a bit longer, but with persistence and a piece of apple on the end of the stick, we got her out and back into her cage.

By the time I cleaned up the dog again and started a new load of laundry, it was past lunchtime. We ate grilled cheese sandwiches and the remains of Chloe's split pea soup. Then Monnie had to dress and dawdled over her clothes till I came in and grabbed some and playfully pelted them at her. We made her bed and after checking on all the animals again (and giving them snacks) we headed outside.

The afternoon was almost past and there was a sad, darkening cast to the air, not twilight yet, but the weakness of a sun that had moved westward across the sky and now only hinted at its former brightness. I made Monnie walk briskly down the road because it was cold and because, suddenly, I felt slothful, wasteful of the day. When we got to the park, I suggested a quick dart into the woods, beyond which the sun was beginning to set, but Monnie said she was cold, so we started back along a parallel street. Monnie liked to look at the Christmas decorations but I preferred looking inside the houses just now at the hour when the occupants were switching on lights and revealing their lives for the brief interval before the husbands returned and the curtains were drawn.

Back home, I felt irrationally virtuous. We ate a hearty dinner, read a long story, and both of us were in bed and asleep by 8:30.

At 9:30 Dan called. I was so deeply asleep that I wasn't even sure where I was.

"Hello?" I said into the phone.

"Polly, listen, I can't believe I forgot to tell you this, but Monroe can only drink one glass of milk a day. You can give her Tums for calcium at other points—"

"What?" After a while I understood. He was anxious about early puberty, which he saw as coming from too many dairy and meat products.

After we hung up I sat thinking for a while. Was Dan afraid of

Monroe becoming a woman, or anxious over a world full of change? I didn't think it was better for her, Dan's world. It was so safe, so sheltered and artificial. He controlled everything. I could do it, I thought, I could be her mother.

The next day we drove the hour and a half to visit my sister, Elena. I hadn't seen her since Herbert's funeral, but we had spoken on the phone a few times. It turned out she hadn't been pregnant after all. Her symptoms had been caused by an ovarian cyst, which had been removed two weeks before Christmas. I'd talked to her a few days after the procedure—she was in the middle of frosting cupcakes for Marielle's holiday party—and she sounded a bit down. When she heard I would be staying with Monroe for a few days, she practically begged me to come visit them.

Elena lived in a large new house that had been set down into what I could tell, even on a gray January day, must have been until recently very pretty countryside. It was one of Roger's developments and as we drove down the brand-new road, past frozen dirt lawns and jutting pipes, it seemed like a ghost town. She had told me it wasn't doing as well as he had hoped and it looked less than half full. A number of houses appeared stalled in midconstruction, and the finished ones showed few signs of habitation. There was nothing wrong with these houses, I supposed, except they were huge, swollen almost, each decorated with stone or timber to be slightly different from its neighbor, and they depressed me.

On the inside, however, Elena's house was surprisingly nice. She'd decorated the whole thing in blue and white, with lamps and throw pillows in yellow.

"You found us!" Elena made a big fuss of kissing Monnie and then me. "Come in, wipe your feet, it's unbelievably dirty out there. I don't know when they're going to be finished, if ever." Her daughters hung behind her, shy. Monnie was shy too. I was glad

Elena had arranged for Roge to be at a friend's house. Monnie and Missy eyed each other warily, until Missy said, "Do you want to see my room?" And Monnie said, "Okay," and off they went, Marielle running on short legs behind them.

Elena and I went into the kitchen. "Tea?" she asked.

"Please."

She poured water in the kettle and spooned black tea leaves into a pot. I sat at the table and looked around. It was a child's paradise, everything clean and bright. One wall had hooks just at child height, and another had bookcases in which books, games, and plastic boxes full of toys were neatly organized. "This is kind of amazing," I said. "This is basically the antithesis of what we had growing up."

She grimaced. "I vowed when I had children that I would know where the scissors were. I just didn't want my children to grow up in the same kind of chaotic household."

The kettle sang and she filled the teapot and set out flowery mugs. "You take milk, right? Sugar?"

I shook my head. She looked thinner than ever as she sat beside me. After three kids, I would have expected her to look more like Chloe. Around her neck was a gold chain with a chiseled dark red pendant. "How was the cyst removal? How are you feeling?"

"Okay, I guess. Kind of dumb. I'd wanted to be pregnant so badly. Though what right I had to think I deserved or could manage another child." She looked away, twisted her necklace. "The procedure was fine." She wrinkled her nose. "They kind of vaporize it out of you." She blinked, stared at her knitting basket on the window seat. "And then, when I was recovering, I did a ton of knitting. I'd already knit so much this year: matching sweaters for Roger and Roge, and a hat and scarf for Missy, a scarf for Mother, and mittens for Marielle."

"I love the scarf you made for me last year," I said.

"Thank you. Anyway, I was so stupid," she continued. "My left wrist had been bothering me forever but I kept ignoring it. Finally it got so bad I went to the doctor, and it turns out I have carpal tunnel." She pulled back the sleeve on her forearm and showed me her brace. "The doctor told me I had to stop doing any repetitive motion. No knitting. Can you imagine?"

I could. "That's terrible."

"I've tried drawing." She shook her head. "No good. I need to do things, but I'm not creative. Do you know how sad that is? I have been doing some ironing, though. That helps a bit. But I can't keep making wrinkles."

I laughed. "What about poetry? You used to write."

"Oh, but that was years ago. The muse has left the building."

I sighed and sipped my tea. I wanted to say more, encourage her, but I also feared another trap. Then Marielle came downstairs and clambered around, wanting attention. I held her on my lap for a bit and she showed me her cloth house full of little kittens. "You smell so nice," I said, and squeezed her. She giggled. I pretended to chew her neck and fingers.

Elena got a sponge and wiped off the table. She seemed preoccupied.

"I don't usually do this," she said, and started a video in the TV room for Marielle. "Okay," she said on her return, "we have twenty-four minutes." Her hands were trembling.

"What is it?" I said.

"Roger. And Christmas. Well, no, backup." She took a deep breath and began talking, not to me, exactly, but to a spot over a child's yellow smock hanging on the wall. "As you've probably realized, I never minded traditional roles. I wanted that. Mother seemed able to put up with very little emotional comfort from Herbert, and I guess I thought that a reasonable expectation from a marriage. In fact, years ago she encouraged me to break up with my college boyfriend, do you remember him?" Of course I remembered Joe, a sweet, not terribly ambitious boy. Of course he wouldn't have seemed good enough. "And I took her advice and broke both the boy's heart and my own. Not that I blame her or anything."

"Why do you think you gave her so much power?" I said after a minute, the way I thought a therapist might.

"Because she was my mother," she said, half laughing. "She was supposed to know."

I nodded.

Roger had been a good catch. Everyone had thought so. He was a good provider. He'd worked hard for everything he'd achieved: after his father had abandoned the family, Roger had put himself through school, built his developing business from the ground up, supported his mother until she died. Whenever Elena felt his coldness, she reminded herself of that. Because, as I'd already guessed, he wasn't the easiest person. Okay. So. Then this Christmas. The children had opened all their presents, and Roger his, and Elena was walking about picking up the wrapping paper strewn on the floor and stuffing it into a garbage bag when it occurred to her that no one had given her a gift. She had not received one single Christmas present. She could forgive the kids, but Roger? She'd been pretending for so long, making excuses for his grumpiness: he's tired, he's hungry, he works so hard. So she'd said, "There's something different about this Christmas. Does anyone know what it is?"

The eldest two had looked at her blankly. "What, Mommy?" Marielle asked.

Roger was acting as if he wasn't part of this conversation, or even the day. When she and the girls were listening to Christmas carols earlier, he had come in and plopped himself down and turned on the TV, as if they weren't there at all. Now he stood looking out the window, his fingers in his back pockets. Elena sensed him scoffing. "Isn't it funny," she said, "no one gave me a present."

Her girls felt awful; they told her they were sorry and Marielle sat down to make a quick drawing. Missy raced to her room and returned with a miniature bottle of perfume in a little purse.

"That's okay, lovies, thank you so much."

But Roger had walked out. Elena bit back the urge to ask him where he was going. It was getting darker now and as Elena reached to turn on a lamp a blue flash came from it and the light-bulb blew. Elena started to cry. She tried to hold the tears back but it was too late. You're not supposed to cry in front of your ten-year-old son. In the way Roge stiffened, she saw suddenly the choice he would have to make between love for her and his need to be like his father. "Roge," she began, but before she could say more, he'd left the room.

She had wanted Christmas to be nice for the children, but despite her efforts the day had not been a success. Roger had almost been daring her, it seemed, pushing her to see how far she would go. "Come baby," she'd said to Marielle, "let's you and me look for a lightbulb to fix that stupid old lamp."

Elena cleared her throat. "So we walked upstairs, hand in hand, and it was the oddest thing. I did not know where I began or ended, I had so little sense of myself. My eyes kept tearing up, not just for the day, or my situation, but for the futility of it all." She sighed. "Who you marry is really so arbitrary, and yet you stay together because you're married. Does that make sense?" She looked at me and I nodded. "I'd tried so hard and Roger was just a bear." She bit her lip. "I'm sorry to dump all this on you," she said, "but there's no one else I can tell. No one else I feel safe with."

"Of course," I said.

They'd fixed the lamp, and Marielle had found Missy and persuaded her to play house. Elena was on the way to the washing machine with a load of Christmas linens when she passed Roger's office. The door was not quite shut, and he was on the phone. With a certainty that surprised her, she realized he must be having an affair. In fact, weirdly, she began to hope he was. She didn't feel as weak and teary as she'd expected. She felt powerful. She crept closer and listened. He said a few things that she couldn't quite catch the meaning of, and then she heard, "I told you, I'm not going to be here forever. You need to act on this. I don't care what you have to do." So he *was* having an affair. She felt vindicated. Sick too. Then he added, "I haven't told her. I'm sure she'll agree with me." Then he said something confusing. "You're right, absolutely . . . piece of prime real estate just sitting there . . . what's that flake head going to do with it?"

"Oh God."

Elena nodded. "Maybe you can guess what's coming. I couldn't. I stood in the doorway and asked who he was talking to. He ignored me. I repeated the question and then he said to the person on the phone, 'I gotta go.' He hung up and told me it was Russ."

"Russ?" I stared at her. "I don't believe you."

"That's what I said. But he said, 'Believe me. He says Merry Christmas.' So immediately my mind fills with concern for Russ. Was he alone and not with his daughters. Should I have invited him? But then I remembered he and Melanie were spending Christmas with Mother. So I asked what they had been talking about."

"Oh no," I said.

She nodded. "I'm not going to give you the whole conversation blow by blow, but basically they want to contest Mother's gift to you. They want to develop the island, get some big backer involved."

"But they can't do that, can they?" I asked.

"I don't see how they can. Mother still owns the island, and they can't do it without her permission."

"But Mother gave the island to me. Everybody heard her. I have no reason to think she's changed her mind." It was true she hadn't mentioned it in our last two phone calls, but that didn't mean anything.

Elena took a sip of her tea, then glanced at me. "I don't want them to develop it. But you can't be thinking that it's right for you to accept it, can you?"

I looked at the rows of matching kitchen cabinets. "I don't see why not."

"Because it's not fair."

At that moment Marielle's video came to an end. "Excuse me," Elena said, and went into the next room. When she came back, she sat and smoothed her hands over her lap.

"So what happened with Roger?" I asked.

"I got mad at him. I told him I hoped he wasn't telling people I wanted a development on the island. He called me a fool. I called him a jerk." She said this without emphasis, as if she were reading an address. "He said I was so oblivious it was frightening. I said if he felt that way, I wasn't sure I wanted to be married to him any longer. He asked why I didn't leave. I told him it was my home. On the contrary, he said, it was his house. He paid for everything. I reminded him about the children, that I did everything for them. He told me a nanny could do what I did. He was practically spitting." Her voice broke slightly but then she was calm again. "I asked if he wanted a divorce. He said it sounded like it, didn't it? I said I hated him and he smirked. God, how could I ever have thought he was handsome? And then I asked if he was having an affair. He just laughed. I told him it was much too serious to joke about." Elena started crying. "I asked him when he had become so cruel, and he said, 'When did you become so annoying?'" She sobbed.

"Oh no," I went round to her and hugged her. She wept on my shoulder. "And do you know what I did?" she said, between tears. "Well, first I washed my face. And then I went to where the kids were. And you know, they were playing together, for once. And so quiet. You know how we used to be when our parents got volatile."

I nodded.

"And all three of my children looked up anxiously to where I stood in the doorway of the room. And I acted as if everything was normal and I asked them, 'Shall we have some more Christmas music?' "

"Oh, honey," I said.

At that moment I saw Marielle glance up from the other room. She seemed about to come to us so I went in and tickled her a bit and slipped in a new video.

When I came back, Elena was drying her eyes with the hem of her sleeve. "You know, for years I kept pretending everything was okay. I mean, I have been happy too, with the kids and my projects."

"Are you thinking divorce?" I almost whispered the word. "It might be the right thing."

"I don't want to get divorced." She started sobbing again. "I'd probably have to get a job."

I nodded sympathetically. "A job's okay."

"Not for me it isn't. I've never worked. What would I do?"

I saw the trap of lifestyle, of self-misconception. "You were always so smart. It's a shame you—" I stopped myself. "Don't worry. It will be okay. You can get a job, a job is easy. Plus you'd get support. And if you want a career, maybe you could go back to school." I handed her a tissue from a box on the counter and she blew her nose. "Do the kids have any idea?"

She shook her head, shrugged. "I don't know." She dabbed her eyes. "All I ever wanted to do was be a good mother. Isn't that stupid?"

"No," I said, "it's not stupid. You are a good mother. You're a great mother."

"Do you really think so?" When I nodded, she said, not looking at me, "The confusing thing is that two days after Christmas, two days when we'd hardly talked, he gave me this necklace." She pulled her chin back and held out the pendant. "He said he's been under pressure, that he was sorry. It's a ruby. It's pretty, don't you think?"

It was pretty, but I didn't understand how she could wear it. When had her life lost its urgency? Where was she, herself, that person who had wanted to do things, wanted to *be* things? When had she become the person who wanted jewelry?

She glanced at me but I couldn't meet her eyes. "I've wanted to apologize for what I said at Herbert's funeral, about your choices."

I shook my head. "It's okay." Neither of us said anything and then I whispered, "Guess what? I think I'm going to try to get custody."

"Oh, Polly! But are you really sure you could handle it? It's a lot of responsibility." Then she said, "That's wonderful. Why not? You do that."

She stood up and took our mugs to the sink. I followed her with the teapot and creamer. She hesitated. "I'm also sorry about what I said about Colin, that night." She opened the dishwasher and loaded the mugs inside. "You know, it's confusing. In one way the island is pure, but in another way it's the opposite. It *was*." Elena closed the dishwasher and sponged off a small wet patch on the counter. "Sometimes it seems like there's so much corruption in the world, nothing will make it clean again."

She seemed to be speaking to herself but I said quietly, "Colin was pure."

"He was defiled." She said it almost savagely.

My heart began pounding. "What do you mean?"

"Russ gave him *drugs* when he was ten years old. That's disgusting. That's immoral."

"I was only eleven," I said in a small voice.

Elena began unloading the cutlery basket, placing each spoon perfectly on top of the one underneath. "I couldn't protect you," she said in a soft voice. She sounded sad and defeated. But then she squared her shoulders. "Luckily you two had each other."

"I used to think, if I could have Colin, everything would be okay. And then he died."

Elena hesitated. She glanced at me quickly, then away. "Was there ever . . . this is so crazy. I used to wonder . . . you guys were so close." My face flushed. I bent over the cutlery basket. She took it from me absently, shaking her head. "Never mind."

"I really loved him." Tears pricked my eyes. "I feel like it's my fault he died."

"Oh come," Elena said, hugging me. "Of course it's not your fault. It was an accident."

And so she absolved me, saying what I had always heard, but which I had somehow never been able to believe.

As I drove away at the end of our visit, Monnie and I waving to Elena and her daughters out the car windows, I contemplated kidnapping my child. We could drive to Maine, I thought. I could just take her with me. I looked back at her face, her honey-colored hair, listened to her talking to herself. Do it, I said to myself. Then I remembered the animals at her house. Who would feed them? I imagined Mme. Manet lying stiff in her pen. Of course, she could be anyway. Chloe had given me a big plastic bag and told me to keep the body in the deep freeze if she died while they were away. No, I thought, turning south on the highway instead of north, I'd have to fight my battles some other way. And so I drove back to Dan and Chloe's house. And all the while I thought of what I was going to say to my ex-husband when he returned.

Monroe was asleep, but I was waiting as Dan and Chloe's car purred to a stop. They carried the sleeping boys in and upstairs and I helped with their luggage. Chloe didn't come back downstairs but when Dan did I told him I wanted to speak to him. "Can't it wait?" he asked. "I'm exhausted."

I followed him into the living room. "Dan, I want custody."

"Absolutely not." He looked through the mail I'd put on the coffee table. "That's out of the question."

"Absolutely not—just like that? Who died and made you God?"

"I'm sorry," he said, looking at me. "I have custody and you don't. That was determined six years ago when you abandoned your child."

"But I've changed. I'm different now." I could hear myself pleading. "I've got the island now. My mother gave it to me."

Dan rolled his eyes. "That island. When are you going to grow up?"

I despised him. "I have," I said. "Don't make me fight you."

"I'm not making you do anything." Now he was straightening up things in the living room—folding a blanket, stacking books neatly—as if I'd left the place a mess.

I went and stood right in front of him so that he had to face me. "I'm going to fight you on this," I said. "I have a lawyer too."

He sighed. "Don't do this, Polly. Don't waste your time and effort and money—and mine too, I might add—on this fruitless struggle, just to make yourself feel better. Monnie is happy here. Don't disrupt that."

By now I was so angry I could barely speak. I was afraid of what I might say. So I just said, "You'll hear from me, Dan." I walked out of the room, then remembered I was sleeping there, that earlier I'd moved my sheets down and put fresh ones on their bed. I waited in the kitchen until Dan finally went upstairs to bed. The next morning I woke up early to have breakfast with Monnie. It was a dark morning, and the boys were cranky from not enough sleep. Chloe and Dan bustled around getting breakfast and Monnie sat with me while I said good-bye to the animals, Mme. Manet with her bleary eyes and stiff tail, and the two squealing guinea pigs. Then I hugged Monnie tightly, promised I would both call and write, and slipped out to the rental car to begin the long drive north.

Seven

~

January was a cold, bitter, dark month. I went to work and crept home. I slept ten and twelve hours a night. This half-hibernation happened every year, and every year it surprised me. But even if I was staggering through my days only semi-awake, somnambulistic, plans were taking shape inside me: how to ensure that the island was mine, how to regain my daughter. What Elena had told me about Russ and Roger worried me, but I figured if I could just make my mother's decision final, I would not have any problems. Unfortunately, when I talked to her about it, she was vague and hesitant. She said she didn't feel well, that the cold was in her bones. She could barely get out, and it was lonely without Herbert. I knew if she was telling me that, she must feel very bad indeed. I asked her about Florida and she said, Oh, someday. That it was just a fantasy, she wasn't sure she had the money. But it's your dream, I said. Not everyone's dream comes true, she said. On the good side, however, she said, Russ was coming over a lot. He'd moved his papers into Herbert's office and he was taking care of some business for her. What kind of business? Odds and ends. About the island— Could we please not talk about the island for a while? She couldn't even think of it now.

As for pursuing custody of Monroe, I hemmed and hawed for a while, and then finally arranged to see my old friend Wally, the lawyer who had advised me after Dan and I split up, down in Boston. He had to reschedule our first appointment and a blizzard postponed our second, so it wasn't until toward the middle of February that we finally met.

I took the noon bus down to Boston. From the bus station I took the T straight to the hotel Wally had recommended. The hotel was part of a chain that had branches in Maine, but this one was glitzier than I was prepared for, all gold lights and potted plants, and a waterfall down one red stone wall. Upstairs, the accommodations were decidedly less glitzy. It reminded me of a woman whose face is perfect but whose neck is scrawny and forgotten. The windows didn't open in my room, the bedspread was made of some prickly synthetic, and the room smelled faintly of smoke.

"I'll take you out," Wally had said after I'd told him I needed some advice. It did cross my mind that he could have invited me home, and did not, but then I thought he was probably working late, maybe this hotel was near his office.

The funny thing was that I had arrived early at the bus stop in Augusta and spent the time shopping, and now I was glad because at the last minute I'd bought a new dress. It was a curious kind of dress, not my usual thing at all. Double-breasted, a matronly navy with largish gold buttons that made it appear conservative, except that the neckline plunged far lower than I was used to. I showered and put it on. It was flattering, I thought, but I felt odd. Like someone else. I had time to spare, so I padded around in my stockinged feet, doing my nails and watching television, relieved to be feeling utterly unlike myself.

Our meeting was set for 6:30 but by 7:00 he still hadn't shown up. I was tired of waiting and went downstairs. At the bar, I ordered a seltzer with lime and then sat at a small table. I felt funny in my dress, but I looked right at home—there were many men having dinner with secretaries. I shifted uncomfortably. I had been the other woman once or twice. The false grandeur of the bar, the pretentiousness, the hush and tinkle of bad lounge music brought it back. For a minute I wished it was Steven I was meeting, though I couldn't imagine him being comfortable here. And then I remembered the lingerie I'd bought in the fall (now shoved permanently to the back of my drawer) and flushed.

When Wally walked toward my table, he was unmistakable. He looked good. All the typical things too: stouter, balding, somewhat florid, but he looked so homey and adult in his business suit, his tie, his life, which I knew so little about, my friend since high school. We hugged and exclaimed and when I sat down he pulled out my chair for me. I stared at the dark hair on his wrist, caught between the gold of his watchband and the crisp white of his shirt, and had a feeling he would take care of me.

He ordered a gin and tonic and I tried not to think how much I would like a drink. Instead, my heart pounding, I attempted to explain what I wanted from him. In my nervousness I fiddled with the buttons on my dress. Wally, help me, I'm drowning, I wanted to say. But nothing came out. I searched my purse for ChapStick, spread it over my lips. My throat was dry. I reached for my glass and by accident took a sip of Wally's drink. Gin and tonic. I gulped air. Man, that was good.

I drank several large swallows of seltzer and began again. "I mean, I don't even know if I want this."

"Jesus, Polly," he said, "calm down. What is going on?"

I took a deep breath. "Okay," I said. "I know it would be hard. But what if, what if I wanted to maybe try and get custody." It was out. I froze, expecting him to laugh me out of the room or turn a horrified gaze on me. He did neither. He loosened his tie. He looked tired but kindly. He was just a bit older than me, but he looked so solidly a man of the world, with his thick gold wedding band and his dark suit and striped tie.

"Well," he began in an understanding, avuncular way. "In cases of this kind, you've either got to fall on the mercy of the parent with custodial rights, or you've got to prove that that parent's unfit in some way."

I sighed. The former was undoubtedly the more reasonable way to proceed, yet it stuck in my craw.

Wally stood up. "Freshen your drink?" I nodded automatically. When Wally came back from the bar he carried two identical glasses, both beaded with condensation, both with lime on top. Mine didn't look like seltzer water. Tell him, I hissed to myself. Could it be he'd forgotten I didn't drink?

"Cheers," he said.

"Cheers." And I took a sip.

It tasted so good—sweet and tart, wet and dry at the same time. Intoxicating, but I knew for me it was toxic. I wanted to pour it down my throat. He told me to drink it, I reasoned. He knows I'm drinking it, so it must be okay. But I knew that was specious, like the credit card argument: "But they kept sending me cards, so I thought it must be okay."

I took another sip, tiny, just enough to wet my lips and tongue. The same delicious forbidden taste.

Meanwhile, Wally had been talking and I'd missed what he'd said. I put my hand on his sleeve. "Wall, I'm sorry, I was distracted. Can you start again?"

"I was just saying, even though you did forsake custody rights, I certainly think you could open up custody arrangements again. You could push for longer vacations with your daughter, a month or so in the summer, for instance. How serious are you about this? Would you consider moving back to Philadelphia? Then we could get you in for alternate weekends."

"Wally," I said, "I want custody."

He kept talking as if he hadn't heard me. "In fact, if you become a bona fide resident, you could try for every other week."

I took a gulp of my drink, for courage. Already my head felt kind of light. "No," I said. "Full custody. I want Monroe to live with me, in Maine."

He coughed, splattering his drink. "I'm surprised. I mean, what's changed?"

"Well, I've got a steady job, cooking, you know. For a retirement home. And I make quite a bit of money selling my pottery, especially in summer. I've got an arrangement with a store in Rockhaven and one in Camden. And I've been asked to join a pottery collective. I was mentioned in the local paper."

"Good, good." Wally was taking notes. "Recognized by the community."

"And," I said quickly, "I joined AA."

"Excellent," he wrote. "Good sign." He didn't seem to make the connection with the drink he'd placed in front of me. I took another tiny, tiny sip, barely moistening my tongue. It tasted a bit poisonous and I put the glass primly back down and pushed the coaster away. "I also don't want my daughter growing up with Dan. I don't want her to have his values. Plus," I remembered, "he keeps porn in his study."

"Does he now?" Wally asked, leaning forward. What was it about men and pornography? "What kind?"

"Erotica, I guess."

"Oh," he said, disappointed. "I should have known naughty photos from the 1890s would have done it. Though I suppose that could be considered pretty kinky in this day and age. Okay." Wally became businesslike. "But none of those things matter. They're not going to make a difference. Can you get some character references to speak for you? Landlord, employer?"

I got depressed thinking like that. I imagined my neighbor Mrs. Kerrey telling everyone about my weed-strewn garden, Stella counting the times I was late to work or didn't smile.

Wally must have sensed my discouragement because he said,

"Polly, you're young still. Why don't you marry again and start a new family?"

"And what about Monroe?" I didn't tell him about getting my tubes tied.

"She's fine where she is, you know that. Why disrupt her life? Don't get me wrong," he added, "of course I'll help you, but think about what you want and why you're doing this."

"I just think she'd be better off with me." I had no idea if that was true, but for my own sake I had to pretend it was. I slipped off my shoes underneath the table and sighed.

Wally sighed too. "Let's eat," he said. While we'd been talking the restaurant had become crowded.

"Don't you have to be home?"

"Nah." He checked his watch. "The kids will be asleep already. I missed bedtime again. Bad Daddy." He pulled a snapshot out of his wallet, smiled as he passed it to me.

"They're adorable," I said.

"Two more G and T's," he told the waiter, "and dinner menus." Now's the time, I told myself. Say no. And didn't.

"Steaks," he said, when the waiter stood by our table again. I wondered if Wally was a tiny bit drunk. I could have told him I didn't eat meat or that I liked to order for myself. But it had been such a long time since I'd sat in a restaurant like this, with a dress and hose on, that I demurred. When our food came, I sliced my meat and ate it. Meekly I sipped my drink. And when he ordered another round, I didn't say anything.

"On the phone you said there were two things you wanted to talk about. What's the other?"

I explained about the island, how Herbert had wanted to sell it, but that my mother had inherited it and said she'd give it to me, but hadn't in fact done it, and how my brother wanted to develop it. "I guess I wondered if there was anything I could do about it."

"Hmm. Very interesting. How much is it worth?"

I told him. "About three quarters of a million. Maybe more."

"The problem is, even if she promised it to you, you have to have it in writing. And she's entitled to change her mind. Still, let me think it over. Maybe we can come up with something."

And then, in the Ladies', by sheer force of habit, I swiped my underarms with paper towels, put on lipstick, and finger-combed my hair. In the fluorescent lights my face looked swollen.

"Catch up," he said when I sat across from him again.

I held the drink and took three large gulps. "There, is that good?" I asked.

"More," he said.

I leaned my head back and swallowed. Fire and ice down my throat. I was quite tipsy but I didn't feel as good as I had expected. Apart from the guilt, I didn't feel high or fun-loving. If anything, I felt kind of down. But there was no turning back.

To his credit, he didn't put his hand on my knee. I was the one who initiated, but I swear to God it felt like my hand was there because he wanted it to be. We left our half-mangled steaks and leathery potatoes and I brought him up to my room, snarfed with him on the chair in the corner and finally the bed. But when he'd passed out, his breath like a gin mill, I went into the bathroom and threw up. I scrubbed my teeth, then drank three tumblers of water. I didn't want to have to go back out there, face him. I felt sad and shitty. I thought of Steven and Dan, and what they would think of me if they knew. And some of my good feelings for Wally were gone. I wasn't sure I still respected him, or that I trusted him. Or could work with him.

When I finally did go back out there, he was asleep on the bed, wheezing a little, the hair on his chest rising and falling. And suddenly I did feel tenderness for him and a line from an old Marvin Gaye song came into my head: "We're all such silly people, let's get it on."

It wasn't a crime to be lonely or to have sex, I told myself. Wally *was* married, though, now that I thought of it. Of course I'd thought of it earlier too, but had figured that if he wasn't worried, who was I to be morality cop? At least I wasn't involved with anyone.

And so I kissed his shoulder and when he roused himself we made love again, more tenderly and more satisfactorily and it seemed we were an old married couple, come together after an infidelity, wary and resigned and forgiving.

"Oh Polly," he said, kissing me on the lips. "I've wanted to do that for years. Get into those hot little pants of yours."

And that could have grossed me out, but it made me feel good, and when he suggested a drink from the minibar, I said, "Wally, you've got to go home."

He looked at his watch and said, "Shit, yeah."

"Aren't you happily married?" I asked, stupidly.

And he said, "Oh, we're all right, I guess. You know how it is, the kids, the mortgage, the dog."

"Oh yeah," I said. "I keep forgetting about the dog."

"Polly, I'll work on it," he said, blowing me a kiss from the door. As I turned the lock behind him, I thought about how I'd have to get a new lawyer.

I held my breath when I asked for my bill the next morning, even though I had my credit card ready. I needn't have worried; Wally had paid for everything. And upstairs, shoved into the wastepaper basket, was the navy blue dress.

After I got back to Rockhaven I had a frenzy of house cleaning. It suddenly seemed imperative that I sort through old boxes and throw out sweaters I hadn't worn in years. Some of them dated back to my time with Dan. And then I remembered my old car, cleaning her out after those weeks when she'd been my home, when I finally decided that the booze was the problem, not the answer. The car was not big, and yet I'd found fourteen bottles of alcohol, in varying sizes and states of emptiness, from the gallon jugs of cheap white wine in the trunk to the whiskey flasks under the seats to the airport bottles I'd stowed away in the glove compartment.

I thought about leaving Rockhaven, moving down to the Main Line. It didn't have to be the Main Line, after all; it could be Philadelphia. I could start life over: get a job, an apartment. Monroe wouldn't have to leave Dan and Chloe, but she could spend weekends with me. I imagined visiting the Liberty Bell, picking apples on weekends, wholesome activities. I saw myself standing on the soccer field, hands in my pockets, and I wanted to puke. The panicky feelings started again. But I believed it was cowardice not to try.

I walked the dirty streets of Rockhaven, the salt and slush mingling together. This was no place for a child. This was no place for me. I gazed out to sea. It was in me now. The wind, the water. I dreamed of the island. Cool and quiet and still. All this was just a distraction. But still, I wondered what made me think she'd be better off with me, I who spread destruction all about me.

Later, when I was home, something Wally had said came back to me. It was after we had sex the first time, just before he crashed. Lying on his back he'd laughed and said, "Dan told me once that you'd sleep with anyone who moved."

Even when you knew it was just about the sex, there's still a sadness that that's what it's about. I didn't expect romance. But maybe I did. Maybe I was just as corny and misguided as the rest of them.

I had gone down to see Wally on a Thursday. On Monday, my mother called. I knew by the way she said hello that something was amiss.

"Hello, Mother, how are you?"

"Someone horrible called me this morning. He said he was your lawyer."

"Wally?" I said.

"He was very threatening. He said I had to give you the island, that I'd promised it to you and that was binding. Russ has explained to me that of course it isn't. And that your lawyer must know that."

"Oh, Mother, I'm so sorry. I can't believe Wally did that. He didn't check with me."

"Well, I suppose it only makes it easier to tell you what I have to tell you." She cleared her throat. "You remember how I said the island was yours? Well, it seems that there may be a problem. Russ has been explaining it to me."

I caught my breath. "What kind of a problem?"

"Well, you know, financial. I've been talking with your brother, who, you know, is good with financial things. He seems to think that selling the island is a good idea."

"And tell her," I heard Russ say in the background, "we're not really selling it, we'll still be in charge."

"I know you love its beauty—we all do—but I think we have to accept that the world is full of change."

"Wait. Wait a minute," I said, trying to gather my thoughts. "Mother, you can't do this. You gave me the island. That's completely asinine."

"Polly, please don't speak that way to me. Russ has been explaining to me that you'll all still be able to go there. It won't be so bad, will it?"

"It'll be terrible—"

"Hold on, your brother wants to speak to you."

It probably should not have surprised me that my mother called to say the island was not to be mine after all. Caitlin was not the kind of person who could be counted on, we all knew that. It wasn't that she was deliberately dishonest or malicious, it's just that in her remote way she was capricious. Unreliable. But this time I'd really wanted to believe she was behind me.

"Hi, Polly," Russ said. "First of all, I can't believe you got a lawyer involved. That's very disloyal of you."

"Disloyal? That's such BS. I'd say what you're doing is very disloyal. Mother promised me the island."

"I know you want to believe I'm the big bad wolf, but it's not me. It's Herbert's estate," he began. "I'm afraid things don't look that good." He explained that Herbert was not in great financial shape when he died. "Things are actually pretty precarious for Mother. If we're going to keep her out of the poorhouse, we're going to need the equity of the island."

"But that can't be," I said. "He would have mentioned it to her. To someone."

"I think he was embarrassed. Look, I've got the papers right here. You want, I'll show them to you line by line."

I sighed. Part of me knew I should go down there and take a look. It wasn't that I didn't trust Russ, but still. I didn't, entirely. On the other hand, I wouldn't know what I was looking at. I didn't understand financial things. But I could ask Wally to review them, I thought. "I think my lawyer should take a look," I said.

"Wally?" He said it as if that was the biggest joke he'd ever heard. "Of course, sure. If that's what you want. I'll send them to him. It's all in black and white, though. Plus, he's going to charge you for it. You know that, right?"

"Of course I know that."

"I'm not making this up."

"Mother says you've taken over Herbert's old office?"

"Yeah, it's perfect. Got my wingtips, got my cigars. I even found a set of Herbert's old irons, so I've been able to practice my golf a wee bit."

He said it in a jokey way, but I suspected he was serious. And then something occurred to me that I hadn't realized before. All of this was playing into some vision he had of himself. Some vision of Mr. Big.

I tried a different tack. "How can you want to do this? Big noisy boats and people everywhere?"

He said, "But we always used to dream about motorboats—that's what we wanted."

"We also wanted a kilo of cocaine—oh, that's not the point. The point is that if you bring motorboats and tourists and build up the island, you're going to wreck it. What makes it special is its pristine quality."

"See, I just don't get that. Here's a prime piece of real estate going for the begging. This entire family is broke—Mother's situation is serious, Elena and Roger need money yesterday, I've got major expenses, you're basically useless—"

"Hey, wait a minute, I'm not in debt at least."

"No, but if you crack thirty grand a year it'll be a miracle."

"Well, what about you? You've flubbed up plenty."

"That's my *point*. We need the island."

"But Russ," I said. "What about Colin? All our memories?" I stared out the window at the empty bird feeder. "All you care about is money. If you loved the island, if you wanted to be there, that would be different."

"No, you listen to me. What you don't understand—and I shouldn't have to spell this out—is that I do feel a loyalty to the island, to Herbert, and, yes, to Colin, to treat it with respect. This resort is my way of repaying any debt to the family I might have. If I even have one, which is debatable. Once you see the end result, and reap the considerable benefits, I might add, you'll recognize my brilliance." He paused to catch his breath, then said, "Why do you feel your vision is better than mine?"

"Why? I'll tell you why. Not only would you ruin our island, but your resort idea won't even work. Look around. Do you see exclusive resorts in Maine? No. It's because they don't exist. Maine's not Florida, you know. Be real, Russ. Maine is a place of hardship and deprivation. The hunting's spotty. There are environmental regulations. The weather's iffy. I know you mean well, but your idea is, to say the very least, misguided."

"No one appreciated Einstein either."

"Russ, what happened to you?"

"What do you mean? Nothing."

"Will destroying the island really make you happy?" I asked.

"Oh, don't be so melodramatic. I'm not destroying the island, I'm making it better. So, what about the papers? You want me to send them to Wally?"

I gazed out at the snow-covered lawn through the plastic-sheeted windows. I thought about fighting, but I knew it was futile. He would always find some way to defeat me. "No, it's okay. Forget it," I said.

"One other thing. As I explained to Mother, I'm going to need power of attorney, to take care of some of the little tricky matters."

"Surely that's not necessary," I said. "Mother's of sound mind. She's right there."

"Of course she'll be involved in every decision we make."

"Let me talk to her again." I waited while he covered the phone with his hand. Then she came on the line. "Mother? Is everything all right? I feel like you're being bullied."

"No dear, don't worry about me. I feel quite taken care of."

After we hung up, I sat, stunned. All the objects around me seemed to have changed. They were filled with a mocking quality now, a loathing. The mugs and plates and pitchers mocked me. Even the flat wooden tabletop scorned me for trusting anyone.

It was amazing how easy it was to start drinking again. All I had to do was go to the package store one or two towns over where I didn't know anybody and buy a six of beer. I'd expected thunder and lightning, diabolical reactions. Nobody said anything. Nobody cared. I'd feared my sponsor might somehow magically know, but Joan and I hadn't talked in a while. She'd probably been as convinced of my sobriety as I was.

I lasted the drive home before opening the first can. Later that evening I said, I'm just going to finish this six-pack. But then, mysteriously, I found myself driving twenty miles to the all-night convenience store for more.

This happened four, five days in a row. But as the week began to end, I told myself I'd stop. You've had your fun, I said. Week's over. I planned to stop, I truly did. But I couldn't. I thought about attending a meeting, checking in with my sponsor, telling her what was going on. But I couldn't. I didn't drink on my shift, and I didn't drink first thing in the morning. But whenever I could squeeze a drink in, I would. I was starting to get bored with beer too. You had to drink so much to get a buzz on, plus it was fattening and made you have to pee all the time. That's when I started supplementing with gin. A little here and there. Not very much. I always bought small bottles because I wanted to finish what I had in the house; it seemed unlucky to leave additional booze around—that would just tempt me to drink. That would be like condoning it.

And on that second Thursday night—I think it was a Thursday, the days were all sort of starting to run into each other—when I'd already finished my six-pack for the day and was well into the gin, and it was only dinnertime, except I wasn't eating, I never had an appetite anymore, I sat on the couch in my living room with the phone on my lap. I wanted to call Steven. What would I say? I love you. *I love you?* I must be nuts. I hadn't talked to him in weeks. I put the phone down. There was half a beer left.

The phone rang, and I lunged at it.

"Mom?" Monroe. Shit. I'd already missed one of her calls earlier in the week.

"Hi, baby."

"You sound funny."

"No, baby, I'm fine." I could tell I sounded bad, slurred and stupid.

"Mom, Mme. Manet died." She started crying. Her grief appalled and petrified me. She started telling me the details. I tried to sober up. I stood up (head rush) and limped (foot asleep) into the kitchen to get some ice. There was no ice in the freezer, so I stood outside on my little porch, the receiver tucked under my ear, and grabbed a handful of grimy snow from the railing, to rub around my face.

"Mom? Daddy wants to talk to you."

"Oh no, honey, not now—"

"Polly?" Quick, what could I do? Hang up the phone? "Are you there, Polly?"

"Yeah, I'm here, Dan."

"Wally called me." My heart sank. Another drunken wave rose inside me. "I don't know what kind of game you're playing, but threatening me isn't going to work."

I slurred something in response.

"Are you okay?" he asked. "Did I wake you up?"

"Yeah, so tired, lemme call you tomorrow."

I could just hear him when he got off the phone saying to Chloe, She sounded like she'd been drinking. Or, I hope she hasn't been drinking. And then he would pour himself a jolly old glass of brandy or sherry or what have you, smug in the fact that *he* didn't have a problem.

I sat down on the couch and shut my eyes. I must have dozed off because I woke with a start. I'd been dreaming of Steven. We'd been kissing, hugging. I longed for him. Surely he knew that?

I reached for the phone. I shouldn't call him. Instead I dialed Audrey. "Audrey? It's me. You want to go bowling?"

She objected to the fact that it was almost 8:00 at night. "Are you all right, Polly?"

"I'm fine, just a little sleepy."

"If you're sleepy, why'd ya wanta go bowling?"

"To wake me up."

"You're crazy, girl. Get some rest. I'll see you tomorrow." We hung up.

I had that feeling of being on the outside, watching myself. Maybe Steven would go bowling with me. I picked up the phone yet again and dialed his number. It rang once and then I hung up.

I thought about calling Wally. He'd left me a bunch of messages. I tried his cell phone and got his voice mail. I was not calling him at home. I remembered his wife and kids and shame spread over me.

I grabbed my coat and car keys and went out.

Tonight I didn't care if everyone knew I'd started drinking again. Tonight I was going to the bar. Life was a lot more fun when you were drinking with other people. I'd forgotten that.

The Hornblower was loud and smoky. It felt good, all those warm bodies bumping against each other. It was surreal, though, to be back in a place like this. Eddie and Mack were there, bellied up to the bar. I hadn't seen them since that afternoon in October. They welcomed me with a smile and cheers. "What're you drinking, my girl?"

"Beer."

"Beer with a tequila chaser," Eddie said.

"You chase her," Mack said, and burst into uproarious laughter.

I laughed too, even though it wasn't funny, even though it was stupid. I was just so glad to get out of my house. See, this was normal. People hanging around making stupid jokes. Laughing. Drinking. Enjoying themselves. What was so wrong with that? After a couple more drinks I made my way to the pay phone, fished out a quarter. I knew Steven's number by heart.

"Hello?" He sounded like he'd been asleep.

"Oh, shit, did I wake you up?"

"Polly? What time is it?" Then, waking up more, a touch of worry in his voice, "Where are you? Are you okay? Do you need me to come get you?"

"Oh, Steven. It's nothing like that."

"What?"

"I said, it's nothing like that. I just wondered if you wanted to come have a drink with me."

"Jesus, Polly. Where are you? What bar?"

"Forget it. Mistake. Sorry I called."

"Me too."

We hung up. *Me too.* Did he have to be so mean?

Eddie and Mack were waiting at the bar, and for a minute I considered not going back in there. But then there I was nestled up between them and, when Eddie put his arm around my shoulder a drink or two later, I didn't flinch. Part of me could see myself clearly, this terrible mistake I was about to make, and part of me was just there, drinking and not caring. Sometime after that Eddie and I were in the corner near the phone booth and his hands were everywhere and Mack was kind of standing guard, kind of watching us, and Eddie said, "See, Polly, you can be friendly when you want to. Why are you such a stranger?"

But a little later, I said, "Eddie, I'm sorry, I can't do this."

"Shit, Polly, not a-fucking-gain. You are such a goddamn tease."

"Eddie, get off me. Let me go. Right now." I pulled away from him, fumbling and straightening up as I went. In the parking lot I tried to open the door to the Green Hornet but missed and was surprised to find myself sitting on the hard ground. My breath spun out in whorls. Behind the cars, black trees slashed against the sky and I shut my eyes because they kept moving. From the Hornblower's entrance a blast of noise burst out. I jolted myself upright, yanked open the door, and slid inside the car. I managed to puke half outside on the ground and half on my boots. I was scared Eddie had followed me, but there was only the sign from the bar flashing on some snow and the faint light of the crescent moon.

The car wouldn't start. "Goddamn it," I muttered, and pressed hard on the clutch, turning and turning the key, listening to the engine cough over. I knew what I was doing wrong, I just couldn't seem to do it right. I rested my forehead on the wheel, forced myself to be calm, and tried again. Finally she ignited and slowly, jerkily, I made for home.

The next morning, I began drinking in earnest. Vodka in my coffee, that kind of thing. It seemed inevitable: the only solution, the only choice. I wouldn't drink forever, I promised myself—I couldn't, I would die from it—but I didn't know when I could stop.

Here's the thing: Drinking didn't feel good anymore, or exciting, or even naughty. It certainly wasn't fun. It was stressful. I was constantly thinking about alcohol, how I could get more, when was my next drink. Even while having a drink I thought about the next one. There was no present for me, only future. Only want and deprivation. The only time I was happy, or felt reasonably content, was the moment before I tasted a fresh drink—that one moment, the drink up in the air, tilted toward my throat. I was happy then.

Three weeks later and I was drinking on the job. Out behind the dumpsters. A slug or two. Just enough.

Of course, Audrey caught me.

"Jesus, Polly, what are you doing back here?"

"Just sneaking a smoke."

She sighed. "You and I have been friends a long time. It's hard to say this. But I can't keep quiet. You're drinking again, aren't you?"

"No, of course not." Even as I looked into her face I was thinking about when she would be gone and I could take another slug. "How can you say such a thing?"

She gave me her severe look, the one she must give her children. "You know, you and alcohol don't mix."

I knew the only way to get her off my back was to argue with her so I said, "Audrey, that fucking pisses me off you would even think that."

"I just hope you're checking in with your sponsor."

"Why should I? You're so nosy, always in everyone's business. Why don't you leave me alone?"

"Well, I wouldn't a' said anything if I knew I was going to get my head bitten off."

After that day we ignored each other. I loved her and I knew she wanted to help, but just then it felt too much like interference. And she must have realized she couldn't help me because she didn't try again.

One day in the midst of all this, Melanie called. I was half drunk, a fairly common state for me though I could definitely pull off sober-seeming if I needed to. At least I thought I could.

"Polly, this is Melanie."

"Hey, girl. How's your hubby?"

She took a deep breath. "I'm not actually living with Russ anymore."

"What?"

"I'm staying with a friend for a little while. He hasn't told you?"

"No," I said, sitting down. I remembered Melanie in their large glass house, sitting alone at the table in her black kimono.

"You've always been such a friend to me, which is why I wanted to let you know."

Nothing could have made me feel worse. I took a sip from my drink and said, "What's going on?"

"I'm so confused. I feel like I don't know Russ anymore. I used to think, when Russ talked about his ex-wives, that it was their fault the marriages didn't work out. They didn't understand him, maybe, or they didn't want to work hard enough."

I made polite, listening noises.

"But now I wonder. I have a different perspective."

"Well, it's so hard to know what goes on inside someone else's marriage. But what happened? You guys seemed so—" I searched for the word. It wasn't *happy*, it wasn't *well-suited*. "Settled."

"It was a façade."

"What about the baby stuff? I know you guys were trying—"

"There will be no baby," she said. "Russ doesn't want to keep trying. He says he's done." She began weeping quietly. "He cares more about money than human life. And the horrible thing is, I knew that about him. But I thought he would change. I had to leave him. I can't even tell my parents. They will be so ashamed."

"Oh Melanie, I'm sorry."

"And then I found out what he'd done to you. I don't know how you can take it. My family is not like this. Loyalty is paramount."

"I'm a little confused. Are you talking about the island?"

"Of course."

"Well, I guess Russ feels he knows what's best for the family. I guess Herbert had some pretty severe debts and Russ feels developing the island will solve the problem." I hated being in the position of having to defend my brother. But something made me. It was like we were children again, all banded together. I don't know why Melanie talked about loyalty. I was loyal to a fault. "Oh Melanie, I'm sure your parents will understand. They love you."

She snuffled.

"Please let me know if there's anything I can do to help."

"No, I just wanted to say good-bye."

I felt helpless. "I'm so sorry," I said again. By the time we hung up a few minutes later, I was already sipping a new drink.

That Saturday I drove out to the large discount store outside of town, the one I called "discontent store" in my head, the one everyone disparaged and said had ruined the local shops, but that everyone shopped at anyway. It was huge, cheaper than the other stores, and provided jobs, and it did this by coming into a community, offering cheaper prices and products and greater selection. But then, when the competition had been hobbled, the store raised its prices.

Nevertheless, there was something seductive about the aisles and aisles of things, the bulk items, the plastic and jugs. Every area of life tackled. Outside were little garden houses and supplies, the promise of spring more than the reality.

It was not my job to do the shopping, but Stella had asked me and I had to stay on her good side. Normally I liked doing errands on company time—it made a nice change—but today, not only was I hungover and dehydrated (I'd been in bar—a new bar, not Eddie's—till closing last night), but I also had the headache of trying to deal with a misplaced order. Instead of prime rib, I would have to make chipped beef, which I hated, and so did everyone else. Saturday night was supposed to be special, but due to an error (on my part, I hated to admit—wouldn't, in fact, admit to Stella), I would have to cook the worst meal on the menu.

I found the dish drainer and the vats of dishwashing liquid we needed at the home, and then I wandered up and down the toy section. Monnie was now seven. What did she play with? I thought of Barbies and dress-up clothes and fluffy bunnies. Here were mother and child dolls, both princesses. Still thinking about the chipped beef, and how stupid I was to have not ordered the right meat, I put the dolls in my basket.

I stood on line. Before I noticed, the salesgirl had rung up the Barbie with the stuff for the home. It was not that big a deal, I could square accounts later. But then I remembered the warning

Stella had given us, about not mixing private purchases with company ones. And I realized the Barbie set was deluxe, and priced at $29. I really didn't want to spend that kind of money on trash. So, apologizing to the people behind me, I told the girl I'd made a mistake and could she take it off my bill.

"I'm sorry," she said. She was bovine-looking. "I can't do that."

"What do you mean?"

"You've already paid for it. You'll have to go to the returns counter."

"Oh fuck me," I said.

"Could you please watch your language?"

People jostled behind me. What a life. What a fucking life. It would probably be easier to take the stupid dolls with me. But I dreaded trying to return them later. Stores like this always sucked energy from me. I was already craving the nip I'd swallow in the car. And suddenly I was in it, the crazy rage that used to happen to me. "Jesus Christ," I said loudly. "What kind of a fucking store is this? I don't want the dolls." And I took the box and flung it on the floor. People started scampering, convinced I was a terrorist.

A pudgy security guard trotted up to me. "Ma'am—" he started.

"I just want to return the fucking dolls," I told him. "What happened to 'the customer is always right'?"

"Ma'am, if you would lower your voice, I will escort you to a customer-care representative."

"Customer care! Customer care, I don't give a shit about that, I just want to return the goddamn dolls."

He escorted me over.

"This is outrageous," I said. "Making me stand in two lines with *incompetents*," I shouted.

"We are going to have to ask you to keep your voice down or we will escort you from the building," the security guard said.

"Here," a young woman with dyed black hair behind the

counter said nervously, "I can help you with that." She rang it up and made me fill out a form and in two minutes we were done.

"That's all I wanted," I said.

"You have a good day, y'hear?"

"You have ruined my day," I said. "Just give me the receipt."

Outside, it had started to rain. Family groups of fat people and children whining around gumball machines lingered under the store's awnings. Some of them nudged each other when I went by.

As I walked out into the parking lot, I saw Steven. My stomach turned over. We hadn't talked since the night I'd called him from the bar. Skippy ran to greet me. Steven saw me and for a moment he didn't have any expression and then he smiled, not a big one or anything, but still a smile. I couldn't help myself, I grinned back. And then the picture filled in around him and I saw his truck, an oversize cart full of bright plastic things and, beside it, a woman I knew was his wife.

"Polly," he said. "You remember Debbie?"

We nodded at each other. She was thinner than I remembered, almost bony. She probably bought her pants in the teen department. She was pretty in a hard, scrappy way, her hair short and artificially colored. That he would pick a woman like her seemed absurdly a rejection of me. On the other hand, he *had* picked her.

"Well, you have quite a haul here," I said, referring to the boxes of snack food, the liters of soda, and the toys.

"Birthdays coming up," Steven said.

"Left the kids at Grammaw's." Debbie laughed huskily, wiped a fleck of tobacco off his cheek. She continued to groom him, straightening his collar, removing a hair from his shoulder. I wanted to ask after her father, remembering he had cancer, but what if he'd died?

"How are you?" Steven asked.

I shrugged.

"I've meant to call you. Check on you."

"It's okay."

He looked like he wanted to say more, but couldn't. Debbie glanced from one of us to the other, her eyes both shrewd and wary. She was jealous of me. I was shocked, and then I felt naïve. "Sucky weather," I said.

"Terrible," she agreed. She reached over and took a drag off Steven's cigarette. She was nervous and Steven was embarrassed by her. That made me not like him. He was weak, I thought, not able to push for what he really wanted, not able to embrace what he had.

It was awkward standing in the parking lot, unable to think of anything else to say. Finally, we said good-bye and I pushed my cart on, unloaded my rubber products, made sure to return it to the cart corral (the prices would go up, a sign threatened, if attendants had to chase around the lot after carts), returned to my car, opened the door, and got in.

Dirty snow lay bunched around the parking lot and under the wispy hedges, mixed with bits of sodden litter. I stared at all the filthy cars, salt-encrusted, grimy. The gray sky. I looked at the key in my hand and couldn't remember what it was for. I put it in the ignition and a horrible noise burst out. I turned the engine off, grabbed my flask. Steven had been my friend for years—I did love him—but he had his own life. He had a wife who looked at me with suspicion, and children who expected plastic toys on their birthdays.

Come on, I told myself after I'd drunk some, snap out of it. I started driving, got to the home, and performed my duties in the kitchen with only a minor burn to my wrist. And all the while I thought, Steven isn't the answer.

I woke at four in the morning, when the low blood sugar kicked in, disoriented, anxious. I had passed out in the living room again. Everything was awful, inside my body and out. I remembered a time when Monnie was seven or eight months old and I had to renew my driver's license. The place was packed with lines of people. She was such a squirmy baby that I'd put her on her stomach on the floor and someone almost stepped on her and a guard had yelled at me. My heart pounded, remembering how close she had come to being trampled. Another time I'd let a door slam on her finger. I looked around the room and saw broken things needing to be fixed: a clock that had stopped ticking, garbage overflowing, a shattered glass I hadn't bothered to clean up. The gin bottle was by the sofa, the top not even screwed back on. I wrinkled my face, ready for the first slug, but the smell nauseated me. I persevered. The gin wouldn't stay in my mouth; it dribbled down my chin. I thought of Wally, how he'd harassed my mother, how I'd slept with him and how wrong that was. Russ had taken the island, and I deserved that. I'd lost Colin and it was my own fault. I took a deep breath, ready to force myself to swallow. And then, even as I couldn't bear to admit it, I knew I was ruining my life with the booze, getting further away from the things I wanted. I'd alienated my mother, my sister, my brother, my friend, my ex-husband, and my child.

And an image of Bride Island came to me, the dark pine trees rising from the water, the rocks ringing the shore. How quiet and contained it was. I thought of the house and the cemetery, the pond and the field, the mental stillness I would find. I needed to go there. More than ever I needed to go there. No matter that it was March, that there was still snow and ice. It was go there, or die.

But how? I couldn't ask Steven. For one thing, his boat was out of the water until spring. For another, I knew he wouldn't take me now. I took a slug of gin and thought. Two towns up there was a marina with a pretty good rental business: kayaks, canoes, small sailboats, even a few whalers. I didn't know if they would be open in the off season, but I would try.

Before work the next morning I went up to the marina. In the store window, I caught sight of my reflection and for a second I didn't recognize myself. My hair was dirty, my eyes bloodshot, I was wearing a stained polar fleece jacket that should have been washed two weeks ago. I hesitated before going in, tried to finger-comb my hair, and zipped up my jacket.

A young, bald guy behind the counter nattered into the phone. I stood a moment, waiting. His shirt said "Virgil" on it in script. He kept talking, so I wandered up and down the aisles, past all the coils of rope, the bolts of sailcloth and racks of foul-weather gear, the hooks and clips and compasses, the little bins of nails and such. The gear. I loved stores like this.

In one of the aisles a sales attendant sifted through a box of nails. He was about forty, with a curly dark beard and, like most people around here, a reddish, weathered face.

"Hi," I said.

"Hiya." He kept sorting through the nails.

"I'm looking for a boat," I said.

"That's a good thing to be looking for." He didn't sound like a local—probably he was a transplant like me.

"I wondered if you would have any advice."

Now he looked at me. "You probably don't need advice. You probably know what you want and should go and get it."

"Follow your heart's desire, eh?"

"That's right." He smiled at me.

"Well, it's not always that easy," I said. "Knowing what you want is one thing, knowing how to get it is something else."

He leaned back on his heels and looked at me. His eyes were blue. "Indeed."

"So, do you think you could advise me?"

"You really want me to?"

I was torn between amusement and exasperation. Then an idea struck me.

"You don't work here, do you?"

"Nope."

"Aha."

"But there's a nice guy up at the counter. He could probably help you out."

"Virgil," I said.

"That's right."

Something held me. Maybe the fact that he made me laugh. Or the fact that he looked at me so kindly. "I guess I'll go up there."

He nodded. "Good luck."

When I arrived at the counter, Virgil quickly got off the phone—I had a feeling he'd been talking with his girlfriend—and after I'd explained what I was looking for, he said, "We're not doing rentals now."

"Look, a whaler, anything. I need to get out to an island. Bride Island."

"I'm sorry, I can't help you. Come back in May, and even then we're not really open till June."

"Do you think I could get out there in a sea kayak?" Maybe I could buy one. I wondered how much food and gear I could carry, how safe it would be. "How much are they?"

"A good one'll set you back about two thousand, maybe eighteen hundred." I sighed. "And this is not the season for paddling out to no island."

The other man came up to the cash register with his box of nails and was trying not to listen. Virgil cocked his head at me and said to him, "She wants to kayak out to an island. Told her it's not safe."

"It's okay, I can't afford it anyway." I shook my head, ready to leave. I'd begun craving a nip.

"You could take her out," Virgil, lowering his voice, told the bearded man. "You've got the boat."

Something flashed between them, some nonverbal exchange, and the bearded one nodded.

"No," I said, "I didn't mean—"

"Oh, he don't mind," Virgil said.

The bearded one asked me when and where. I told him I was thinking of heading out next Friday, for the weekend. I held my breath.

"Sure, I'll do it," he said, more to Virgil than to me. He scratched his chin. "There's a cove just up from the marina here—do you know it?"

I nodded.

"I'll meet you there Friday midday."

"You will? You'll do it?"

He nodded. "I can come pick you up on Sunday too."

"Oh, perfect," I said. I cleared my throat, looked away. I hated this part. "Of course, I'll pay you." I was suddenly conscious of my unwashed hair and bloodshot eyes. I wondered if he could tell I'd been drinking. At the same moment I thought longingly of my bottle in the car.

He told me we'd work it out. He told me his name and immediately I forgot it. When I offered to give him my number, he shook his head and wouldn't take it. "I'll be there," he said.

"Well, at least give me yours," I said, "in case something comes up."

He shrugged. "Call Virgil at the marina here. He'll know how to get in touch with me."

I looked at him more carefully. He was on the tall side, with dark blue eyes. His beard made him seem big, but he was actually kind of slender. I wanted to ask him his name again, only after what he'd said I felt I couldn't. "Okay, then," I said. "I'll see you on Friday."

He smiled again. "Come hell or high water." Even the cliché didn't sound bad in his mouth. And for a moment, less than a moment, I quit longing for a drink, and I just stood still and felt this friendly gesture.

Eight

A week after my visit to the marina I set foot on Bride Island. I don't set foot so much as lurch, almost fall. I'm a bit wobbly, partly because I'm pissed off, and partly because I'm pissed. Woozy. Tipsy. Inebriated. All right, drunk.

The bearded one says, "Are you sure you're okay to do this? How much did you actually drink?"

"I told you before, I'm fine."

He sighs. Condensation steams out of his mouth like smoke. "Please, tell me there's someone else here. Tell me you're not camping out, that there's a nice warm house here, preferably with central heating, not a stove or a fire, or something that can do serious damage to suffocate or poison you. Please tell me that."

"Could you pass me my things? Or get out of my way." The wind whips the words out of my mouth.

"I can't leave you here like this. I really can't. Apart from anything else, if something happens to you, your family would sue me."

I sigh loudly, exaggeratedly. "Nothing is going to happen to me. Besides, they won't care. They won't know." I haul bags. I've borrowed a tent from Audrey's husband, Bill, and the most high-tech winter gear he has. All my stuff is summer-weight. He's lent me a little cook-stove, as well as snowshoes and a sleeping bag. I have a thermos of tea and, in homage to Chloe, one of pea soup. I have chocolate bars and energy bars and dried fruit and nuts. I also have oatmeal and beef jerky. "Okay," I say, once I've lugged all my stuff onto the dock. "Thanks for the ride." Then, as a friendly reminder, I add, "You can go now."

"I can't let you do this. It's not safe."

"You can't stop me."

"Don't be crazy."

"I told you, go." Something in me snaps and I'm pushing at him as hard as I can, at his chest with my arm and at his boat with my foot. "Get the fuck off my island," I yell, and part of me knows this is totally ludicrous, only I'm in it and can't get out. I don't even hear what he says, my head is hammering so loudly. But it works. He starts his motor up and reverses his boat, shaking his head as the boat moves away.

I am so drunk, I can barely believe I got here. But I had to get drunk, I remind myself, since it's my last time.

My plan is to camp on the island for two nights. In my bones I know I need this, this chilling and enduring. I know other people have therapy. Other people don't need to go out into freezing temperatures and do this. But I do. And it's the only way I can think to stop drinking.

If I have expected any signs of spring, I am very much mistaken. Snow mounds the island. Banks of old, windswept, sandy snow. My knees tremble but it's not the cold. I don't feel the cold. I'm not even wearing my warmest clothes and I'm hot. Intellectually, I know I have to be careful, that the cold, and my obliviousness to it, could be dangerous. No, what makes me tremble suddenly is the folly of this. What was I thinking? The sheer, obstinate stupidity of what I'm doing attacks my bowels and I feel a surge of panic.

Instinctively I turn around and look for the boat. It's nowhere in sight. I scour the water, and finally make out a tiny speck that turns out to be a seagull. He really has gone.

I turn back to look at the beach. All of my favorite books were about children who survived solo. How did they do it? They were plucky, those children. Plus they lived in an ultimately benign universe.

The enormity, the craziness of what I'm doing hits me again. I gag, then bend over and breathe deeply. And then I do what I always used to do. I pretend to be sober.

The first question is where to put the tent. There will be a spot in the lee, I promise myself. But right now there doesn't seem to be anywhere not ravaged by the wind. None of the trees have leaves. Much of the island, of course, is coniferous. Pines, spruces, firs. But still many of the trees are deciduous, almost the whole understory of shrubs and bushes. Without leaves, it gives the impression of being much lighter than in the summer.

It's 3:00. Two hours, perhaps, till sunset, and I have a lot to do. First I drag my kit up the beach and behind a big rock. I need to find a campsite. The air is sharp with briny wind, the thrashing trees sound like helicopters. I have a spot in mind. So, grabbing my pack, I turn away from the path to the house and head toward Indian Cemetery and the clearing by the pond.

I pitch the tent on my third try, which seems reasonable considering my depth perception is off and my fingers are having problems grasping the thin poles and latches—though whether from the cold or my drunken state I'm not sure. I put down the mat and the air mattress, set up the stove, and start a small fire with exaggerated care. To focus myself, I imagine the lonely inhabitants of other islands seeing my fire burning. I am filled with excitement, suddenly, and the feeling that this is going to work out. It's going to be splendid.

Once the fire is going, it is easy to make a simple meal on my stove. The beef stew, plus the pea soup, revives me and I feel better, pleased with myself. I wash out my dishes in the snow, tidy up, make everything shipshape. Oh, Bearded One, I think, I wish you could see me now. For a moment I regret telling him to fuck off.

Pleasantly full, I sit inside my tent as darkness falls. It's snug in here, out of the wind. I've arranged everything. Now I have nothing to do but wait quietly until it's time to go to sleep. I sit and wait. Wait and sit. The air in the tent begins to feel close. I peer out through the flaps. The sun has almost disappeared. The island looks so different now, the landscape so much harsher than in summer.

When I step outside, the cold burns my face. The ground is frozen and bumpy, uneven. Down at the point, the wind whips my ears even through my hat. This time of year, it's as if summer is a distant memory, civilized life completely overridden by the wildness of winter. I remember the old fable of how the island got its name, a woman abandoned by her lover, who promised to come back for her and never did. How did she manage? Or any of those other people who lived on islands year-round. Well, for one thing, they farmed a bit—vegetables, berries, and so forth. They dried and conserved. They fished and raised some livestock. But the sheer effort of constantly maintaining the fire, or cracking open the well water, of the long, lonely winter—how did they manage that?

I reach the shore. The tide is low and I walk on the rocks, black, slippery rocks, out toward the sea. The sun has set but there is a last blaze of pink in the sky, and a few opalescent clouds. The air is cold and wet, wind flicking bits of spray.

Had she a daughter, that mysterious bride? Had she been pregnant when her young husband left? If she had, the baby might have died in childbirth. Or perhaps, miraculously, the woman had delivered a healthy baby who survived that first terrible winter, and then the years after that. How that child would have been cherished. But that was impossible. The bride's body had been found in the spring by a neighbor who'd come over to investigate on the first day fit to sail. Or so the story goes.

As I pick my way over the rocks, I try to imagine that poor young woman, scanning the horizon every day, searching desperately for a sail. How her heart would sink, only to become hopeful again each morning.

And yet she must have known, once the seas became too choppy, that there was little likelihood of him returning. She must have surveyed her meager rations and wondered what she would do. Colin and I used to speculate about the bride: Had she just given up, or had she struggled to survive? Had she eaten bark, and leaves, and other dried things? We fantasized about living together on the island, what we would do, how we would survive. Because we were sure we would survive.

And now I remember his eyes beseeching me, Colin's brown eyes that turned darker when he was angry. I shake my head as if to clear it of the vision and then, looking at the waves washing up on the rocks, I see where I am. In the twilight I have come to the cove where he drowned that night. I don't remember making the choice to walk down here. It's not a place I want to be particularly, not now, not ever.

I stare out at the oily blackness of the water, only a few slippery rocks away from me. Colin didn't fight the water that night. He wasn't a fighter. He wasn't a fucking fighter. My eyes tear, or else it's the wind. Colin drowned because he wanted to. Didn't he? The waves splash and gurgle at me. The inky darkness lures me. I feel muddle-headed, as if I were submerged already. It would be so easy to slip in. I would freeze, probably, before I would drown. Fishermen hereabouts say it's better to not be able to swim, that swimming only prolongs the agony.

"Colin," I call. His name shoots away from me, over the water and into the wind. My eyes tear. I stand on the rocks, neither trying to remember nor forget the night he died. The dark chaos, the wet, the noise. We'd been drinking, Russ, Colin, and I. We'd dared each other to jump into the freezing water, icy even during the hottest part of summer. There was something wild about swimming in the cold darkness, not knowing where you were going, what was in front of you, the thrilling ickiness of swimming into seaweed, how we screamed. It was dangerous, like drinking on New Year's Eve and wandering around outside in a T-shirt was dangerous. But none of that mattered. Immersed in life, energy, risk, I'd felt sorry for Elena, up in our room with a book, sorry for my mother and Herbert for being old and clueless.

Only that night there was an edge to our wildness. Russ, who was leaving the island soon, goaded us into drinking more than usual. He also sensed the weirdness between Colin and me, but didn't know its cause. "Drink up," he said, "it's like a fucking funeral."

I tried to hug Colin but he shrugged me off. He grabbed the bottle, took a long draining swig, and threw it out to sea. Then he stripped to his jeans and dove in.

"Wait," I called.

"What's with him?" Russ asked.

"Nothing," I said. But I knew.

Colin was swimming so fast I couldn't catch up. I yelled at him to cut it out, to come back. He yelled something in reply and I thought he sounded unhinged. It was mayhem in the water, the three of us yelling and cursing, and when I got back to the shore and struggled to pull my clothes on over my sticky, salty skin, I thought how this would be one of those wild nights we would laugh about later. Russ emerged next and together we waited.

How long before we knew something was wrong? By the time we got the boat and paddled out, Russ rowing, me holding the flashlight high, it didn't matter. We didn't see him again.

"Colin," I whisper.

But he is not here. Or if he is, he has been transmuted into something else, something impersonal. Not unkind, not unfeeling, exactly, but uninfluenceable, like a tree or rock or body of water.

Abruptly I start back, I cannot go quickly enough. I scramble over rocks slippery with icy seaweed. All I can think of is a drink, something that will warm me, that will help me to not think, to forget. I imagine all the drinks I have known and loved, all the fancy cocktails, the homey beers, the crisp white wines, the sharp tang of lime and mint, the earthy red wines, the sweet, fruit-filled novelty drinks, the deliciousness of champagne, the bubbles. Every summer my mother and Herbert would bring cases of alcohol onto the island, fighting with us to leave things at home so that there would be room in the back of the car. I remember a picnic in the rain one time, with another family and the cheers that greeted Colin when he found the tomato juice because otherwise the grownups would have been forced to drink the vodka neat.

Why am I the one? Why could everyone else manage to drink, not have to give it up entirely, and only I was so fucked up by it? It isn't fair. I deserve to drink. Deserve to be fucked up. I already am. My whole life is evidence of that. I think longingly of a little nip. Not much. Just something to tide me over. A couple swallows. A couple burning swallows of gin. I can taste it. I am almost at camp now. I pass the trees, the wind rustling through the dead leaves, burning my face. The walk has warmed me up some and as I stride across the field to my campsite, anxiety suddenly clutches me.

Just get back to camp, I tell myself. Just get back and everything will be fine. But now I'm wondering, did I bring the gin?

Part of me knows I didn't. I deliberately did not bring the gin, because now I must sober up. I must. But then suddenly I think that I did bring it after all, I must have, because what if? What if I couldn't quit? What if some part of me knew drinking *was* my savior? What if some part of me wanted to drink myself to death on my island? A neat ending to it all.

I arrive at my tent, unzip the flaps. In my mind I can see the bottle. I know I brought it, packed it, slipped it in when my other self wasn't looking. I make a desperate search of my gear, checking the obvious places first: backpack, food sacks. Only someone devious could have hidden it so well. Only I could have hidden it so carefully. At first methodically, and then more haphazardly, I search through my things, tearing my bags apart, knocking over the gear, unpacking, rummaging, turning over and under. I dismantle the stove and check the inner cavity; I even take my knife and slash open the inner pockets of my bags.

And there is no bottle. There is no bottle.

Then I remember the house. I have to slow down and breathe because suddenly I remember the house. My mother and my stepfather, those old reprobates, of course they must keep alcohol in the house. And already I'm on my feet, flashlight in hand, and walking across the field, past the woods and toward the house, past the frozen pond, through the drifts of snow. The moon is coming up, nearly full, with an orange circle around it. I sniff but can't smell snow. I turn off my flashlight.

In the darkness, the house emerges like a ghost house, shrouded, lumpish. It appears empty and abandoned, as if it has never been used. The sight of it shocks me a little, seems to diminish my craving. The cold air does too, now that I'm not moving.

The door is locked. All the doors are locked, of course, I double-checked them myself last October. I pat my coat pockets. And now I remember. The key is at home in a bowl. I can see it clearly. Still, to be sure, I check, carefully taking out the stuff of one pocket and transferring it to my other hand. I do not have the key.

I scout around. I try to open a window, but they are all completely sealed shut and I have done such a good job of painting them that they will not budge. The only way is to break a window. I scuffle around in the snow and find a rock. I could smash the pane of glass, knock out the glass shards, slip my hand in, and turn the doorknob. Relatively straightforward. Afterward I can tape up the hole with garbage bags and duct tape and come out early in the season and replace the glass. My hands rub the stone I've selected, feel its heft and weight. Suddenly I am tired. All that, for what? For a bit of alcohol that might or might not be in the house? I think of an older woman I met once at rehab who confessed to drinking perfume, spirits, even rubbing alcohol.

This craving for temporary intoxication is so irrational, so chemical. It makes no sense. I must just wait and I will get through it. But why? Why not drink every day, lull myself through the days and years left of my life? Who said impairment was so bad? Whole segments of society make it a way of life.

The rock in my hand is smooth and black and shaped like a lop-sided kidney bean. It has been on this planet for millions of years. I stand with it in my hand and tap the glass. Alcohol is ruining my life. And as long as I keep drinking, this is what my life will be. I will only come to this point again, some other time.

I take a deep breath and throw the rock away. It thuds, the sound half-eaten up by the snow.

By now it's close to 10:00 and bitterly cold. The wind comes up from the water, the trees groan and creak. I make my way back across the frozen path, so cold, so sad, so down, that from step to step I can hardly believe I'll take another. But I keep going, plodding along, my flashlight bobbing across the snow, and round the corner. And there is my campsite, utterly vandalized. Clothes, gear, foodstuffs, all strewn about. The tent flap gaping open. For a moment I truly think someone else has been here. And when I realize it was me, a wave of shame and horror and also compassion breaks and falls over me and my legs buckle and I think I'll have to sit down. But behind that comes another wave, this one of panic.

I drag all the stuff back into the tent, which remained standing through my wild search. Fortunately, my sleeping bag is lying on some of my other things, and is only partially wet. Everything else, though, is soaked from the snow. I need to make some decisions about what can stay outside and what I'll need inside, but my head aches and throbs.

I start sorting the foodstuffs, and end up just hurtling everything into a stuff bag except the stove. It's so cold my fingers are turning white. All the bones in my head ache. I take off my boots and like a good camper put them at the foot of my sleeping bag and crawl in after them. At first I don't move. I am so cold I think I will freeze. Then I start shivering. I must finally drift off to sleep because I have strange, unpleasant dreams.

When I wake up my throat is parched and my head still aches. I'm wedged into my sleeping bag, every part of me covered. I don't feel the chill at first, wedged in as I am, my boots down at the bottom. I've slept in my clothes and I don't intend to change. I ease myself out of the sleeping bag, my bladder bursting, and when I unzip the tent flaps, I gasp. Blankets of new snow cover the ground. Everything is white, muffled, clean. I don't know what time it is, but it must be early. Sunrise is probably still several hours off. In the bluish light, mist is coming in over the snow, creeping in through the trees and bushes, rolling around rocks. It seems to me that surviving is the bravest thing I've ever done.

I layer myself up—coat, gloves, boots, etc.—and find the spot I've designated as a toilet. I am so glad to be awake, I wouldn't mind what the world looked like, but to find a clean, new world feels like a blessing. An irrational optimism floods me and I set to making coffee.

When my coffee is ready I sit and listen to the predawn sounds, the muffled rush of the waves, the lowing of the wind in the trees, the thick stillness of the snow. I wonder how much has fallen on the mainland, and am anxious for a moment that my ride will worry and feel he needs to come get me. But I shake that off. This is my day. Mine alone.

I sip my coffee, enjoying the smell and warmth. I contemplate making porridge from an instant packet, but eat a protein bar instead. I clean up my campsite, organize everything tidily, hang my sleeping bag from a branch to dry out. I am so relieved to have escaped the demons of the night before. When everything looks shipshape, when the damage of the night has been hidden and the sun is just beginning to rise, I take a mug of coffee and set off. I plan to spend the morning walking the island, looking and listening. Already the fog is lifting and some lightness coming out of the sky.

I am hungover, quite badly, but I ignore it. If I can keep walking, even sweat a bit, I will be okay. Even though the island is not large (to walk clear across it takes only twenty minutes), to walk its perimeter will take me hours. I start at the front beach. There is so much to see and hear: the creaking of the ice, a soft plop of snow falling, enormous frozen puddles, bird tracks, a tree with its arms outstretched. I have brought with me some things to eat, raisins and nuts, slices of dried apples. I walk and walk and walk.

After some time I am back at Colin's cove. This morning, with the sun up and shining, the snow and waves glinting, it is an altogether different place. I wonder if he is here now. "Colin," I call. There is no answering call, of course not, but I sense some presence in the crisp air, the chill sunshine, the frothing water. I remember his sweet brown eyes, his lithe body and smooth skin, his shoulders just beginning to broaden. I remember the smell, like cloves and hay, on the back of his neck, the weight of his arm on my shoulders. Colin was my best friend, my brother, me if I'd been a boy. We shared clothes and books, we walked arm in arm. We wrestled and lolled. So much was sensual on the island: the sun and the breeze on our skin, the plum juice dripping down our chins, the dried salt we licked from each other's knees. When we kissed it was the strangest sensation, almost like kissing your own self. "We were kids," I whisper. I feel a bit awkward speaking aloud, but also less lonely. "We loved each other. Was it so wrong?"

But even as I ask, I know. We were so alone on the island and sex, the promise of it, was everywhere. Of course it was wrong. And when he wanted more, I said no. I pushed him away and his brown eyes showed hurt and confusion, and anger too.

And then he died.

On this beautiful, fresh snow-covered day, snow that is already melting in the sun and the lapping waves, I want to crumple with sorrow and self-loathing. For a moment I almost retch with guilt, and then I am so angry suddenly at my mother. How could she not have known? Her silence, her alcoholic fog, permitted it. And what about my father? How could he have abandoned us? How stupid and irresponsible.

It is because of this that I want to drink, this and every other failure of my sad and blighted life. "Colin, I'm sorry," I call. But whatever spirit was here has moved on.

I walk. Several times I pass within close proximity of my campsite and once I go there and take down my sleeping bag and put it back in my tent. I get more food and keep walking. It is not until I am well into my second loop that I consider the Bearded One might not come back for me. That I've been an asshole, and no self-respecting person would subject himself to such treatment, particularly when he was doing said person a favor.

But he wouldn't just leave me here, would he?

I would, I tell myself. For sure. Wouldn't I? Okay, I might not just clam up about it, I might casually mention to someone else that an asshole was waiting for a ride back from an island—mention it cozily over beers, and then laugh, thinking about that poor dumb fuck trying to thumb a ride back to the mainland.

But that would make me an asshole twice, wouldn't it?

Maybe people who aren't assholes don't behave like people who are. I have to hope he is one of those. Of course, Audrey knows where I am, and if I don't come into work on Monday, she'll investigate. I don't need him, I tell myself defiantly. Meanwhile, my little fantasy has got me thinking of beers. How good one would taste. The thought of the Bearded One cozying up to the bar almost makes me cry with self pity.

I pull out my stash of peanut butter cups, tear off their outer packaging, and eat six of them. My legs are tired, my feet sweaty, and also cold. All of me is starting to feel cold now. I decide to head back to camp. Time for hot chocolate with a slab of butter melting in it.

I make an early dinner. Despite all my snacking, I have not eaten much today. I feared nausea if I put too much into my stomach. But now I need nourishment. I've brought two dinner packets, chicken and beef, and I decide to eat both of them. The plastic envelopes with their dubious contents remind me of my mother's cooking. They are the kind of thing she might have fed us, thinking they were wholesome. I remember our house, how dark and unhomey it was, how plain and disorganized. More than disorganized. Chaotic.

As I spoon the warm gloop into my mouth, the handi-utensil clanks against the tin bowl as if I were in prison. Afterward I boil snow and make tea in my tin mug. It is 4:30. There is perhaps another hour of daylight. Already the light has a darker, weaker cast. A chill breeze whips up. The tide is coming in, the waves swelling. The warmth, the transitory warmth, has sped south.

The evening is before me and tomorrow I go home. I half hope I'll sleep and sleep for hours. I feel as if I could go to sleep now and not wake up again till morning. I rinse my plates with snow and secure my trash. I put on a scarf. If I'd brought a Walkman I could listen to music. Instead I breathe deeply and listen to the island. As I stand there I have the sense again that I am being watched and I turn, sharply, to look over my shoulder. Of course, no one is there. But it's more than an immediate feeling; it's a larger feeling. Something to do with the sky.

And now I know. Colin is there, watching me. I feel him. It is not unfriendly or scary or ghostly, but it is persistent. "What is it?" I ask. Kissing him never felt sexual to me. It was the natural progression of our closeness. It was also just something we did. In one way, I can't believe it happened. In another way, I still don't think we did anything wrong. We loved each other. Is that so bad?

And yet, even as I think this, some other part of me is appalled and deeply ashamed. He was my little brother. I should have known better. I should have protected him. Not made him want more. "Colin," I say, "I'm sorry. I'm sorry I hurt you." The wind riffles through the trees, the sun is setting.

"*Colin,*" I yell. And then, not what I expect to say: "Let me go." But nothing changes.

Night comes quickly. And the moon, wouldn't you know it, is full. And the land that I want to claim as mine is utterly different. Or do I mean indifferent? To own land is such a strange concept. I heard a neighbor say once his island "honed him."

So cold. I cannot even remember what it is to be warm. I lie with everything I own on or beneath me. I want to sleep. Vaguely I remember I should not sleep. But perhaps I should. Maybe sleep is exactly what I need.

The island talks to me and I listen. The wind. The waves. The cracking of ice. It is almost too cold to sleep, but I spend the night in a half-dreamlike state. When I wake I have been semiconscious for several hours. And then the sickness comes. The craving. Now it takes the form of lemon sorbet, the kind that is both sweet and tart, crushed ice. I unzip the tent and grab a handful of snow, press it to my mouth.

Sometime later he is standing by my bed. "You came," I say. Something is off and I can't immediately gauge what it is. Then I realize. My breathing sounds short and ragged. "Colin," I whisper. "Don't leave me. I miss you."

I know he let go in the water. I know he gave up.

And then I think of my father. I remember him, lifting me. I remember the feeling of him, the smell, the touch. Bliss, that. And not enough. It is too cold to cry, but I find I am weeping without shedding tears. My chest hurts, my rib cage hurts. All these people: Colin, my father, and then it's my mother I want, the most basic, most elemental human impulse. "Mama," I say. My heart is breaking. "Mama," I whisper. At the same time, I'm thinking of Monroe, my own Monroe.

I'm aware I'm hallucinating, but I either don't mind or can't stop. I'm speaking in a low voice, a monologue. I might be feverish, only I know it's the cold. I say this out loud. Because my teeth are chattering, it's hard to speak.

My watch says 2:00 A.M.

I must have slept, because now there is early-morning light. The islands are emerging through the fog. And a line from a W. B. Yeats poem comes to me: "And I shall have peace there, for peace comes dropping slow."

I make coffee and when it is gone I wrap the slashed stuff bag tightly, wanting to conceal the tear, the evidence of my craziness.

Later the sun comes out and melts the snow. The ground is shiny and wet. Moss grows on the north side of trees and the birch's bark is white and radiant. I feel fragile, newborn, my eyes weak and unaccustomed to the light. My island has begun to restore me, just as I knew it would.

Before I leave, I walk past the house. It looks small and defenseless. I walk up to the door and press my nose against the glass pane. Everything inside is silent, waiting. Half buried in snow is the rock I threw. I pick it up, wipe the snow away. In the daylight I see it is not black, but gray and speckled. It is smaller than I remember. I hold it in the palm of my hand, then slip it into my pocket.

I'm down at the dock and ready to go, but the Bearded One hasn't come for me. What do I know about him? Nothing. Why am I always dependent on a man to get me to and from the island?

On the dock I feel like Penelope waiting for Odysseus. Twenty long years she waited, convinced he would return. Everyone said she should marry again, and her house filled with suitors eating her food and drinking her husband's wine. She said she would pick a suitor when she finished her weaving. What no one knew was that each night she picked out the weaving she had done the day before. Though this had always confused me. Did she pick out all or almost all of her weaving? She must have had to leave some. She must have had to give the semblance of making progress.

I hear the boat before I see it. Then ripples, and out of the fog he appears.

He has to help me get on, stow my stuff. I am stumbling, every part of my body numb, barely able to move. "God," he says, after looking hard at me. "Do you want some brandy? I have a medicinal flask."

"No," I say. "No brandy."

"What day is it?" he says.

"Sunday." But for a minute I'm not sure.

"Quick now, who's the president?"

"That asshole," I say.

"Everything okay?"

I nod. We start out. Even though he's silent, he's not indifferent. I can sense a kind of quizzical sympathy emanating from him. I turn toward him. "Do you have a dog?" I ask because of Odysseus and the ancient, faithful dog who recognized him disguised as a beggar on his return. But I don't explain this now. My lips can't form the words.

He shakes his head. "Not anymore." There's a story there, asking to be told. But I don't ask.

"How was it?" he asks gently, after a time. My skin feels stripped,

I can barely move any of my limbs, I'm sure I stink. I'm also afraid if I start talking I won't be able to stop.

"Cold."

He nods. "You're strong," he says. "Stronger than I thought."

For the rest of the ride we sit in silence, of which I'm glad. At the dock I ask him how much I owe him.

He shakes his head. "Don't worry about it."

"Thanks," I say, and mean it. "If I can repay you in some way."

"I'm glad I could help you out."

I wait for a moment to see if he'll ask my name, but he doesn't, and again, out of stubbornness, or maybe exhaustion, I don't ask for his and then the moment's over.

"Thank you," I say again, as I start putting my stuff into the Green Hornet to go home. He's still standing there. *Go away*, I think. I don't want him watching me.

"I just want to make sure you can drive," he says.

"Oh yeah," I say. "I can drive." But I can't. I can barely maneuver the key in my hand. But sheer willpower gets me through. And the Green Hornet serves me well, starts up on the first try, a miracle. Using my hand as a sort of oven mitt, I manage to go from reverse to first gear and then second. Then with a last flap of my oven-mitt hand I wave good-bye.

Nine

Night had begun to fall when, dragging camping gear behind me, I walked up the front steps of my dark house. I was accustomed to nothing. My skin felt raw, my ears too. After the roar of the wind, everything seemed quiet. Soundless. I felt stripped down. Even inside, with the heat turned up, the cold I'd endured stayed with me. I put on a heavy sweater and a thick bathrobe and lit a fire in my old cast-iron stove. My feet were numb and a greenish white when I pulled my socks off. I remembered being taken sledding as a child and how cold I would get. Afterward my father would rub my feet between his large, smooth hands. I put on new socks and massaged my feet until the blood returning to them made it painful, but in a way that felt good too.

I had only been gone three days, but everything seemed strange and unfamiliar. I sat with my feet tucked underneath me and took it in: the bookcases, the bead curtain, the shells and pictures, Monroe's drawings on the walls. I tried to imagine her here. Oh, I could imagine her here, could see her sweet face and honey-colored hair. But I also knew I could leave this place. If that's what it took, I could leave, move back to Philadelphia. But first I had to try to get her in my life here. Rockhaven wasn't just a place where people hit bottom and washed up. I liked its hardscrabble quality, the stony but deep-rooted friends I'd made. I wanted to stay here, if I could.

That first Sunday night, sober again, I sewed Bill's stuff sacks with tiny mouse stitches. Those first few hours when I craved a drink so badly my teeth ached, I sewed. Luckily I had finished the booze before I went to the island, so all I had to do was rinse out the bottles in preparation for recycling. I had many calls to make— there were so many people I wanted to apologize to and reconnect with—but they could wait till morning. The only person I called that night was my sponsor, Joan. I told her what had happened, that I'd meet her at an AA meeting tomorrow, after I got off work.

Monday morning I got my house in order. I woke up early and before anything else, I filled two paper bags with the liquor bottles I'd rinsed the night before, and stowed them in the trunk of the Green Hornet to take to the redemption center on the way to work. I ate an enormous breakfast, oatmeal and bacon and eggs, with several cups of strong tea. I washed the dishes, sponged off the counters. I stared at the phone. I had to tell Wally I didn't want to work with him anymore. My throat was dry. Outside two squirrels tussled over something and one raced up the bird feeder. A car passed by, then another. People were driving to work. It looked cold, a bit slushy. A perfectly ordinary day. I straightened some papers on the kitchen table and there was my island stone. I picked it up, traced its smooth contours. I wished I was like that stone, hard and without feelings. But maybe stones had feelings? Maybe they were miserable all the time. In one of the Greek myths, Niobe is a queen who thinks more highly of her eight sons and daughters than the gods. She boasts of the strength and beauty of her offspring, and in retaliation for such hubris, the gods kill them all. Niobe's grief knows no bounds; she weeps and laments until finally the gods take pity on her and transform her into a stone. And even then, water-falls crack through and course out her sides.

That was the part that amazed me: the ancient brand of compassion, so harsh, so magisterial. You thought she was going to get help—have her children restored to her, perhaps, or be given new ones—and all that happened was that she was shut down. Literally turned to stone.

Anyway. I had to be brave. With my free hand, the one not holding the stone, I picked up the receiver and dialed.

"Wally King speaking,"

"It's Polly."

"Hey girlie! I've been trying to reach you. Didn't you get my messages?"

"Yes, I did—"

"I know, I know. Your busy love life. Did you tie one on this weekend?"

"No, I—"

"Got a wee bit of a headache myself this morning." He laughed. "Okay, where do we start?"

I glanced at Monroe's collage on the refrigerator. "We need to talk. I don't think this is working—"

"Give it a chance, will you? I need more input from you—"

"No, that's not what I mean."

"If you're not happy with the progress, it's probably because I've met with some unanticipated resistance from—"

"Wally!" I pressed the smooth stone against my forehead. "We can't do this anymore. I don't want to work with you."

The silence was unpleasant.

"You're firing me?"

"No! Not firing. Come on, we're friends."

"I'm sorry you're not happy with my work."

"I appreciate everything you've done."

"You know I'm still going to expect payment," he said coldly.

"Fine, fine, of course."

It seemed too weird to bring up the hotel room. I was scared he would and tell me I'd have to pay for that too. In a way I wanted to, just to get rid of that murky whorish feeling. Luckily he didn't mention it and I decided to let it go.

"I hope you won't regret it," he said.

"I'm sorry it's ending like this," I told him.

"Me too."

When I got off the phone, I wanted to drink really badly. But I tried to sit with the feelings of discomfort. Oddly, the person I most wanted to talk to was the Bearded One. I would have liked to call him, thank him again. Or perhaps, in some obscure way, I wanted to apologize. But of course I didn't have his phone number, or even his name for that matter. And so I decided to put him behind me, to think of him as a kind person who helped me in my time of need.

My shift started at 11:00 and I got there a few minutes early so that I could talk to Audrey. I waited in the parking lot, blowing my breath and flapping my arms. It was a clear, windy day, the sky swept clean of clouds. Audrey's dirty light blue station wagon bounced up the drive. I gestured like a madwoman for her to stop.

She rolled down the window, nodded at me.

"Audrey," I said, "I need to make it right with you."

I'm sure I was a sight, with my nose running and everything. But she just looked at me and smiled. "You're back."

I knew she didn't only mean from my weekend. "I'm so sorry," I said.

"Let me just park," she told me. When she got out of the car, her arms were open and we hugged each other.

"I've been a jerk," I said.

"Oh, Polly."

We were not mushy types, so after a few moments of this we were reduced to patting each other on the back and clearing our throats.

Stella loomed. "Are you two coming in?"

"Oh go suck an egg," Audrey told her.

I couldn't wait to get to work. Suddenly I loved my job, loved feeding all these people. What could be better than feeding people?

At home that evening, after work and the AA meeting, I called Monroe. It had been two weeks since I'd talked to her, and much longer since I'd talked to her sober.

She picked up, happy and eager as always. "Hello? Lerner Family."

"Hi sweetie, it's Mom."

"Oh."

"How are you?"

"Fine."

"How's school?"

"Fine."

I asked about her brothers, her guinea pigs, her best friend. She answered each question the same: fine. I knew I deserved it, but still it made my heart break.

"The snow's finally beginning to melt," I said. "I went out to Bride Island over the weekend. It was so cold. Brr." I shuddered exaggeratedly. "I'm thinking about summer." I paused. "I miss you."

There was silence, then she finally mumbled, "Miss you too."

I didn't want to force her any longer so I asked to speak to Chloe. When Chloe got on, she was mad at me. "You know, Polly, I go to bat for you all the time against Dan. But lately you've been a real flake."

"I know," I said. A dozen excuses came to mind, people or things that I could blame, but I resisted. "I'm sorry. I really am."

When I got off the phone with Chloe, with an apology accepted and a time set up to talk to Monnie, I called my mother.

"Hello?" Caitlin's voice was wavery. She sounded as if she hadn't spoken in some time. I imagined her sitting alone in the dark, in her dark house.

"Are you all right?" I asked.

"Fine."

"Did you have dinner?"

"I'll fix something later. I'm not hungry now."

"Mother, I've been doing a lot of thinking. I'm sorry about everything. I'm sorry about Wally harassing you. I never meant to be ungrateful. If anything, I wanted to show you how much the island meant to me." My voice cracked. I wanted to tell her I forgave her. I wanted to tell her that whatever the island offered was inside me now. But I couldn't figure out how to articulate it, and anyway, she probably wouldn't understand.

"I know that, dear. But it's out of our hands now. Russ will take care of everything." What did she really feel? It was impossible to know. Fossil-like, over the years she had settled deep into herself. And then it came to me that she was afraid of feeling. That this whole stubborn carapace—the drinking and remoteness—was a way to avoid connecting.

"There's one other thing you should know. I'm reopening my custody agreement."

"Are you really?" she said, sounding more alert than she had the entire conversation. "Good for you."

After we hung up, I called Elena. "I just spoke to Mother. She didn't sound great. I'm not sure she's eating."

"What can I do about it? I can't just drop everything and go up there and take care of it."

"No, of course not. I didn't mean that. I just thought maybe you could talk to Russ. He's the one who lives nearby."

"Try counting on Russ for anything." Her laugh sounded like a bark. "He's useless."

"Is everything okay?"

"Fine."

"Maybe *I* should call Russ," I said. "He must feel pretty bad about Melanie leaving."

"I don't know why she wanted to marry him. She needed to have her head examined."

"Really, Elena, what's up?"

My sister sighed. "Oh, it's Roger. Same old problems. I don't want to bore you. He's being a jerk. And not just to me. To the kids. He complained because they all needed new sports stuff. All our credit cards are maxed out. And on top of it, he's never here."

I didn't say anything.

"And when he is here, we fight all the time—mostly about money. He says I'm bleeding him dry. Whenever I walk past his office he hides the screen he's on. I've begged him to come to counseling with me, but he won't. He's always talking in a low voice on the phone. I'm convinced he's seeing someone."

I imagined Elena's pretty, careworn face. "Would you ever think about leaving him?"

She sobbed. "I think about it every day. But I can't. I just can't. Sometimes I feel so bad for him. He seems so unhappy."

"But he's making you unhappy."

"I know, and then I hate him and I think maybe we'd be better off if he'd just leave. Get it over with."

I didn't know what to say.

She sniffed. "I tell myself it'll be okay, things will work out. This is just a hard patch and life is full of those. Maybe it's a test of some kind. He really is a decent, caring man."

I couldn't help myself. "Why do you protect him?" I asked, though I knew the answer: because otherwise her life would be unbearable.

"I don't. Haven't you been listening?"

The tension was uncomfortable, though neither of us seemed to want to hang up. It was the same when we were growing up. We'd fight and then she'd come back, wanting to reconcile. I guess I counted on her to do that. She was my sister. "Have you started knitting again?"

"The doctor told me to wait. I've been cooking a lot. And I'm thinking about quilt making. I've got all of the girls' old dresses. I thought I could make a pattern with them—a pattern filled with something safe and happy."

"That sounds pretty."

"Anyway, can you call Russ? I cannot deal with him right now."

Reluctantly I agreed, and we said goodnight. I promised to call her again soon.

That night I sat under a blanket on my nubbly sofa. It was dark, but my house felt safe. Rich yellow light spilled from the lamp over the arm of the sofa and onto the floor and even the darkest corners of the room felt warm and unmenaced. I curled my feet under me and thought about my family. And it seemed to me that we'd been whole once, but that the deaths of my father and, a few years later, Colin, had been like an amputation. We'd survived, but we'd been crippled. No, it was more insidious than that. Some kind of wasting disease that had corrupted as it deformed. None of us had ever fully recovered.

When I reached Russ the next day, he sounded upbeat. Things were going great. His house was great, his life was great, he loved working with Roger, he'd had interest from quite a few ladies—he couldn't help it, women just found him attractive, he guessed.

"Russ," I said. "This is your sister, the one with the built-in lie detector."

There was silence. Then, "I don't know why she left. She had everything she wanted."

"Well, she wanted a child."

"Melanie was infertile. What could I do about that? I tried. I did everything I was supposed to do. Her body didn't want her to have a child. Is that my fault?"

"Well no—"

"You know what else is weird? Melanie said she was leaving and it was like she was going to the store. With Jesse it was tears and all-night-long heart-to-hearts and with Teri it was screaming matches and smashed dishes, but with Mel it was just a quiet . . ." he paused, searching for the word. "Deflating. I can tell you, it made me feel middle-aged. And now the whole house is falling apart. Let's see." He inhaled and then said in a rush, "Disposal, oven, dishwasher: not working. Parquet floor? Popping up, plus the edges are dark brown from water rot. Roof? Leaking. Baseboard? Rotting. What else? There's a hole in the fence and there's something chewing up the lawn."

Despite myself, I laughed, he sounded so much like a demented salesman. "Maybe the house is protesting her absence."

"And I have no money to fix it. I've already got a second mortgage. Meanwhile, I've been trying to do what she wanted me to. She always insisted on a healthy breakfast. So after she left, I loaded up on organic produce and nutritional supplements at the health-food store, and the food's pretty much rotted ever since."

"Oh, Russ," I said.

"Even my daughters don't come by anymore. Their mother's moving them to Pittsfield—only an hour and a half away, for sure, but still, too far for me to go regularly. I guess I'll show up every three weeks, or maybe every month and take them out to dinner and try to talk to them." He sighed. "Maybe I'll do that."

"What about the island?" I said.

"Roger thinks he's got it all figured out. Between you and me, some of his contacts give me the willies."

"Why don't you just not work with him? Stop this whole thing."

"Are you nuts? That's the only bright spot on my horizon. Plus we've set up a corporation. No, no, we're way beyond the getting-out stage."

Suddenly I didn't want to talk to him anymore, didn't want to listen to his bullshit. It was too painful. "Listen, I'm calling about Mother. She's not well. Are you checking on her at all? Because you need to. Today."

"All right." He sounded grudging. "I'll swing by—I have to check some stuff at my office anyway." He chuckled. "The Monstrosity. Get this: Judy says we could probably get a decent price for it."

"Judy?"

"My friend the Realtor. We've become . . . close."

"You're sleeping with the Realtor?"

"Don't be prudish. It doesn't suit you. Melanie left me, remember?"

I sighed in exasperation. "What does Mother say about your wanting to sell her house?"

"She doesn't care. She wants to move to Florida."

"Don't do anything without telling me and Elena, okay?"

He mumbled something.

"Do you promise? Do you?"

"*Okay.*"

I didn't have a good feeling about any of this.

Two days later I met with Jenny Freeman, the lawyer who'd been recommended by Audrey's sister-in-law. Jenny was trim and pretty in a no-nonsense kind of way. She worked out of a sunny storefront office in Camden, the next big town over.

"I rarely come to Camden," I told her, sliding my palms along the dress pants I'd worn for the occasion.

"It's touristy, but I like it. All right, I know this is expensive, so start talking. Let's go over everything."

I told her about the island. How my mother had said she would give it to me, but then my brother had discovered Herbert's debts and persuaded her to let him develop it. Jenny interrupted me. "What kind of debts?"

I shrugged. "I don't know. He said my mother would be in the poorhouse."

"Have you actually seen the papers?"

I shook my head. I felt sheepish. "I can get them for you if you want them."

She nodded. "Absolutely. What about your mother? What does she want?"

The question stopped me. "What do you mean?" I asked.

"Well, presumably she inherited the island from your stepfather. Does she have wishes of her own? Or," Jenny said, seeing my confusion, "if we could solve your stepfather's estate problems in another way, would she be open to rethinking the future of the island?"

I had to admit I didn't know anymore. "I do know she gave my brother power of attorney."

Jenny grimaced. "That's too bad. Did she actually deed it over to him?"

"I don't know. I don't think so."

"Okay," Jenny said, writing. Then I told her about Monroe.

"Okay," she said again. "Sounds tough, but I admire your perseverance."

"I want my daughter," I said.

She looked at me. "Are you really ready for this?"

I thought for a minute. Part of me, a tiny but panicked part, wanted to say no. But I didn't listen. Instead I nodded.

Jenny promised to get in touch with Dan, to open the custody discussion again. "It's too bad," she said when I told her about Wally. "But we can work with it. Trust me, I've seen a lot worse. I'll find a way."

After seeing the lawyer, I felt buoyed up. Purposeful. I was finally taking action. I couldn't help but think something positive would come from all of this. I went about my daily work with enthusiasm. I began a new project in the studio. I spoke to Stella about cooking classes for the seniors, and she even agreed to let me offer an afternoon workshop in baking, which, as she liked to remind me, she didn't have to do. And meanwhile spring was creeping in. Daylight saving time came and the landscape began to change. First, small brown buds appeared on the trees, then the flowering fruit trees erupted into blossoms of white and pink. It wasn't at all warm yet; in fact, it was still quite chilly, but you knew there was no stopping spring now.

Several weeks earlier, Audrey had invited me to a party at her cousin's place. It was to be a supper party, early on a Sunday evening. She told me I had no excuse for not going. "And do me a favor," she said. "Dress up a bit."

Monroe told me I had to wear lipstick and a pink top. "You'll look nice in that."

"It's not a party party," I told her. "No cake and candles."

"I know that," she said with dignity. "It's a grown-ups party."

Finally the day arrived. I tried on a skirt and the pink top. Then I took off the skirt and put some pants on. I didn't want to wear stockings and it was too cold to go bare legged. I put on a necklace and a pair of dangly earrings. I felt overdressed. This is silly, I told myself. Finally I put simple silver stars in my ears and said enough's enough. As I walked to the car, I realized what a pretty evening it was. A thin coating of green covered all the trees and the air was crisp and poignant. I loved this moment in the day, the crossover time between late afternoon and evening when the sky flooded with surprising light.

The cousin was an antiques dealer and lived in an old clapboard captain's house on the waterfront. The first person I saw, planted in the very middle of the walk, was my neighbor Mrs. Kerrey. I'd managed to avoid her for most of the winter, but somehow she was always invited to every social event, opinions loudly on hand. Now she was telling an elderly man that he needed to have a spot on his face checked for melanoma. I walked quickly past them, averting my eyes, and dodged through the front door. The party was already quite large. In addition to Audrey and Bill and members of their family, I knew a few people, and recognized quite a number of others. But after I'd said my hellos, I couldn't seem to settle into a lengthy conversation. I exchanged some words with the woman who ran the bookstore and chatted with Audrey's daughter Maggie about her summer plans until her boyfriend made her go outside with him. I stood at a discrete distance from the buffet table, trying not to eat too many brie crackers, and talked with Ben, one of my coworkers. Then I roamed around for a while, reading the book titles on my host's shelves. I pulled a book called *The Maine Islands* off a shelf and turned to the Penobscot Bay area. No mention of Bride Island, though the author, Mrs. Dorothy Simpson, wrote about the quarry at Vinyl Haven and the summer colony on Isleboro. Then I loaded my plate with lasagna and salad and looked for a place to sit. People had gathered around the table in the dining room and also on chairs in the living room. Mrs. Kerrey was bearing down on me so I darted into the kitchen and found a seat next to a middle-age couple. They were neighbors of Audrey's cousin, they told me. We chatted comfortably—it turned out his mother resided at the home—and when I'd finished eating, I stacked my plate with some others in the sink. It seemed to me I'd put my time in and could now leave.

The kitchen opened onto a terrace and paved garden. A few brave souls were eating in the chilly air outside. I went out too, smiling at them, and wandered around the garden. Little was up yet, but everything looked neat and orderly. I'd worked on my own garden that morning, raking and weeding, thinking about what I wanted to plant: a row of sweet peas up the side wall, as well as poppies and snapdragons in the beds. Another rose, a yellow one, and maybe some more lilies. Back on the terrace, I stood a moment more breathing in the brisk, promising air. Their wisteria was coming in much better than my own—it was probably decades old, while mine supposedly wouldn't even flower for two or three more years—and I was gazing at it enviously, when I heard Audrey's voice behind me. "There you are, Polly. There's someone I want you to meet. I'm sure you have a lot in common."

I turned.

He had shaved his beard. He gave me his hand. It was smooth and dry. It seemed strange I'd never touched it before. "Owen," he said.

Owen. "Of course," I said. "So what do you do when you're not giving strangers rides to islands?"

Audrey said, "You know each other?"

Owen laughed. "We've met." He was wearing jeans and a red button-down shirt. One of the flaps on his collar stuck upright. "I'm a guide. I take people fishing." He handed me a card. Owen Brown, River Guide.

"Oh," I said. "So you do have a phone number."

He laughed.

"I didn't realize you'd met. Small world," Audrey said.

"Tiny," I said.

Bill came to the door of the terrace and waved energetically. "Goodness, is that my husband needing me again? I only just got away from him. Will you two excuse me?"

We watched her go, then I said, "What happened to the beard?"

"It's a seasonal thing."

"You look better without it."

"You look better not half frozen."

"Oh, yeah," I said. "I forgot about that." We smiled at each other, and then I had to glance away. "How do you know Audrey?" I asked.

"Actually I know her cousin."

"Small world."

"Tiny," he said.

Suddenly I was embarrassed, remembering how we'd fought when he didn't want to leave me on the island. I cleared my throat. "You really helped me at a tough time."

"It was my pleasure." We stood a few moments then he gestured at my glass. "Can I get you a refill? What are you drinking?"

"It's only seltzer and I'm fine, thank you." I wanted to keep talking but I didn't know what to say. My face felt flushed. "I should get going," I said. "I told my daughter I'd call her tonight, tell her about the party."

"How old is she?"

"Seven." I thought I should clarify. "She lives outside of Philadelphia with her dad. We're divorced."

He nodded. "Do you have a picture?"

"As a matter of fact, I do," I said. I opened my purse and pulled out a snapshot of her from last summer.

He held it up. "I recognize that place." He looked at the photo again. "She's beautiful," he said. Then, raising his head to me, "She has your smile."

His steady gaze made me uncomfortable. "Well, I hope I'll see you again," I said, "now that I know your name. Again, I mean."

"I'm around. We'll probably run into each other at the ATM or somewhere. The Donut Shoppe."

"See you," I said. We shook hands again. I liked his hand, I decided. It was warm and calloused and dry.

The next day we did in fact meet at the Donut Shoppe, but we only waved at each other. I was late for work and leaving as he came in. Then suddenly Owen was everywhere. At the bank, at the supermarket, having dinner at the clam shack. Often we just nodded at each other; sometimes we exchanged a few words, nothing special, just a bit of banter. But it was nice. He was nice. Cute, too. Cuter than I'd thought at first. I found myself thinking about him often—how he looked in his jeans, his red shirt with the collar turned up like a dog's ear, how kind he'd been when he'd picked me up from the island, how his silence had felt like solace.

Then there was the time we noticed we were waiting on parallel cashier lines at the hardware store.

"What are you doing here?" he asked.

I gestured at the packet in my hands. "Buying screws," I answered, and blushed. Quickly I added, "What about you?"

He pointed to a long, bulbous hose-type thing. I didn't even know what it was used for, but I felt mortified, drenched suddenly in sexual innuendo. "I gotta go," I said.

"Don't you want to pay?" he asked.

I'd forgotten where I was. "It's okay, I'll come back later." I tossed the screws on the counter and headed out, my cheeks burning.

It wasn't just that I was horny—since Wally I hadn't had sex—it was that I found Owen attractive. I felt warm around him. I almost couldn't believe it—the Bearded One! But he, however, seemed to have no such reciprocal interest in me. He was friendly, kind, jokey—I could tell he was amused by me—but it was not more than that. He never asked me anywhere, or seemed to want to pursue a friendship, much less a relationship.

And then, just as suddenly, I stopped seeing him. A day went by, two, a week. He was not at any of the usual spots. At first I felt disappointed, but I adjusted. After all, I told myself, I was very busy, working my shifts and in the studio and meeting with Jenny and talking with Monroe, my sister, and my mother, and basically rushing from here to there. But there were times when it was hard to sustain my optimism. My world seemed to be growing smaller, not larger: no child, no island, no lover.

In early May my mother came to visit. This was unprecedented. Though she and Herbert had come to Maine every summer, they almost never stopped by Rockhaven—they were always in a hurry, or had too long a drive. And my mother had never come simply for a visit. But in one of our phone conversations, she'd said in her wavery voice that she would like to. I found her a cheap flight from Boston to Portland, and told her I'd be waiting at the gate.

My house had two bedrooms, mine and the small one I thought of as Monnie's. The day before I picked my mother up in Portland, I did a thorough cleaning. I scoured the inside of the stove and wiped down the fridge; I took the tools out of their box and organized them again neatly; I sponged my bead curtain and dusted the circular-saw collection. I laid a pink quilt over the bed in Monnie's room and arranged my nicest ceramic vase with lilac branches on the dresser. Frankly, I was scared to have my mother to stay.

Her flight was delayed, which gave me the opportunity to really panic. For one thing, I was worried about her drinking. Would she bring her own booze? Would having it in the house prove to be too much of a temptation? "Let Go, Let God," I murmured, as I saw her small figure heading toward me.

"Polly." She reached up to clasp both of my ears in her hands. We didn't kiss, but she gazed at me. "It's good to see you."

My eyes teared up. "Good to see you too." We hugged. She seemed so small and slight. It was strange to think I'd been afraid of her. I took her suitcase. In the car on the way home, I reminded her that I had to work, which meant she'd be on her own the bulk of each day. She patted my hand on the gearshift and said that was quite all right. She hoped to do some reading, perhaps some drawing. She also had plans to visit the museum and the antiques shops. Oh, and she was interested in meeting the lawyer I'd mentioned. There were a couple of things she wanted to ask her about. Baffled, I said I'd give her Jenny's number. And then my mother turned away from me and fell asleep.

"Isn't this lovely?" she said, when I brought her inside the house. I recognized her "being polite" voice, but as I glanced around I thought how, for the witch's cottage, it didn't look so bad.

The next morning my mother and I had coffee and sticky buns at the Donut Shoppe and then walked over to the post office. My mother wanted to buy stamps, and I had a letter for Monroe. She and I were writing again and talking regularly. I had begun to feel somewhat hopeful. Jenny had been laying out my options—she thought we had a fair to good chance. But she warned me it could be expensive. I wasn't sure that a legal battle was what I wanted, even if I could get the money together. What I really wanted was for Dan to include me in decisions and to share our daughter. Even though part of me wanted Monroe for myself, another part knew that I could accept having her only some of the time. I wanted her to be more in my life. I wanted her to know me, to know the other half of who she was. Most of all I wanted the chance to be a good parent, a good mother.

I kissed the letter and slid it into the slot. I knew all the pick-up times by heart, but still I checked to be sure hers would go out by 10:00.

"Important letter?"

It was Owen, looking slightly sunburned.

"My daughter," I said. "Hey. Haven't seen you around."

"No, I've been on the river."

"Fishing?"

He nodded. "And other things."

Something clicked. "Is this one of those therapy-type things?"

He shrugged. "For some."

"So what, people just get out their poles and go yak, yak, yak."

"Basically. If they feel like it. Sometimes you just sit there in silence, waiting for a bite. It's an opportunity to connect."

"And people pay you to do that?"

He raised an eyebrow at me.

"I can't imagine how that would help."

"Can't you, Miss Island Girl?"

I laughed. "But that's different. I was alone."

"Imagine the same experience with someone else along."

"It wouldn't be the same then."

"You should try it sometime. Isn't there someone in your life you'd like to work something out with?"

"No one who would consent to go fishing with me!"

My mother had finished her transaction and stood a few feet away reading the "Have You Seen This Child?" posters. I introduced them.

"Pleased to meet you," Owen said.

"My mom is staying with me for a few days," I said.

"It's wonderful to meet Polly's friends," my mother said. "My husband and I spent twenty-three summers on a nearby island, but I don't know Rockhaven nearly as well as I should."

"Would that be Bride Island?"

"Why yes, do you know it?"

"Just by name."

"It's very sad that those times have come to an end, but times change. Life goes on."

Owen obviously didn't know what to make of this, so I said good-bye, that we'd be seeing him.

Outside my mother turned to me and said, "He seems very nice."

"He's just a friend."

"Did I imply anything?"

I smiled at her. "You don't have to." I linked my arm in hers. I suddenly felt so happy with her. This was the most time I'd spent alone with her in years. She seemed gentle, defanged. Maybe now that Herbert was gone, now that she no longer felt caught between her husband and her children, we would become close.

"You should find out if he's seeing anyone," she said.

"I'm sure he is," I told her. "They always are."

"Though I wonder if he's quite professional enough," she continued. "Do you suppose he makes a good living?"

On another day, in another mood, this would have irritated me, but now I only laughed. "He probably scrapes by," I said, "like the rest of us."

As we walked down the street, I thought about what Owen had said about the river trip. What if Dan and I were to go together, with Monroe? What would that be like? No, it was crazy. He'd never go for it, plus what would be the point? What could we possibly accomplish? Still, I thought I might run it by Owen. I had his card in my purse. Owen Brown, River Guide. The problem was, I did kind of like him. If we went with him I wouldn't be able to date him. Oh come on, I chided myself. He's not interested in you.

"Such a pretty day. The Maine air is wonderfully fresh." My mother squeezed my arm. "Look, someone's waving. People are so friendly here."

"That's Audrey," I said. We watched her dodge the traffic.

"I'm glad I ran into you," she said, puffing a bit.

"Mother, this is Audrey, one of my colleagues and closest friends." She beamed and reached out to shake my mother's hand. "My mother, Caitlin Robbins," I said.

"Oh, not Birdswell?"

"No, I took my late husband's name. The children retained their father's."

"Polly, while your mother's here? Bill and I wondered if you would like to come over for supper one night?"

"That would be lovely," I said.

"How 'bout Thursday?"

I turned to my mother, who nodded.

"Perfect. That's my mother's last night."

"Oh, and Polly, I thought we could ask Owen."

I blushed. "That would be very nice. I mean, if you think he wants to come."

"Why wouldn't he want to come?" my mother asked. "Such a lovely invitation. Really, Polly." She looked at Audrey, who only laughed.

After we said good-bye, I walked my mother to the antiques shop, showed her a café where she could have lunch, and told her I'd see her later that afternoon. I offered her the keys to my car, but she refused to drive the Green Hornet. "I don't think I'd feel safe in your *vee-hicle*," she said, kissing the air by my cheek.

All that afternoon at work I started when the phone rang. It took me a while to figure out that some small, irrational part of me expected Owen to call. First I ignored that part, then I gave it a sharp talking to, and finally I broke down and found his card. When I phoned, I told him I'd been thinking about our conversation in the post office that morning, which was true, and asked if he could spare a few minutes to talk more about his job. He seemed glad to and we made a plan to meet Wednesday morning.

That night my mother and I went out to the Inn for dinner. It was a nice evening. Caitlin had only one small sherry and a glass of white wine. She was more relaxed than I'd ever seen her and I thought she looked beautiful. At home she asked about my pottery, in which she had never before expressed interest. I took her out to the studio, demonstrated how the wheel worked and and the waxes and glazes I used to make patterns. I showed her the tiny electric kiln in which I fired bisque. I told her about the big pieces I wanted to make and pulled out an early attempt. She was still interested when we went back into the house, and asked to see some of my older pots and vases. "You made these?" she said, running a finger over the glaze. "They're beautiful. There's so much beauty here, in your life." She looked at me as if surprised, as if seeing me for the first time.

Two days later I met Owen over in Rockport by the sculpture of Andre the Seal. Perky little white-capped waves and a wind made the water look greener than usual. Daffodils bloomed in the town square. We took our coffee and sat outside in the sun, shoulder to shoulder because the air was a little nippy.

"So, Owen," I said.

"Yes, Polly?"

"Can you tell me more about river guiding? Is it where people shoot the rapids, then sit around on sandbars, drumming on buckets and chanting to the moon?"

He laughed. "They do that kind of thing in the West. Here in the East, it's quieter, a lot more mellow. It's all about being quiet, letting the river do its work. No drumming, no chanting."

"No music whatsoever?"

"Well, different guides might have something—a harmonica or a—"

"Guitar?"

He smiled, looked abashed.

"Lucky guess. What's that for? 'Kumbaya'?"

He laughed. "Sometimes."

I laughed too. "I guess I always had a soft spot for that," I said. "Something you said the other day gave me an idea. The truth is, there is somebody I want to work stuff out with. It's my ex and my daughter. I want to get a new custody agreement." Normally when I talked about my past, I simplified the story. I just said that Monroe lived with Dan. I didn't go into why or that I'd left her as a baby. But with Owen I felt that I could. That I wanted to. "I thought she'd be better off without me," I told him. "I was afraid I'd harm her. I had to spare her as much as I could."

He listened carefully. "It can't have been easy, doing what you did."

"You don't judge me for it?" I realized his good opinion was very important to me.

He shook his head. "I don't judge you, Polly. But it sounds like people, including yourself, have been hurt. And that's hard. But no matter how many other people forgive you, it's how you feel inside."

"Oh shut up," I said, covering my ears. "I mean, I know you're right."

"Sometimes people don't forgive you, either because they die, or because they just don't—and you have to find a way to go on, to be at peace with yourself."

I nodded. "But do you think this could help? It's not that I don't like my lawyer—I mean, Jenny's great—but I just wondered if there's another way."

"If your ex was willing, I think it would help. Yeah, absolutely." He paused for a moment, then he said, "You're strong, Polly, and you're brave."

I had to look away. The wind flapped the new daffodils until they dipped down deeply and then flew back up. Bright sun lit every corner. I glanced across the square. A man stood outside a storefront, his hand shielding his eyes. Steven. My heart did a funny little flutter, even as my head wondered why. At first I thought he hadn't seen me, but then he came toward us. "Excuse me," I said to Owen and stood up. "Steven? What are you doing here?"

"Hi, Polly." He squinted at me.

Owen also got up and the two men faced each other. Steven was broader and fair, Owen taller and dark. For a minute I missed his beard. I wondered if I would know him when it grew back.

"Owen, this is Steven."

They nodded. Steven seemed hostile, Owen uninterested.

"Haven't seen you in a while," Steven said. He reached and fingered a button on my jacket, then let it go.

"I know, I—"

"Heard your mother's in town." He was standing directly in front of me, forcing Owen to one side.

"Yeah. What are you doing here?"

"Had to get something for the boat."

"Owen is a river guide."

"That so?" He glanced briefly at Owen, who nodded, then back at me.

"Polly," Owen said, "I should get going. I hope I answered your questions."

I turned toward him. "Actually, I did have a couple more."

He shrugged. "I'm around. Give me a call."

Steven said, "Polly."

"And we're seeing each other tomorrow, right?" I said. "At Audrey's?"

"That's right," Owen said. "See you then."

"I look forward to it."

"I need to talk to you," Steven said to me.

Owen started to walk away.

"Bye," I called after him.

He turned and waved in reply.

"Polly," Steven said again. He held my forearm.

I focused on him. "What is it?"

"I was going to ask if you wanted coffee, but I see you already have some."

"I could have more."

We went back inside and he ordered two cups, his extra light and sweet. While he paid I found a seat by the plate-glass window. He came and sat beside me, and then followed my gaze to where Owen was getting in his truck. "How'd you meet that guy?" he asked.

"Through Audrey."

"He your new boyfriend?"

The way he snarled the word caught me by surprise and I looked at him sharply.

"First of all, he's not. But why do you say it like that?" I gazed into his face. "What's up with you?"

He looked miserable. His eyes shifted about and he coughed. He also looked like he'd put on weight and been living on snack foods and soda. "Nothing," he said.

"I'm going to see if Dan will come on the river with me, as a way to work out our differences. What do you think?"

Steven snorted. "Good luck." He looked around, rubbed his lips with his fingers. He tapped his cigarette pack, then crumpled it up when he saw it was empty.

"Steven, what is it?"

He leaned over and kissed me. He caught me just as my head was turning, so his kiss landed on the corner of my mouth. He sat back, embarrassed. I was embarrassed too, and almost couldn't look at him. We sat in silence for a minute. I resisted the urge to rub his kiss away. This was Steven, I thought, my Steven.

"Let's get out of here," he said.

I followed him outside, into the bright light. I didn't know what to say or do, so I said, "My car's over there." I had parked in the town parking lot, a block away. We walked together. Halfway to the car, in broad daylight, he pulled me to a stop and kissed me again, his lips dry and tentative, but insistent too. I was so surprised, I could barely respond. Then suddenly I could. I had to think fast. There were probably a few things I could have done, but what I did was pull him into a thin alley that ran between two sets of buildings and start making out with him.

This was Steven, my Steven. We kissed and hugged and pressed ourselves tight against each other and it was perfect, like old times, familiar and warm, full of the same smell, touch, saliva. I grabbed his hair and he buried his face in my neck. He pushed my back toward the wall and ground himself against me. For one wild minute I thought we might have sex there, his groping was so insistent but "Steven," I finally said, breaking off. "What's going on?"

"Don't you want to? Don't you?" Both of us were panting.

"You know I do. But what about Debbie?"

Now he pulled away, as I had known he would. His leaving was an absence and I felt the invisible strands between our bodies snap apart. "We had a fight."

"You've had fights before."

He turned and rested his back against the wall. We were facing another brick wall, with garbage cans below and barred windows above and seagull droppings over everything. "I know. But I don't love her, not the way I should. I shouldn't have married her, you know?" He glanced at me, then away. "I tried. We had Scottie, then Timmy. You think you're doing the right thing."

"I know that feeling," I said.

"But you're not."

I sighed, rubbed his arm. "Let's get out of here," I said gently. "It smells pretty bad."

I led the way back out of the alley and onto the sidewalk. I didn't look around. No doubt someone had seen us go in together. Outside the Green Hornet, he grabbed my wrist. "Let me go home with you." He breathed into my shoulder.

After all these months. "Steven," I said. "I love you, I really mean it. And God, part of me would hop into bed with you right this minute. It's a pretty nice offer. But I can't help but think you'll regret it."

He wouldn't look at me. He mumbled something about not regretting it, and I thought what a boy he was. He reminded me exactly of the boy he'd been, and some odd combination of feelings—magnanimity and compassion and confusion—came over me. "Oh Steven," I said. I squeezed his hand. "You're like a brother."

"What about your brother? Didn't you sleep with him?"

It was as if he'd poured ice cubes down my back. "What?"

He shrugged, miserable. "Colin said—"

I detached myself from him. "What? What did he say?"

"Nothing. I just always thought . . . There was something weird between you two."

"No. Never. He wanted to, but I said no." I stared at Steven. My face burned. "You mean, all this time, you've thought we . . ."

He lifted his hands in a hopeless gesture. "Oh, I don't know. I thought it, but then it's like I forgot about it."

I hugged my arms to myself. My hands were icy. "I have to go."

"Polly—"

"I'm sorry." I got into my car. He stepped back and I drove off.

By the time I got home, I felt bad. Bad that I'd left Steven so abruptly, bad that I'd made out with him, bad that his revelation had affected me so much. It was plausible Colin had talked to Steven, I thought. I knew that he was freaked out by what we'd done—I knew that at the time. I was freaked out too. Sitting in the Green Hornet in my driveway, I wanted to go back in time and help those children, our younger selves. At the very least I wanted to talk again to Steven, hear exactly what Colin had said, what frame of mind he'd been in. But then I thought of everything that had happened between Steven and me this morning and I felt exhausted and headachy. And my mother was inside, waiting for me.

The past was over, I told myself.

My mother had been drawing. Before her on the table was my vase with the lilac branches I had arranged. I glanced over her shoulder at her still life. "That's nice," I said.

She looked at me. "What's happened?"

I was about to shrug it off, to answer her in some irrelevant way, but there was something about her gazing at me so calmly with her intelligent gray eyes that undid me. "Oh, Mother," I said. I sank onto the sofa and actually buried my face in my palms. "I'm so confused."

She sat down next to me. She held out her hand with its beautifully kept nails and I placed mine inside it. She squeezed and I squeezed back. I wanted to rest my head on her shoulder, be enfolded by her caress. "It's about Steven," I said. She nodded. I paused. I had to tread lightly. "He wants to leave his wife." That seemed the simplest way of explaining it.

She waited a moment, then said, "Do you think you could be happy with him?"

"I did," I said. "At one point." A blossom dropped from the bouquet on the table. I stared at Monroe's face attached to the fridge. "Do you ever feel that things run so deep, there's no chance of moving on? Of having a different life?"

"I used to feel that," she said. "I used to feel that you just had to hunker down and bear whatever was dealt you. But now I think you can make your life what you want it to be." She reached over and stroked my forehead. I breathed in her perfume, the Chanel she'd been wearing since I was a child.

"Really?"

She nodded. "I think if you and Steven love each other, you could make a go of it."

"But I don't," I blurted before I realized what I was saying.

Neither of us spoke for some time. She continued to stroke my hair and I continued to sit and fight back tears.

"When I was your age," she began. "I had Russ and Elena. They were three and one. Your father and I had bought our house and he was working steadily. Then I found out your father was having an affair." She shushed me. "It wasn't the first, but it was the most serious."

"But I thought he loved you so much."

"He did, I suppose, but that didn't stop him. People hurt each other all the time. And your father was younger. He was a handsome man and absolutely charming." Her voice was soft. I remembered pictures I'd seen of my parents, dressed to go out, elegant and formal. "I knew he was like that. Men were, in those days. Maybe still are. Don't think it didn't hurt. But I had you children to think of."

"Not me," I said.

"No, that comes later. And his lady friend grew tired of waiting, I suppose. And then your father came back to me and I had you and then your brother. How I loved you children. You were our second chance. Those were glorious years."

I squeezed her hand. I had guessed, without knowing, that there had been something like this between my parents. It didn't shock me. And yet it saddened me. Despite everything, I wanted to believe in something untarnished. Except that, no matter what, our childhood was not "glorious years." At least that had not been my experience growing up. The booze, the chaos. And it was the alcohol, that great rose-tinting element, that fueled both the fantasy and also the chaotic reality.

And yet this moment existed, here, between my mother and me. Such moments were not so common that you could ignore them. I thought of Monroe, resting her entire weight on me, the soft trust of that, and how she, after what I'd done to her, could still be so vulnerable, so trusting.

"I love you," I said to my mother.

"I love you too," she said, surprised. In my family, we almost never said that.

"Russ is a bit like Daddy," I said, after a time.

She was quiet a moment. "He would like to be. I'm afraid Russ is more calculated. Your father's charm was not something that could be turned on or off."

"What do you mean?" I asked, though I thought I knew.

"Russ had been having a flirtation at work."

"Is that what got him fired?"

"I don't think so. But apparently the girl called Melanie."

"Oh God," I said. "That's why she left him."

"In part. They'd been trying to have a baby together." I nodded. "But it turned out Russ had been sabotaging many of their attempts."

"How? What did he do?" For a second I remembered what he had said about the hamster egg, and the hamster baby with his face on it.

"Really, Polly, I don't know the details."

"How do you know all of this anyway?"

"Melanie told me. I think she wanted to explain why she was leaving. She's a very dutiful person and leaving him broke her heart."

Again we sat in silence. Then I said, "Why did you let them take the island? Why didn't you trust me? I would have done everything to help you."

She looked sad. "I know you thought you were right. But Russ needed it, in a way you didn't." She stared across the room. "He needed it to be a man. Can you see that? I couldn't help both of you."

"And so you picked him."

She didn't say anything, but we both knew it was true. "I'm sorry," she said at last.

This conversation—this intimacy—was so unexpected. "Mother," I said. "There's something else, something I never told you. About Colin."

Her hand stopped on my hair, then resumed. "Maybe," she said, her tone light, "if you've never told me, you don't need to tell me now."

"But I want you to know," I said like a child. "It's about what happened."

She sat back on the couch, her hands in her lap. "Maybe that's water under the bridge."

"Please let me tell you."

She stood up. "It's not necessary. Don't you think we've suffered enough?" She walked over to the table and began examining the pages of her drawing pad. "I'm not happy with the perspective on this."

In despair I said, "You know Russ is the one who messed him up first."

"Polly, it does no good to go over these things. When you reach my age you will understand that." She turned another page. "I rather like this one. Don't you?"

Why did I think anything could change? I stood up, glanced at the lines she'd drawn on the page. "Mmm, it's pretty," I said. "I'm going to make some tea. Would you like some?"

"Lovely."

When I handed her a mug a little later, she said, "You should focus on the future. That's what I do. You know, mistakes were made by everyone."

All afternoon at work I replayed the morning's events: Steven, Colin, Russ, my mother. The intimacy that was and was not there. She had told me I had to focus on the future. It was useless going over the past, I thought as I hacked an onion in two and started chopping. More than ever, I thought as tears stung my eyes, I had to focus on my daughter, on getting her with me. I chopped the onions and, giving in to the fumes, cried and cried, and afterward I felt better.

On my break I called Dan at his college office. "Is this an okay time? I need to talk to you."

"Polly? Wait a minute." He placed his hand over the mouthpiece and murmured to someone. I'd had to chew a wad of gum to get up my courage and now I spit it out. "I can give you a couple minutes. What is it?"

"I've made a lot of mistakes," I said. "And I'm very sorry for that." He didn't respond. I drew a breath. "I know it's hard for you to believe it, but I've really changed. And I want my daughter back." I tried to lighten the tone. "You can face thousands in lawyer's fees, or you can meet me for a river trip with Monroe."

"A river trip? What the hell is that?"

I started to explain how traveling the river could be therapeutic, a great way for people to talk, but he interrupted and said, "Polly, I'm just not interested. Is this like a couple of years ago when you did your personal report card—"

"Inventory. It's called personal inventory."

"Whatever. And called everyone up and thought if you said you're sorry that would do it? Well, it doesn't cut it. 'I'm sorry'? You know, Polly, it's not words, it's actions." He was breathing through his nose, snorting almost. "You humiliated me. You left me in the beginning of a new semester with a child who could barely walk. And God knows why, but all she wanted was her mother. She kept asking for you. 'Mama? Mama?' She could say five words and one of them was 'Mama.' There's a hole, Polly. A hole where you used to be and she's always going to have it."

"I'm sorry," I whispered. I didn't know what else to say. "I'm really sorry. Please give me another chance. I'm not the person I was then. I've grown up." I was blubbering. "I think I can be a positive influence in her life. Please, Dan, give me a chance."

"No, Polly, it's too late." He hung up.

No, Polly, it's too late. The words pierced me. Part of me was furious at him and hated him and wanted to blame him, but part of me knew he was right.

I wanted to call Owen, hear his friendly voice, and tell him what had happened. He would understand, plus he might have other ideas. But I knew I had no right to burden him with my problems.

I thought about talking to Audrey, but I could hear her down the hall discussing something with Stella. So I picked up the phone again and dialed Elena's number. It rang and rang and I was just about to hang up when she answered. "Oh Elena, thank God. I'm so upset. I just got off the phone with Dan," and I launched into an account of our conversation. "And Dan said no," I ended, sobbing.

There was a long pause. "Well, Polly, what exactly did you expect?"

Shit, I thought. I should have known she'd be judgmental. A dozen defensive, slightly nasty things leapt to mind but I tried not to blurt out any. "Well," I said, "I guess I wanted him to see that I've changed. That I'm responsible now."

She paused for a minute. "You're right. You have changed. But still, Polly, how does he or anyone know that? I mean, your behavior's been so erratic."

"I know," I said. "But I'm going to be Miss Consistency now. You'll see."

"That's good." She sighed. "I have to go."

"How are things with you? You sound down."

"Things are a little crazy here. Let me call you later."

After work I picked my mother up and took her to the clam shack. She was a little soggy, but it wasn't too bad and we got through dinner okay. Both of us shied away from any more revelations and the conversation we did have was brief and factual. Back at home, I was beginning to think it was a good night for early bed when the phone rang. It was Russ, sounding alarmed. Had I heard from Roger? When had I last spoken to him?

"Roger? I never speak to Roger. Why?"

"He's missing."

For a brief second my mother hovered in the doorway of her room in her nightgown and then the door shut.

"Doesn't Elena know where he is?"

"He left her yesterday."

I sat down. "Yesterday? But I talked to her this morning. She didn't mention it."

"I'm driving down there, I'm halfway there now. Don't panic, I'll take care of everything."

"What do you mean Roger left her? Left their marriage?"

"As soon as I figure out what's going on, I'll fill you in. I can't tell you more than that. Look, hang up now, I want to keep the line clear."

After I got off the phone, I tried Elena. No one answered and finally I gave up. I stood outside my mother's door. It seemed to me I could hear her breathing, and that she was awake. I tapped lightly, and then a little harder. Nothing. "Roger's missing," I told the door. I waited for a reaction and when none came, I went to bed although it was hours before I fell asleep.

The next day, Thursday, was the last full day of my mother's visit. Since we were having an early dinner at Audrey's, I'd switched to the morning shift. Mornings were usually low-key, but one of the seniors had had a heart attack in the night and though he'd survived, there was a great deal of commotion. On my break I snuck off to call Elena. This time she picked up. "Russ told me," I said.

"I can't talk about it. I feel like such a failure. I keep saying to myself, My children live in a broken home."

"What happened?"

"I haven't told anyone except my friend Penny. When I drop the kids off at school, I feel like a fraud. Everyone still thinks I'm part of a marriage. Ooh, if I can find that bitch, I'll scratch her eyes out."

"Do you know for sure there's another woman?"

"What else could it be? No, all the signs were there."

"Have you heard from him?"

"I've never been the other woman, never once been tempted. What makes someone unfaithful?" She began to cry. "I loved my children, loved, or tried to love, my husband."

"Maybe it's for the best," I said weakly. "Maybe it brings things to a head."

"Don't you understand anything? At least when we were together, no matter how difficult Roger was, there was always the possibility of things being better. And now he's gone."

"What happened?"

"We had a fight. Not even really a fight. I got a call earlier in the day from a credit-card company—more and more they've been calling, I barely even answer the phone anymore—and when I went up into our bedroom to talk about it, I saw him looking through all the sweaters I'd knit for him. He had taken them out of the closet and laid them all out on the bed. He was picking through them and weeping, and he was furious that I'd found him. I asked what was going on. I said, 'You're leaving me, aren't you? You're having an affair.' I started throwing things at him. He said, 'I can't live like this,' and walked out."

"He just walked out?"

She began to cry. "He didn't even say good-bye to the kids." I murmured sympathetically. "How could he leave his children? How can somebody? Tell me Polly, I really want to know."

That was painful, to feel that Roger and I might be somehow alike. "I guess when someone gets desperate enough," I said. "Look, my break is nearly over, I should call you back—"

But Elena had begun to talk. She talked about her mixed-up feelings, she needed to hear that she'd tried, she'd done the best she could, and he had blown it. What was it about marriage? There had been affection and humor between them once. When they first met, she'd been in a constant state of excitement, to the point of throwing up before they went out. In the evenings she used to read him poems and he would brush her hair. "Our troubles started small," she said. "Then it was like a cold war that just grew and grew. I always thought that we could overcome whatever had gone wrong, that it would never get so bad we couldn't overcome it. But something had happened to us."

She admitted she was being obsessive. It was as if she was hoping that if she kept realigning the facts, she would end up with a different picture, some way that it would come out differently. I told her something I remembered from rehab. "It sounds like you wish you could undo it. You can't. You have to accept that it happened."

"I know, I know," she said. Then, "But I can't help thinking, if we hadn't moved into the big house. When Roger got involved with those new developments, that's when it all started to go downhill. And then, that first night without him, I felt alive, energetic. I couldn't sleep for the longest time. I felt I was transforming—" She laughed. "I know this sounds weird, but I felt my outer skin was cracking open and peeling off, revealing some much tougher being. But when I woke up the next morning I was back to being lost and despairing. It makes me sick, the things I'd worried about before— the children, the Parents' Association, what to serve at a dinner party. I went out for breakfast and had no idea what to order. Do I even exist if Roger isn't there?"

"Of course you do." I glanced at my watch. My break had ended twenty minutes earlier. "I really have to get back to work. I'll call you later."

"Okay." She started weeping again. "He didn't even say goodbye."

When I came home that afternoon and my mother wasn't in the house, I panicked. I felt certain she'd left, abandoned me. But I checked and saw that her suitcase was still there. Then I worried that she might have forgotten about Audrey's dinner. Where could she have gone? I made a rhubarb pie, and while it was baking I went to get changed. I was exhausted from all the commotion of the last few day. I thought I looked tired and tense. But I washed my hair and dried it and then put on a summery dress.

The phone rang and it was Monroe. "Hi darling," I said. I couldn't help thinking about what Dan had said the day before. About what might have been. "Listen," I said, "would you like to go on a river trip sometime?"

"What's that?"

"Oh, you go down the river with canoes and look at the wildflowers and go fishing—"

"Would Skippy go?"

I laughed. "No, neither Skippy nor Steven. Hey, do you think I should get a puppy?"

"Oh yes, please."

We talked about which breeds we liked best, and then we hung up. I tried Elena again, and then Russ's cell phone, but neither of them picked up.

I was starting to get really concerned about my mother, when I heard voices on the street outside. My mother, dressed in her best clothes (a rose-colored linen dress and matching jacket), and Mrs. Kerrey stood on the sidewalk, chatting. I watched them a few moments—twice Mrs. Kerrey brushed my mother's arm—and then they waved each other good-bye.

"You look nice," I told my mother when she came inside.

"Thank you." She would be way overdressed, but I didn't know how to tell her that. She'd had an appointment, she said, and on her way home she'd met Mrs. Kerrey, who kindly invited her over for tea.

"You went to her house?"

"Why not?"

I was too stunned to answer. Mrs. Kerrey's house, to which I'd been invited several times before she gave up on me, was one of the most uncomfortable places in the universe. She had plastic covering the furniture and always kept the curtains shut so the sun wouldn't fade the upholstery. No matter where you sat down, she'd make you move because you'd picked her "best" chair. I always ended up perched on a hard little wooden stool, though even there I had to be careful because it was "an antique."

"She said you could be a good girl if you wanted. She also told me to tell you your cherry tree needs lime. And also that whatever mistakes you've made are not my fault."

"You do realize she's crazy?"

"She seemed sane to me."

"Oh," I said.

"Pefectly sane." And that was all she would say. Except that she'd also been out and bought a bottle of gin, she said, to give to Audrey and Bill as a present. I glanced at her, sharply. Her breath didn't smell, but nor did she seem entirely sober.

"Well, let's go then." I packed the pie in a basket and we left. Despite my apprehensions, despite everything else that had happened in the last twenty-four hours, I was looking forward to the evening. I was looking forward to seeing Owen again.

Bill and Audrey lived out by the edge of town, too far to walk. We drove the Green Hornet, sunroof cranked open. It was a pleasant, warm evening, and as we cruised through Rockhaven I gave my mother a little tour, pointing out some of the finer houses.

"It's so funny," my mother said, "all those years we drove through here to get to the mail boat. I never imagined people really lived here."

I laughed, assuming she was making some kind of self-deprecating comment. Then I realized she was serious. "All the people coming tonight live here," I said.

"I realize that."

We pulled up at Audrey's house. She and Bill lived in a small clapboard house with a wraparound porch. Audrey's sister lived down the street. She and her four kids were milling around outside when we arrived and the two middle ones ran down and banged on the door of the Green Hornet.

"Hey Norbert, hey Justin," I said. They scowled.

My mother got out of the car slowly. I introduced her to Audrey's sister over the sound of Norbert and Justin shooting imaginary guns at each other.

"It's all right, Mrs. Robbins," Audrey's sister said. "I'm taking the young ruffians home. Come on, rabble-rousers," and she smiled at her boys.

"Let's go inside, Mother." I ushered her through the porch and into Audrey's comfortable living room, with its oversize beige furniture. Many a time I'd come over to talk to Audrey and fallen asleep on the couch, one of her dogs sprawled on my lap. Audrey had made an effort, I could tell: the newspapers had been picked up and the dog hair vacuumed. The dogs themselves were nowhere in sight, though I could hear faint whines and scuffles from an upstairs bedroom.

Bill waved us into the front parlor, a more formal room where no one ever sat. Their daughter Jen was there, without her boyfriend. Jen was considered an attractive young lady. Her plump breasts had been corseted into a low-cut blouse; her skirt was about four inches long. Everything about her was fringed and pleated and ornamented. Much was made of her boyfriend's absence by Bill, with Audrey reining him in when his teasing got out of hand. I settled my mother on the sofa and followed Audrey into the kitchen to deliver my pie.

"How's the visit going?" Audrey asked, squatting to look into the oven.

"Well, it was going fine." I tried to think how much to tell her, but it seemed so complicated. "Then my mother had tea with Mrs. Kerrey."

"At her house?"

I nodded. "This afternoon."

"Oh dear." She rose. "Do you think she was poisoned?"

"I'm sure any poisoning she can do on her own."

Audrey laughed. "Nice bottle she brought us. Do you think I should offer her some?"

I glanced toward the parlor, where I could just see my mother sitting primly on the sofa. "Let's just stick with wine for now, okay?"

Audrey lifted the lid on one of her pots and steam billowed out. "So," she said, not looking at me, "Word is you and Steven got together."

"Oh, Jesus." I said. "Who did you hear that from? No, never mind. It doesn't matter."

"There's always somebody willing to shove their nose in your business, right? Anyway, is it true?"

I laughed. "We did kiss, yes, for about a second."

She raised her eyebrows.

"It was nice but . . ."

"But?"

I sighed. "Steven and Debbie had a fight. He's never going to leave her."

"Never say never."

I was about to tell her my feelings had changed—yes, of course I still loved him, as a friend—when Bill arrived in the kitchen. "Stop yakking," he told Audrey.

"We're just about ready," she said. "Polly, do me a favor and pick a couple sprigs of parsley. You know where it's growing, by the front porch?"

I nodded. And so I happened to be outside when Owen arrived. He wore a deep blue shirt and with his dark hair it made the blue of his eyes stand out. "Hello, handsome," I said, then felt horribly foolish.

He laughed, then said, "You look very nice yourself, Miss Island Girl."

I curtsied. I did feel young and pretty in my summer frock. But then I remembered the way I'd looked the first time we met. A wave of hot shame overcame me and in confusion I yanked at Audrey's parsley.

"What are you doing to that poor plant?"

I brandished a large sprig. "For your information, I have an extremely green thumb."

He scrutinized me. "I can imagine that," he said.

I felt myself flush. "I mean, I'm not some whiz gardener or anything."

"Well, that's okay then."

I looked at him and we both laughed. "So," I said, "were you out on the river?"

"Today, no. I've got a big trip this weekend though. Three siblings and their spouses. And I've just found out the two brothers aren't talking to each other."

"Sounds like fun."

"It will be," he said. Then added, "Eventually."

We stood there for a minute in silence. Why was it that sometimes the people you wanted to talk to most were the people it was hardest to talk to?

"Have you had a chance to think about our discussion?"

I nodded. "Actually, I've already talked to my ex. He didn't sound so keen."

"What did he say?"

I looked down the street, at the children playing ball on the sidewalk. "Basically he told me to go away. That the damage was done. Et cetera, et cetera." With my fingernail I picked at a bit of peeling paint on the ledge. "Boring, boring, boring."

"I'm sorry." We both waited a moment. "Maybe he'll change his mind."

I sighed. "Maybe."

The porch door banged open and Audrey's daughter materialized. "Are you Owen?"

"I am indeed."

"I'm Jen." She giggled. "My mother wants to know if you plan on coming in."

"Well, then let's not keep her waiting."

"I doubt Audrey's the one who's waiting," I muttered.

He tapped me on the arm. "You have to be positive."

"I know." I made quotation marks in the air. " 'Pollyanna' and all that. Didn't you hate that book?"

"Is your name really Pollyanna?" Jen asked me.

"Not usually," I told her.

Owen said, "The movie was better. Anyway, that isn't what I meant." His fingertips grazed my back as we went inside.

The mood in the front parlor was awkward. Bill had cut dozens of tiny cheese cubes and was arranging them in the shape of a pyramid. My mother sat on the sofa, her handbag held upright on her lap. Even Audrey, in her nice skirt, seemed ill at ease and kept wiping invisible flecks of dust off the arms of her chair.

"Yes, it's been an interesting visit," my mother was saying as we entered, an almost empty glass of white wine in front of her. "I suppose I've seen all that Rockhaven has to offer."

Bill leapt up. "Hello, Polly. Again." He kissed my cheek, then shook Owen's hand. "Good to see you."

"Mother, you remember Owen?"

"Why, yes." She held out a hand in a formal way and he clasped it for a moment.

"My mother's leaving tomorrow," I said, for something to say.

"And where are you off to?" Owen asked.

"New Prospect, Massachusetts." It wasn't what she said that was rude, it was the coldness of her tone, as if she were surprised to find herself here. She drank the last few drops of wine in her glass, and Bill quickly refilled it.

Owen nodded. "I've heard of it."

"Get you a beer?" Bill asked Owen, and seemed grateful to be able to step out of the room.

Jen pulled on Owen's arm and asked if he wanted to see her parents' cacti collection. "It's famous hereabouts," she said, and giggled.

"In that case," he said, and let himself be led away.

"Where is the powder room, dear?" my mother asked, and I showed her. I could hear Jen's giggling from the glassed-in porch where the cacti, a bristling landscape of miniature silos and hedges, sprawled out over an enormous table. A set of heat lamps nurtured it in winter. I thought about joining them, but Jen was such a flirt, I didn't want to compete.

When my mother returned, and Jen and Owen reappeared, Jen still giggling, Audrey summoned us all to the table and presented a large dish of chicken and potatoes.

"So, Mrs. Robbins," Audrey said, dishing out potatoes, "Polly says you might be moving to Florida."

"I hope to, yes."

"What part?" Bill asked.

"Down south, I imagine." My mother gestured airily.

"It's a lovely place. Bill and I always talk about spending the winters there. When our ship comes in."

We were quiet, eating and thinking about that ship.

"I spent a year in Florida," Owen announced.

"Did you?" Audrey looked grateful for this conversational lifeline.

"What were you doing?" I asked.

"Alligator rustling."

"No!"

"Actually, no. I was working on the wetlands."

"Hear it's awful hurricane-y down there," Bill said. He poured my mother more wine. I noticed Audrey make a "slow down" motion with her hands.

"Well, yeah. I was inland though. A bit more protected."

Bill carved more chicken and Audrey passed the carrots around. It was a nice dinner. Or it would have been, if my mother hadn't been there.

"Owen," Audrey said, "my cousin tells me you've moved recently."

"That's right. I used to live down by Boothbay, but earlier this year I moved to the peninsula."

"How do you like it here?" she asked.

"Why'd you move?" Jen asked.

"I like it very much," Owen said. "And, to answer your question," he said, turning to Jen, "my relationship ended and it seemed like a good time to make a change."

He's gay, I thought.

"Do you have a girlfriend?" Jen asked.

I choked on my water.

"No, I don't."

I tried to signal to Jen, and Audrey got very busy passing the potatoes, but Jen seemed oblivious. "Do you have a boyfriend? What?" she asked her parents.

Owen laughed. "I was with the same woman for five years, and since we broke up I've been on my own."

Bill said, "So you're footloose and fancy free?"

"That about describes being single," I said. And blushed.

Jen said, "Before Josh and I hooked up, I went out on dates all the time."

Owen said, "I can well imagine it."

She giggled and her father rolled his eyes.

Owen said to me, "I don't think I've ever been footloose in my life, dating or single."

"Really?"

He thought a minute. "No, I don't think so."

"But that's sad," I said softly, so the others couldn't hear.

"It is a bit, isn't it?" He smiled at me and all my insides lit up.

My mother said to Audrey, "Can't you introduce Polly to somebody nice? I do wish she'd get married again. She has such a ragtag life up here."

"Who, Polly? Oh she does just fine," Audrey bustled. "You don't need to worry about her, Mrs. Robbins. We take care of her."

"I can't tell you what a disappointment she's been," my mother said.

I stared at my napkin. Audrey stood up to clear.

"It's almost eight o'clock," Bill told Jen. "You'd better hurry if you're going to meet Mr. Wonderful."

"Well, it was good to see you," Jen said to Owen. "I hope you'll take me out on the river sometime."

"Anytime you like."

When I kissed Jen good-bye, she winked at me, but I pretended not to notice. I gathered some plates from the table and took them into the kitchen. I set them in the sink and said to Audrey, "I'm sorry about my mother."

"Oh, honey." She hugged me. For some reason I hadn't expected this. I don't know what I'd expected—maybe that she'd pretend she hadn't noticed. "You know she said she thought she'd seen all Rockhaven had to offer." She began to giggle.

Owen came into the room with the platter of chicken bones.

"Set that down right here," she told him. "You aren't supposed to be clearing."

She handed me a stack of dishes and some ice cream and put the pie in front of me. "Can you?" she said. "I want to tell Jen something."

"I'll help," Owen said. After Audrey left, we stood together against the counter, me shoveling a piece of pie on every plate and him scooping ice cream over it. I was so aware of him. Of the way his chest rose and fell. Of his separate body. There was a quietness to him, a listening. Different from Steven. Steven's quiet was soft, companionable. Owen was taut. The one time he touched my wrist to help me slide over a piece of pie, my skin burned.

"I've been meaning to ask, was everything okay the other day?" His eyes had long, dark lashes. "Your boyfriend seemed kind of upset."

I blushed. I seemed to do nothing but blush around him. "Steven? He's just an old friend."

"Oh, I thought I saw the two of you—" He broke off, embarrassed.

Could he have seen me kissing Steve? I didn't think so—he had driven away by then. Hadn't he? "Well, you know, we've been friends a long time. I mean, he was my boyfriend way back when. He's married." My stomach was in a knot.

"It's okay. It's not my business." Owen loaded plates along the crook of his arm to take into the next room. "Ready?"

I feared if I said any more, I'd sound as if I was protesting too much. Still, I added, "I'm single. Not involved with anybody." And blushed. Again.

Audrey was at the table with Bill and my mother, silence thick between them. They greeted us with forced cries of delight.

My mother pushed her pie to one side then lapped up her ice cream in small steady spoonfuls. Afterward, she got up to use the bathroom, taking her handbag with her, as she'd done several times earlier, and I realized that she must have something in her bag. A fifth of gin. Of course. And I realized her behavior tonight—distant, overly formal—and her drinking resulted not only from whatever gossip Mrs. Kerrey had told her about me but also from our closeness yesterday. The boomerang effect.

I wanted to lay my head on the table in exhaustion. It was too hard navigating these shoals of intimacy.

Audrey had just asked if we wanted coffee when we heard someone pounding up the porch steps. There was time for Audrey and Bill to glance at each other in surprise and then the door opened. A voice called, "Excuse me? Sorry to bother you," and Steven burst into the room.

Not again, was my first thought. My second was, maybe he really does like me. My third thought was something must be wrong. And indeed, he appeared distraught.

"What is it?" I said, rising, my napkin falling out of my lap.

"I'm sorry to interrupt your dinner." He turned to my mother, "Mrs. Robbins, there's been an accident."

My mother paled, stared at him.

"What's going on?" Bill asked.

"It's Roger, he's been killed."

"Oh my God," I said.

"That's your sister's husband?" Audrey asked.

I nodded. "What happened?"

"It was a car accident," Steven said. "Appears he crashed. I guess Elena tried to reach you at your house. She called me. Actually, it was a friend of hers, Penny, I didn't speak to your sister directly. And I remembered I'd heard you all say you were having dinner here."

"Thank goodness you did," Audrey said, her hand on her heart.

"There's more—Russ is in the hospital with a broken nose."

"A broken nose?" I said. "What happened?"

"Penny didn't know. She thought he'd been mugged."

"Roger? Russ? There's an unholy alliance," said my mother. I expected her to sober up, as she normally did in a crisis. Instead, she appeared to get more incoherent. "My Elena, is she safe? Tell her not to worry, that I'll be there."

By unspoken agreement we ignored her. For a moment I felt as if there had been a large rent in the fabric of the day—that all that was normal was just behind us, I was feeling for it still, trying to gauge how this affected me, how involved I should be—but even as I was thinking these things, I realized everything had changed.

It was Bill who was the most practical. He called the airlines and arranged for us to fly down to Lehigh Valley the next morning.

Owen offered to take us home, but I told him I had the Green Hornet. "At least let me drive you," he said. "You're in shock."

I wanted to let him but Steven, who was supporting my mother down the porch steps, told him he'd take care of us.

"All right, then. Call me when you get back." And he hugged me. All my reactions were delayed and before I could respond, he let me go. I tried to put my head on his shoulder, but already he was pushing me away, down the stairs, and turning toward Audrey.

We drove in silence through the dark evening. Stars glittered above the windshield. It had become cold, but I couldn't feel it.

Outside my house, I thanked Steven for coming to get us.

"I'm sorry I had to be the bearer of bad news."

"It was lucky you knew where to go."

"About the other day . . ."

I shook my head and he looked relieved. Whatever had been between us would not be mentioned now. We kissed each other chastely good night.

Elena had taken a valium and was sleeping, her friend Penny said when I called. She told me basically what Steven had told us, that Roger had been killed earlier that day. His car had lost control and gone off the road a very tricky intersection. Town officials had known for months it was unsafe. Russ she knew less about, only that he'd been mugged, his face smashed in. She thought he could leave the hospital next day.

We were awake most of the night. My mother packed and unpacked three times. She kept drinking, even when I told her firmly she had to go to sleep. It was a relief when dawn arrived. Audrey came by early with breakfast, which neither of us could eat. We went over some last minute details—I wasn't sure how long I would be away and she promised to fill Stella in—and then I got my mother into the car. She looked a wreck. Her hair was uncombed, her eyes wild. She still wore the rose-colored dress, only now it was crumpled up and down and had a smear of something greasy on it. She muttered to herself as I waved good-bye to Audrey, and then we set off for Portland.

It was a struggle getting my mother on the plane. I thought the stewardesses might not allow such an obviously intoxicated person on board. In the end, they fastened her into a wheelchair and rolled her on. I tried to keep my heart open. I tried to feel compassion but I couldn't. As she murmured and gurgled her way to an old-lady snooze, her mouth open, drool running down her chin, her skirt hiked up, I thought, This was why I didn't have my daughter living with me. This was why, right here.

Ten

"Twenty-seven cards," Penny said, as she and I waited for the suitcases to appear at the airport.

"What?" I said. I had never met Penny before, but she seemed kindly and competent, two things I was much in need of. She had been waiting for us at the gate, had sized up my mother's condition pretty quickly, and sent Missy to accompany her to the restroom.

Now she glanced at Roge, who sat hunched over a Game Boy several yards away, before saying in a low voice, "Roger had twenty-seven credit cards. He was in debt up to his eyeballs. He'd use one card to pay off the next, a round robin that got out of control. Elena had no idea."

My suitcase appeared, followed by my mother's. We grabbed them.

"How did you find out?"

"Elena scoured the house. I thought she'd gone to bed, but she was up all night. She thought he'd been having an affair—" She glanced at me and I nodded. "—and she felt she couldn't rest until she found proof. Instead she found out about the debts. I'll let you convey whatever you think appropriate." Penny indicated my mother, who, holding Missy's hand, had come out of the Ladies'.

Without exactly looking at us, without raising his eyes from the game he was playing, Roge appeared to know it was time to go and slunk over. Penny sighed. "I thought it might be good to get them out of the house." Louder, she said, "We're all set here." She indicated the bags.

"Good," my mother said brightly. She had sobered up after her nap, and now, with her hair brushed and her lipstick renewed, she looked quite presentable. "Who wants ice cream?"

Penny said no thanks, Roge didn't say anything, and Missy shrugged. I led the way over to an ice cream bar at the food court and, after receiving no answer to my query of what flavor, ordered four black raspberry cones. Twenty-seven credit cards, his development not succeeding, and now he was dead. I paid and we followed Penny out to the car.

"This flavor sucks," Roge said, once he was buckled up next to me and Penny had started driving.

On my other side Missy said, "My stomach hurts."

I wanted to be able to say something to them. What could I say? What could I possibly say that would make anything better? Instead I ended up eating both of their ice cream cones, in addition to my own. Then, when my mother couldn't finish hers, I ate that as well.

I stared out the window and felt sick. Everything seemed normal and weird at the same time. A thing—a barn, a roadside restaurant—would appear in the distance and then, all of a sudden, it would be behind us, without my noticing. I wanted to ask Penny for more details, to go over the accident, the debt, what had happened to Russ, but I didn't know how much to discuss in front of the children. "I should go to the hospital," I said. "They told me last night Russ could be discharged today."

"I can take you later," Penny said. "We'll stop by the house first."

We reached the town. Gas station, bank, supermarket, flew past. Penny had to be speeding, though maybe it was the way my eyes were seeing things. My teeth ached. I realized I was clenching them and rubbed my gums with my forefinger. I'd barely slept the night before. I thought about Elena, really alone now, with three children. How can she deal with it? I wondered. Being a widow? But I must have spoken out loud because, "Oh, she'll be able to deal with it. You'll see. She's stronger than you think," my mother said from the front seat. "And she has three wonderful children to be brave for."

"Yes, indeed," Penny said.

I tried to squeeze Missy's hand (Roge's was busy with his game), but she gave me such a clear-eyed look of reproach that I immediately felt respect and hope for her, that she wouldn't just swallow whatever bullshit people tried to force on her.

At the house, Roge disappeared into his room. Missy went to find Marielle, with whom she'd promised to play Candy Land. I wondered if they would remember this, years from now, just as I remembered drawing magnetic beards on a cartoon character in the back parlor of the Mansard Monstrosity, Colin leaning over my shoulder, the day my father died.

Elena lay facedown on the flowered pillows of the guest-room bed. Shades obscured the windows, making the room dim and pink, and the air was dense. When she saw us, she began to reach out a hand, then made a fist and jammed it against her nose. Her hair was tousled and her eyes dripped sheets of water. My mother and I held her and rubbed her back. Elena cried and subsided, and then burst out sobbing again.

"It's my fault," she said at last, "I pushed him away."

"Shh," my mother said firmly, "you're not to blame."

"It was an accident," I said.

She sobbed harder. She seemed to be trying to articulate something. "I told him to go."

"There, there," my mother said. "Of course you didn't mean it."
She began to croon one of her ballads, my sister in her arms.

I left them and went to find Penny. On the way to the hospital
I learned she had two kids, her husband was a lawyer. She was a
full-time mother, but she was thinking about going back to work.
She couldn't believe Roger was dead.

"What actually happened?" I asked her. "Were Roger and Russ
together?"

"I don't know. I think not." She changed lanes. "All we really
know is that around four yesterday afternoon he charged through
an intersection—people were always having fender benders
there—and in avoiding a collision with another car, smashed into a
phone pole."

"Was it definitely an accident?"

She grimaced. "Officially, yes. There are witnesses. Unoffi-
cially? Who knows? The least said, the better. Elena's going to
have enough trouble with his creditors as it is." She sighed. "Your
sister is a saint. I hate to speak ill of the dead, but he was not an easy
man. Whatever feelings he had were buried so deep—it was like he
was a rock. A mineral. He couldn't just be kind or giving. When
your sister had that cyst? He wouldn't go. I had to take her. There
were lots of things like that. And yet, I think they would have come
through it." Penny blinked hard. "Poor guy. It just makes me sick."

She dropped me off at the hospital entrance and I told her I
would call her later. A woman at the reception desk gave me direc-
tions and then a slow elevator took me to the sixth floor. I followed
several green-tiled hallways to room number 642. I didn't know
what to expect. Russ, bloodied and bruised? On life support? Legs
in traction?

What I didn't expect was what I saw: Russ in bed, his nose covered by a large white bandage, a pretty nurse holding a glass with
a straw for him to drink out of.

"Any more?" she asked.

"No thanks," he said, though it came out sounding like *No dangs*.

"Look," she said, "you have a visitor. Are you the partner?"

"Sister," I said.

"I'm separated." *Ibe sebaraded.*

"Oh, that's a shame."

"No it isn't." *Isbint.* He winked at her.

"Now, now," she said to him. To me she said, "He's making very good progress. His nose was broken in two places but with a little luck he'll be as handsome as ever. We'll finish up with the paperwork and then he'll be good to go. Well, I'll let you visit and then I'm sure the doctor will want to speak to you."

He shrugged when she left. For some mysterious reason, he would always be attractive to women and he and I both knew it. "Cute kid," he said.

"She's not a kid. Are you in pain?"

"Doped up." The skin under his eyes, what was visible, was black and purple.

I sat in the chair next to him. "What happened? Are you hurt anywhere else?"

"So stupid. Roger and I got into a fight." He sounded embarrassed, but slightly proud too, the way men did sometimes. "He's got an amazing slug." He paused. At first it was hard to understand him but then I got used to it. "It's a bad business, Polly. I don't say you were right, but I was misled. Roger's going to have some explaining to do. I told him that."

"You don't know." My heart hammered. I felt it in my ears. "Roger's dead. He died yesterday afternoon in a car crash."

Russ's swollen eyes gaped, then narrowed, and a small tetching sound came from his mouth. *"What?"* he finally said. "Oh shit. Mary, Mother of God. Dead?"

I nodded.

"Fuck. How?"

"It was a dangerous intersection. His car crashed." If Russ was thinking what I was thinking, that it wasn't an accident, he didn't let on.

"I'm ruined," he said in a tone of wonder.

"What do you mean?"

"He wanted me to cosign. Thank God I didn't. Well, maybe we can salvage something. I don't know how much."

His hand, greenish in this room, lay near mine. I didn't want to touch it, but I couldn't help myself. His palm was damp, and now sweat was breaking out on his forehead.

"Elena for sure will lose everything. But I'll look after her, I promise I will. Polly, you have to believe me. He told me it would be okay, that we would pay back the money as soon as it started coming in."

"Well," I squeezed his hand. I tried to speak with equanimity, "There were Herbert's debts, Mother's well-being. I know you did what you thought was right."

He sobbed, a painful, dry, coughlike sound. "I didn't want to. Roger convinced me. He's the only one who ever believed in me. It would have been stupid not to try. The island was just there, ripe."

"What do you mean?" I let go of Russ's hand.

"Herbert didn't have any debts. Roger's the one who had debts. He had a problem, a cash-flow problem. We rearranged some numbers. It was meant to be temporary, just till things got off the ground."

Something was breaking inside me. Be calm, I told myself. Nothing was irrevocable. But I didn't believe that. I wouldn't have led my life the way I had if I believed that. I stood up and went to the window. A light rain had begun to fall. I struggled with the casement but it wouldn't open. All around the hospital parking lot streaks of pink petals clotted the ground and trees were full of papery green leaves about to unfurl. And meanwhile the news blossomed inside me. "You lied?"

"I would have told you the truth eventually. And I would have given everyone a share."

"You duped us. You lied." I turned to face him. "That's illegal."

"I wanted what was best for the family." Russ blubbered. He looked frightened. "I don't want to go to jail."

You deserve it, I wanted to say. You with your false schemes and grand illusions and selfishness. I wanted to walk out and leave him there. And yet, something held me back. My complicity? I had not fought as hard as I could, had not stood up for what I knew was right.

A family was a big, messy, tentacled thing, all pulling and pushing. Even now while he was spewing out bullshit about sorry and forgiveness, I loved my brother. I wanted to help him, to believe him, to believe that he could be better than he was. And so while his sobs jagged through his broken nose, I stroked his hand and soothed him. "It's okay," I said, over and over. "It's going to be okay."

There was no love lost between Roger and me, but still, it was something to attend the funeral of a forty-five-year-old man. Elena cried through the whole thing. She stood in front, clasping my mother's hand. I wondered if she felt there was some scary recreation of my mother's life in hers. I hoped she would be better off—I expected she would be—but I felt sorry for the children. The three of them stood close to her, Roge in a small suit and tie, the girls with their long hair pulled back and tied with ribbons. They seemed more stunned than anything, far too small to be so bereaved.

Russ appeared diminished, smaller than he'd been at Herbert's funeral. I thought about Melanie, whether she missed him. I'd asked Russ if he wanted me to call her, but he said no, he'd do it himself. He'd said, joking—but with Russ you never knew—that he had a plan for getting her back, and a great black eye over a broken nose was not the way to go about it.

A lot of people attended the service. Elena seemed amazed by the warmth and support. I overheard her whisper to Penny, "I guess people liked him."

"They're here for *you*," Penny answered. "It's a tribute to *you*."

I knew people were talking about Elena, about her terrible story. You could sense their curiosity, the horrified excitement. I wondered again if Roger had killed himself, or if, perhaps in agitation, he'd lost control of the car. I'd seen the site of the accident, a three-way intersection at the foot of a hill marked only by a flashing light. My mother and I had left flowers near the telephone pole his car had hit, our pink roses joining the daisies and carnations already there. The newspaper had run an editorial about Roger's tragic death, declaiming the municipality's refusal to install proper traffic lights. The same paper was planning a piece about Roger's financial woes, his unsuccessful development and defaulted loans. I did not know how my sister would manage.

The morning after the funeral, a taxi came to take my mother and Russ to the airport. Ostensibly my brother was looking after my mother, but with his nose bandage and wrinkled coat, slumped behind her, he looked more like an overgrown child than a man. She supervised the loading of the bags into the trunk; she told him to get in the car.

"Call me tonight," she said at the door. "Tell me how she's doing, how you're all doing." She held me tight for a minute, hugging me, and I hugged her back. She brushed the soft underside of my chin. "What Russ did was wrong. I know," she said, seeing the confusion on my face. "I don't know if there's anything I can do. We can do." She looked at me. She looked as if she was about to say she was sorry, but then she didn't. Instead she said, "It's time to go."

I kissed her cheek. As I waved good-bye, I thought how nice it would be if I could count on her.

After I cleaned up the breakfast dishes, I went upstairs. I thought Elena might be resting in the guest room—her sleep had become so erratic that whenever she did fall asleep, I didn't disturb her—but she called to me from the room she'd shared with Roger. I knew what to expect but still, coming in was always kind of a shock: the dresser drawers gaping open, the closet doors pulled wide. And then, on Roger's side of the bed, a pile—at least a dozen—of the sweaters Elena had knit for him. Some had fallen over and were creating their own new pile.

She was kneeling on the floor, a bunch of paperwork, bank statements and bills and letters from collections agencies, spread out around her. "It's a nightmare," she said. "I feel so stupid, so ignorant. How could I not have guessed?"

"You can't blame yourself. You knew something was wrong. You just didn't know what."

"He was so dutiful." She stood up. "He was always trying to be good. Sending money to his family, paying their bills. It's true, Polly. I can't bear to think how alone he was, that he couldn't tell me what was going on. I hate that he thought I wanted all this *stuff*." She gestured around the room at the matching furniture, the mirrored doors and floor-length curtains. Both of us were quiet. I sat on the edge of the bed and after a moment she sat next to me. We looked at the pile of sweaters she had knit. She fingered the top one, tracing its pattern, then folded it.

"Sometimes I'm so relieved there wasn't another woman," she said, not looking at me. "I don't see how I could have lived through the humiliation of that. But then other times I wish there *had* been another woman, because at least then he would still be alive." Her face collapsed. She clutched the sweater to her and sobbed without sound. Not only for love or loss of him, I imagined, but also the loss of herself. The person who had tried to love Roger, had tried to put a good face on it. Who had worked so hard, put so many hours into trying to weave them together into a tight bond. Who had been innocent and idealistic, who had thought that a hand-knit sweater was love manifest.

But I didn't know, really, what she felt. I couldn't. I could only hold her.

For the week I stayed with her, Elena led a schizophrenic existence. She rose early, dressed, got the kids up and fed, drove them to school and then returned home and collapsed, crying for hours. Then she was up and busy sorting papers, making phone calls, assessing. She met with the lawyer and the accountant. The thing that made her cry hardest was that despite all the other bills he defaulted on, Roger had religiously paid his life-insurance premiums. "He did want the best for us," she said. "He did want to look after us." But at other moments, in other moods, she railed against him, swearing and bad-mouthing him to me. On those days she did not move until the carpool brought the children home. The family kept going—everyone did—but I knew what a strain it was. Roge suffered the most, at least obviously. He had become withdrawn, obsessed with his computer games. Luckily the girls had found each other. Missy seemed happy to play hours of games she'd outgrown, which delighted Marielle.

My last night I offered to take them all out for dinner.

"No more different restaurants," Elena said, "we'll go to one restaurant. But after that, we're staying home. We can't afford to eat out." She had already made a rule that the children had to make their beds and take turns loading the dishwasher.

We found the children sitting on the sofa, staring into the photo albums. "Remember how Daddy always played with us?" Missy said.

Elena looked at me and I knew she was amazed. What her daughter said was so blatantly untrue. I wondered for a moment if there had been another Roger, one neither Elena nor I had seen. One who had spent hours playing with the children, being kind and interested in what they did.

We ended up ordering in and the photo albums were forgotten. But later that night Elena sighed and said, "You know, I've been thinking a lot lately. I thought children would be my salvation. But they aren't. They can't be."

We were in the kitchen where I was cooking a bunch of lasagnas for her to freeze and eat after I was gone. I stopped with my hands full of ricotta and said, "I never thought I'd hear you say that."

"I'm worried about them growing up without a father. It doesn't seem fair."

"It isn't fair."

"I'm going to do the best I can. Anyway, we managed, and so will they."

I hesitated. I never knew how much to say and yet I yearned to be honest with her. But before I could speak she said, "But we didn't manage very well. Did we?"

"No."

We looked at each other and I felt something happen, something grow between us. I said, "I guess, compared to the rest of us, you turned out pretty well."

She paused. "You and Colin had each other, and Russ was kind of the anarchist king—" I laughed because it was an apt phrase. "And all I had were Mother and Herbert. It was up to me to be the good girl because the rest of you were so crazy."

For the first time I saw it from her perspective. "It must have been hard."

"It was. I guess I got lost somewhere trying to be good. Trying to be *appropriate*. I used to think with Roger that if we could just look the image of the happy family, we could be it too."

Unexpected tears came to my eyes. "Oh, sweetie," I said.

"I know what Russ and Roger did was wrong. But I want to forgive them. It's important to me. He's the father of my children. Okay, maybe it's a selfish desire—but it makes me feel better."

I nodded. "I understand."

For a few days after I returned to Rockhaven, I wandered around feeling desolate. I wished Monroe was with me. It pained me that I had been so close to her in Pennsylvania, and yet had not seen her.

I needed to gear up to speak to Jenny, tell her to get more aggressive. But somehow I didn't have the heart to do it. I tried to focus on my breathing, to Let Go and Let God. I recited the serenity prayer. I stood by the shore and looked out. That I would lose both the island and my child seemed almost definite. And it was no more than I deserved. I tried to prepare myself. I told myself it would not be harder than it had been. My guilt and loss would not be greater than what I'd experienced the last five years of Monroe's life. But even as I said that, I knew it was not true. I had changed. Before, I had believed, even if self-justifyingly, that Monroe was better off without me, that I could only damage her. Now I knew better. I knew that, however imperfect, I was not dangerous or harmful. I did not need to protect her from myself. The fact was, now I would have to live without her in all my knowledge—in all the realization—of that loss.

It wasn't as if I would never see her, I reminded myself. I'd still see her in the summer and maybe a few other times. We'd talk and write letters. And she'd grow up and I'd grow older and the world would continue to spin on its axis, the sun rising and falling day after day after day.

And then one afternoon, Dan called me. "Polly," he said, "I'm sorry. All those things I said—I was out of line. I've been so mad at you, with pent-up rage from the past. I can see you're not the same person now. And you know, your leaving caused some good things. Chloe and me, for one. Actually, she made me call. She thinks I need to forgive you."

"Oh, Dan," I said.

"And furthermore, Monroe really wants to go." He cleared his throat. "Your lawyer's been somewhat persuasive too. So," he said, "tell me again about this river business."

Eleven

⌒

The day after Monnie's school let out in June, she and Dan flew to Portland. They spent the night in an airport hotel, and early the next morning, I met up with them. Monroe had grown an inch since I'd seen her last, just after Christmas. Her hair was longer too. She looked so sweet, shy, and cheerful, and I thought, please let me have her for the summer. And when I hugged her, she let me kiss her nose and she leaned into my hug. She had so much to tell me, chattering a mile a minute about her animals, her reading, a school trip to a nature center, I could barely take it in. It was just 7:00 A.M. and she talked all through breakfast, enormous platters of pancakes and bacon that we ate in the dim green recesses of the hotel dining room.

I had been a bit nervous about spending time with Dan, and right from the start he got on my nerves. He was snotty to the waitress, made pretentious, ignorant comments about Mainies, and droned on about his real-estate acumen. When it was time to drive off, he disparaged the Green Hornet, lecturing me about safety guidelines. This is not going to work, I thought. I considered giving up right then and there. But I kept on driving, nodding politely. I tried to draw Monroe into the conversation, but despite her earlier chattiness, she remained quiet in the back, and finally fell asleep. Then Dan, too, became silent, his head tilted up against the side of the car, and he began gently to snore.

We had arranged to leave my car at the ending point of our journey, an unremarkable sandy clearing by the river. The place was deserted, except for Owen's truck and Owen himself, double-checking the knots holding the two canoes fast on the truck's back bed. The river itself was wide and gray and I imagined it stretching out to the sea. We stumbled out of the car, blinking and stretching as Owen came forward to greet us. I introduced Dan and Monroe and he shook their hands. He gazed straight into their eyes when he said their names. I hadn't ever seen him in his professional capacity and my heart fluttered a bit, he looked so handsome and competent. Stop it, I told myself firmly.

"How was the trip?" Owen asked me.

"Fine," I said. I was going to joke that we could just stop right here, now that we'd reached the ending point, but it didn't seem quite the moment. The tongue-tied feeling overcame me. "Fine," I said again.

We transferred our duffel bags to the truck and I said my customary prayer for the Green Hornet and then we piled into Owen's four-seater cab. Dan insisted on sitting in the front next to Owen, and getting out the map and asking questions and being all officious. Monroe and I sat behind them and played hide-and-seek with our hands and her stuffed mouse. We ate a snack bar and then she put her head on my lap and I braided her hair. After a while she closed her eyes and I stared out my window, past mile after mile of the same bristling pine trees, occasionally broken by a small house. Owen had said it would take three hours to drive the same length of river we would traverse in two and a half days. I nodded off for a bit and woke when Owen stopped to get gas.

It was past noon when we reached the landing point we were to leave from. This time the sandy clearing was ringed by pointed firs and there were more trees bunched on the opposite bank too. The landscape resembled the coast, only diluted. The trees and rocks were the same, but without the scale or harsh beauty. The river was narrower here. Two and a half days? Suddenly I didn't see what the point of all this was. I was the one who had got us into this—persuaded Dan and Monnie to come up from Philadelphia, booked Owen, cajoled and organized—and it could be a disaster.

No one else seemed to share my doubts. Owen and Dan were busy unloading the canoes, unknotting and slipping ropes off. Monroe squatted by the water's edge, poking at something with a stick. There was nothing for it. I took a deep breath and tried to be brave.

As we carried the canoes across the sandy ground, Owen said that he would take Monnie, and that Dan and I should go together.

My ex announced his intention of sitting in the back of the canoe.

"But you don't know how to steer," I said.

"Yes, I do." His nostrils flared.

Monnie looked anxiously from one of us to the other. Owen said, "Now, Monroe, let's just let them work this one out. You're sitting in the bow and you can paddle. I bet you we beat them."

They started out, Monnie in the baseball cap with neck flaps Dan had insisted she wear. "Did you put on suntan lotion?" he yelled after her.

"Yes," she called.

"What about bug spray?"

"Yes."

"What about your sunglasses?"

I said, "Dan, will you leave the kid alone? I saw her put them on."

We eased off the sandy, silty muck of the shallow bed, the water the color of strong tea, with foamy bubbles.

"I'm not sure I like this. What do we really know about that guy anyway?"

"You are tipping the canoe," I said between clenched teeth. "You don't know how to balance your weight. If you tip us over . . ." I warned, but didn't finish my threat.

Ours was definitely the noisy canoe. Daniel sat in the back as he'd insisted, but of course, just as I'd predicted, he couldn't steer so I got pissed off because I was putting all this muscle power into it and we weren't getting anywhere.

"You always think you know best," I said.

"And you know better?"

"About some things I might. Do the J-stroke," I yelled at him as the canoe meandered first right, then left, nosing into a bank, then spinning around. "The J-stroke." I demonstrated in the air. He did finally get it, though not well, so we arrived at the flat rock where the others had stopped for lunch a good twenty minutes behind them. I was hot and tired. My 5:00 A.M. departure was catching up with me. Luckily Owen had packed a big lunch.

"These are good," Dan said, biting into his tuna sandwich. "I thought we'd be eating gorp."

"Oh, that comes later," Owen said cheerfully.

I suggested that perhaps we should change partners after lunch.

Owen looked thoughtful. "No, you have to work it out. You each have skills that you bring to the experience."

"Is that part of the healing process?" I said.

"Teamwork is hard," was all he said.

I felt better after we ate. It was high afternoon, the sun golden and glorious. We could not have had a better day. The breeze had no chill edge. We were lucky with our timing, Owen said. A week earlier—half a week—and we'd have been dying with the black flies.

Before we left again I pulled Monnie aside. "I'm sorry I yelled," I said, as I dabbed her arms with sun cream.

"It's okay," she answered. "Owen said sometimes people have to yell at each other to work something out." She'd been looking at some bubbles on the water's surface as she said this, but then she raised her eyes to mine. So clear, so gray in this light. My mother's eyes. Her forehead puckered a little, forming endearingly tiny wrinkles. I wanted to ask her what she wanted, who she wanted. But that would be unfair.

As we prepared to board our canoes again, Dan surprised me by suggesting that we switch places. "Okay," I said. "Sure."

The other canoe was just ahead of ours and I watched Owen maneuver his paddle, his gestures efficient, the minimum movements needed. He must have been watching me too, because he said, "Where did you learn to canoe, Polly?"

I thought. "I can't remember. I feel like I just always knew."

"Polly always was kind of an outdoor girl," Dan said, and it sounded like there was more admiration than grudging. "Good at sports and things."

I shrugged. His compliment pleased me more than I wanted to admit. "What about you, Owen?"

"My family had a cabin on Sebago Lake." He had grown up in Maryland and, like me, come to Maine in the summers.

There was so much I wanted to know about him and so much I wanted to tell him—about Roger and Elena, Russ and the whole sorry business. But I didn't feel comfortable talking about it now, so I focused instead on the paddle in my hand, the rhythm of the stroke, the *plish* of the blade striking the water. The landscape didn't change much as we paddled along. Only a large rock that had been in the distance came closer, and then we were alongside it, and then past it.

Gradually Dan and I drifted away from the other canoe. It was strange to have so much proximity to him again. A host of memories came to me: trips we'd taken, moments in bed, little rituals we'd had. We'd spent six years together, after all, been married four. Here we were, literally in the same boat, and I sat behind him and stared at his Monet-style straw hat. It was just shy of looking

absurd yet somehow it suited him. He was pompous and pretentious, true, but he was also a dedicated teacher. You couldn't say he
didn't love his subject. And more important, he was a good father.
A friend of mine had once told me that you knew how you truly felt
about someone when you saw the back of their head. And what I
felt now was an exasperated tenderness, the tightness in my chest
not entirely gone. He must have just had a haircut because an edge
of pale skin ran under the rim of his hat. And all the while *Ask him,*
ask him chanting in my ears.

I steeled myself and said, "So, Dan, when do you want to talk
about custody?"

"Never."

"Ha ha."

"Ha ha."

I knew that it had to be hard for him too, the thought of shar-
ing Monroe. "Well," I said, deciding to put everything on the table,
"I guess I want to know how open you are to her coming to live
with me?"

He stopped paddling and turned to look at me. "Polly, I'm just
not. For one thing, I don't think she should leave her school. It's a
very good school and was hard to get into." The canoe wobbled
and he faced forward again. "For another, I think she's better off
with Chloe and me."

"The school's just an excuse. You're never going to let her go,"
I said. "I went to all those fancy schools, don't forget, and where
did it get me?"

"Yeah, where did it get you?" I knew he was sighing, even
though I couldn't hear it. "Talk about a waste. You could have done
something with your life."

His comment was biting, but it was also sorrowful. He had
loved me once, after all, had believed in me, had encouraged and
bullied me. I remembered him proofreading my thesis. He had
wanted to make something of me. And what had happened? My old

stubborn self. But also. Once the baby was born, Dan had never loved me quite the same way again. He had found someone new to devote himself to.

"You don't have to disparage me," I said lightly. "I *am* doing something with my life. My work is valuable. My pottery and my job. I'm starting a series of cooking classes for the seniors. And ceramics too, for the more able ones." I wasn't, but I suddenly thought I would like to.

We fell into silence. I wanted to say more, to talk about vacations, but didn't. Perhaps the river was lulling me. Perhaps I wanted to think about this insight—that he had found someone new, someone more perfect, in whom to invest his energies. And that was not to blame him for loving Monroe, or to discount my enormous role in our troubles—just to say it wasn't only my fault, even if I had been the one to act out what we both, perhaps, had felt.

I was still puzzling this over when I noticed Owen signaling for us to pull in at a small pebble beach alongside a low lying, flattish rock. He jumped out of his canoe, helped Monnie out, and then dragged the canoe several yards up the shore. He prepared two long fly fishing rods and when Dan and I beached, he began telling us about the psychology of fish. This time of year they weren't hungry, but we were going to try to trick them into eating our dry flies. He tied the fly and demonstrated the cast. I'd been fly fishing before, and knew what a precise, graceful sport it was, and also how hard it could be. It seemed unlikely we would catch anything and I thought I should warn Dan, but he looked so eager to learn that I kept silent. I had forgotten about his relentless belief in self-improvement.

While Dan practiced his casting, Monroe and I explored the shore. We clambered over rocks and fallen tree limbs, looked into pine-needle covered dens, felt smooth moss. I told her the soft baby fir trees lining the ground were fairy's carpet. When we came back, Dan attempted to demonstrate how far out he could send his fly, and succeeded on the third try in reaching the middle of the river. And Owen showed us the beautiful, speckled, and wriggling brook trout he had caught.

"Dinner," Dan said.

"Unfortunately the mercury count's pretty high up here. I should probably release it."

"Mercury? What's a bit of mercury?"

I laughed. "I can't believe you, Mr. Health Nut, would say that."

"But it's so beautiful," Dan said. "I want to eat it. It's our dinner." He looked so downcast that Owen promised him he could have it.

While Owen killed and cleaned the fish, Dan watching, I started a fire. Then Monroe and I looked for dandelion greens. We grilled steaks and the fish and cooked potatoes in the embers of the fire. Dan exclaimed all through the eating of his fish how delicious it was, but it made me sad how pristine it appeared here and yet how polluted the waters had become. Afterward Dan sat while Monroe showed him how to tell the temperature by listening to the crickets and then we roasted marshmallows. I didn't even think about alcohol, until I realized I hadn't been.

The long evening stretched on for hours and became a beautiful, cold, starry night, the kind you only seem to get in Maine, and the four of us lay on our backs and looked at the black sky spread with pinpricks of light and washes of milky spray. Monroe got under a blanket and snuggled between Dan and me. Above us was the Big Dipper, and below that the Little Dipper. Proudly Monroe showed us the North Star.

Owen pointed out a constellation of seven stars. "See that cluster over there? That's the Corona Borealis."

"Which one?"

"There. Do you remember the story of Theseus and the Minotaur, and Ariadne leading Theseus out of the labyrinth with a ball of magic thread, if he promised to bring her back to Athens? Well, he keeps his promise, but something happens on the way home, and instead of taking her to Athens, he abandons her on an island—" I raised my eyebrows at that, but I didn't think Owen could see in the dark— "and she was all alone and mournful." I coughed, which Owen did notice. "But it all worked out," he continued, "because along came Dionysus, the god of wine, and fell in love with her and married her. Only Ariadne was mortal, unlike the gods—"

"The gods are immortal, which means they live forever," Dan explained to Monnie.

"And when she died," Owen said, "he set her crown in the sky so that the world would always remember her."

We sat in silence when he finished. "I like that," I said. If I'd been alone with either of these two men, I might have asked jokingly if he would have done the same for me. But of course I wasn't and didn't.

"Someone's almost asleep," Dan said.

"Not asleep," Monroe murmured, and Dan reached down and picked her up. He swung her against him with certainty and carried her to the tent, and I was happy that she had such a reliable father. I looked at him with real affection as we settled her into her sleeping bag and he smiled back at me. Together we had made this child; I remembered, with surprise and also gratitude, that we had loved each other.

We said goodnight. We were all tired from the sun, the fresh air, and the paddling. I crawled in beside Monroe—we had two tents, the Gulls' and the Buoys'—and was asleep almost instantly.

In the night I awoke. Monroe was sleeping quietly, but, sitting up, I saw a man—Owen, I thought—head toward the river. I figured he'd gone off for a pee. I waited for a minute, gradually deciphering shadows in the dark. Then, when it appeared he wasn't coming back right away, I got up and lurched around, trying not to kick Monroe or bump into anything. I tracked him down to a rock by the canoes.

"Hey." I sat next to him. "Can't you sleep?"

"I don't want to. There are so many noises. Sometimes I get distracted listening, trying to locate each one. Listen."

I listened. The crickets, and the soft shushing of the wind in the pines, and the water lapping on the shore. And on the river before us, all those radiant sparkles, the stars caught and scattered.

He sat beside me and I felt the body heat emanate from him and without thinking I kissed him. Our lips barely touched and a charge went through me. He pulled away and at first I thought I'd been presumptuous, but then I realized it was because he wanted to see me better. His eyes were dark in this light, with only a tiny reflection from the moon, or the water. My heart was opening and at the same time I trembled with fear.

"You're cold," he said. He put his arm around me. "I'm only doing this because you're cold."

"I know." I was stupid to kiss him. I was his client, and apart from what repercussions there might be for him—could he lose his license?—I was here with my daughter and my ex. If Dan even suspected . . . And yet. I'd never been very good at impulse control. I turned my face so that it touched the canvas of his jacket and burrowed. He laughed a low laugh that sounded more like a moan. His hand reached for mine and we held tightly. His fingers were both calloused and smooth. I longed to touch his face, to kiss him, and for a slow moment I thought I could have him and everything else I wanted and then I kissed his sleeve and squeezed his hand and stood up. "I'm going to bed."

"Good idea." His voice was husky and I was warm between my legs and liquid and wanted nothing more than to stay but I made myself leave. I made myself walk away from him back toward the campsite and Monroe.

Before, I would have taken the risk. And sleeping with him would have been great or sordid, but it wouldn't have been this serious. As I tried to soothe first one hot cheek on the silky lining of my sleeping bag, then the other, I thought about how much simpler my life was now, and how much more complicated. I was proud of myself and disappointed too. It was awful to need people. Part of me wished I could just pack up my stuff and walk away. I imagined stealing into one of the canoes and sliding off into the water, paddling in the dark like a lonesome brave, alone and independent. I craved a drink—my teeth ached for something icy and numbing, something that could obliterate feeling. But I didn't go. I didn't try to find the bottles of beer Dan was saving for the next night. I just lay there and listened. Beside me Monroe clucked in her sleep. A bit later Owen came back to the campsite. I heard him unzip the tent flaps, rustle inside, zip the flaps back up, and, after a moment, slide into his bag. And as I lay there in the dark, I wondered if he was lying awake thinking of me too.

The next morning I woke up late and the first thing I noticed was a slug stuck to the sweater I'd shrugged off last night. Monnie squatted by my head. "Mom? Are you awake?"

I nodded.

"Are you going to get up?"

I nodded again.

"When?" She put her face right next to mine, nose to nose, and stared into my eyes. Then she stroked my eyebrows and rubbed the spot above my nose, something I'd always done for her. I laughed and grabbed her and tried to pull her into the sleeping bag.

The morning was so quiet and still that Monnie's laughs and shrieks might have seemed like sacrilege if they hadn't been so happy.

I walked with Monnie down to the river where Owen and Dan

were sitting and talking quietly. Something about them sitting together, so serious and yet so boyish, amused me.

"Hi, Polly," Owen said. He tilted his head back and smiled at me.

"Good morning," Dan said. He seemed calmer, more relaxed. Looser. "Did you sleep well?"

"Well enough," I said.

"I thought you loved camping out," he said in a concerned voice.

"I do. Just there was this big disturbance in the night." I grabbed Monroe. "This enormous creature—" I began tickling her "—rolled on top of me and *squished* me," I said as she shrieked and writhed on the ground.

"Stop," she begged. "Do it again."

"*Squished* me," I said and tickled her until she crawled for protection to Dan's lap. But he just laughed and kissed the top of her head.

I helped myself to coffee and Owen cooked me a couple pancakes that I doused with maple syrup. Across the river, fog wreathed the outer bank. Closer, though, the water was clear and still except for bugs skimming the surface. A bird sang. A chipmunk darted toward the rock we sat on, and then veered up a tree. The air smelled like pine and coffee and sweet pancakes. On this beautiful fresh morning, with its glorious light and waking-up noises, I sat and ate my pancakes and fed my daughter from my plate. The Buoys began packing garbage and washing dishes. When Monroe and I had finished every morsel and licked up all the syrup with our fingers, I stood up and cleaned my dish. Then she and I began pulling the tent poles out of the ground and folding the nylon tent into the tent bag. Owen said nothing when I handed it to him, just thanked us.

"You're welcome," I said. My cheeks felt warm.

"You've got a good helper," he said, nodding at Monroe, who was now wiping away the slug trails from my sweater with a leaf.

"I know," I said. "Can I keep her? I'm *kidding*. Did you sleep okay?"

"I'm a pretty light sleeper. Easily disturbed."

I rolled my eyes. Monnie announced she'd cleaned up my sweater and held it out for me to see. I thanked her and tied it around my waist.

"God, this is beautiful," Dan said when we were ready to go, and even the fact that he was standing on the rock as if he owned it didn't bother me.

Owen told Monnie and me to go in the lightweight canoe.

"Let's try to beat them," she whispered.

"*Okay*," I agreed. We started off with a lot of vim and vigor, both of us paddling hard, trying to keep our lead over the other canoe. The two men easily overtook us, however, and didn't even seem to notice we were competing with them. Their canoe was much heavier than ours and as they moved by, Monnie paddled valiantly to stay abreast of them. But it was hard work and soon they were well ahead of us. It got hot and we got sticky. The bugs began to bite and Monroe paddled less and less well. We were losing ground behind the others and she and I were getting cranky. She swung out her oar in a halfhearted paddle and sprayed water all over me.

"Watch it," I said, even though I didn't mind the water.

"I'm tired," she complained. "My arm hurts."

I was annoyed with the Buoys. Owen hadn't even looked back. What if we were in trouble here? And Dan, Mr. Super Dad, had just blithely rowed off. I wasn't worried—I could paddle the canoe by myself—but I resented their self-importance and obliviousness. I resented that they couldn't let a little girl win. Probably they would say it wasn't about *winning*.

Monroe cried out and slapped at her arm. "It bit me, Mom," she said.

I told her to stop, take a break. "I can paddle for both of us." I reached into the backpack and pulled out a bottle of Gatorade. "Here, have some of this. You're doing good. You're really strong."

She drank and rested, one hand under her chin, the other flicking the water. She murmured something, talking to herself, and I stared at the back of her head, at her honey-brown hair poking out through her baseball cap, at her delicate neck and slender shoulders. And in that moment something happened. I fell in love. The way I hadn't allowed myself in her early months, the way I'd had to deny when I climbed on that Greyhound bus. She, of all people, was my heart, and because I loved her, I would accept what was best for her. I remembered what Elena had said, that our children couldn't be our salvation. I couldn't be for my mother, Monroe couldn't be for me. And yet. Demeter raged when her daughter was taken from her, destroyed crops and withered growth until that half-yearly compromise was worked out.

Destruction and loss against love and life. My mother loved me, I knew she did, in her own flawed way. Elena had talked about the opportunity to get it right versus damage control. How brave she was, any mother. Any father. If I ever became a mother again, I would love my child so fiercely. I would never let her go. And then I thought, what about this child? It's not too late.

"I need to tell you something," I said. "Turn around a second." I took a deep breath. "I love you so much. I've always loved you. Even when I left you when you were just a baby, it was never because I didn't love you." I had to stop a second because my voice was wobbling and I didn't want to cry. "It wasn't your fault that I left and it wasn't because there was anything wrong with you—it was me. Something was wrong with me and I was afraid," I half sobbed, half hiccupped, "afraid to make something wrong with you."

"Huh?" she said. "I don't get it."

"I know you don't," I said. "It's because it doesn't make sense. I was wrong." I couldn't let myself sob the way I wanted to, so my voice got very tight and tiny. "It's okay," I said. "I've figured something out, something I needed to understand."

She sighed. I got nervous that I'd done the wrong thing, overdone it, dumped everything on her and been hysterical. That I'd damaged her again.

"Mom," she said. "I love you too. I have two families. One is big—Dad, Mommy, Claude and Edouard, and Mme. Manet, only she died, and Berthe Morisot and Mary Cassatt." She drew a deep breath. "And one is small—you."

Tears dripped down my face. Quietly I blew my nose on my shirt. "Hmm," I said, after a bit, "d'you think maybe I really should get a dog?"

We talked about that, about dogs we liked and dogs we knew, the advantages of a young dog over an old dog, the ways in which Mme. Manet had made a good pet (she hadn't needed much exercise). She filled me in on the details of the funeral—Dan had read a poem and Chloe had recited the animal blessing. Then I said, "Monroe do you know any songs? What songs do they teach you in Philadelphia, anyway?"

And so we sang. And the ones she didn't know I taught her. By the time we paddled to the rock where Dan and Owen had bivouacked and were setting up their fishing equipment, we were hollering "Kumbaya" at the top of our lungs.

"Quiet," Owen said, "you'll scare the fish." But he was smiling.

We fished again that afternoon, and unlike the reverence of yesterday, we laughed and joked and cheered each other on. We didn't catch any fish, except for Dan, who landed a tiny pickerel that warranted much jibing and a few photos. Monroe was happy and seemed to blossom before our eyes. She got cheeky, and sweeter, and funnier, and somehow more herself. Dan and I looked at each other, proud.

"Monroe is an amazing child," I said. "You've done a great job with her."

"She is who she is," he said. And then, "She's a lot like you."

I knew how much it must have cost him to say that. "Thank you," I said.

We stripped to our bathing suits and threw ourselves into the water. It was so cold and pure, albeit brownish. But even that seemed to testify to its strength, its iron core. Of course that did not make sense. But I liked thinking it.

Monroe could float but she was not a strong swimmer, so Dan and I took turns playing with her, giving her rides and swirling her around.

"Anyone want to swim to the other side?" I asked after a bit. "I feel like a long swim."

"Count me out," Dan said. "And you too," he said firmly to Monroe who pouted for a second, but cheered up when he told her would read to her from *Charlotte's Web*. "And if I'm really lucky, we'll take a nap."

"I'd better go with you," Owen said.

"You don't have to," I said. "I'm sure it's not part of your job description."

"Making sure everyone comes home safe is," he said.

I glanced at him but he wasn't looking at me. "I don't need a babysitter," I said. "If it seems too much I'll turn back."

"No, I'll go. I could use the exercise."

So off we set. At first I was aware of him and swam hard, with well-formed, powerful strokes. He was a good swimmer and I felt some pressure to stick to the fast rate I'd set. I also knew that we needed to pace ourselves, so that we wouldn't be tired out later. I slowed down. Gradually I forgot about Owen, and just enjoyed the sensation of being in the water, the lightness of my limbs, the physicality of my being moving through water. I rarely got to swim as much as I wanted to. The waters around Bride Island were just too cold for anything more than a quick dip or a vigorous set of strokes. All of us siblings liked to swim. I let the river water slide into my mouth. And then Colin had drowned. Why? Had he been a less strong swimmer? I turned on my back, looked up at the sky. Had it really been on purpose or was it just bad luck? And then because this was almost too painful to think, I flipped around again and dove deeply under the water. I tried to imagine that night from his perspective. Drowning. Going under first. Fighting the water, the air, the current. Not breathing. The panic, the disorientation. My lungs were bursting now, they felt hot and the pressure to breathe intense. How stupid we were. How stupid and useless his death had been, no matter the reason.

I came to the surface, gasping, and shook my head. This was silly. Thinking about it didn't help anything. Colin had died, and I missed him, and that was that. But that wasn't that. As I prepared to submerge again, out of the corner of my eye I saw some whitish mass, like a body, and then I felt a slimy hand coming to reach for me and my leg brushed something in the water, something that felt fleshy, and even as I thrashed in the water, kicking, even as I realized it couldn't possibly be him, I thought how I didn't want death, I wanted life. And I screamed.

In a second Owen was beside me. "What is it?" he asked.

"There, there, in the water." I grabbed him and kicked hard, propelling us away. I didn't want whatever it was to get him too. "Something touched me."

He ducked his head under water. "I can't see anything."

I let him go. "It was round, with a head." I shuddered.

"You must have found a river growth."

We were face to face, so close we were almost touching. His wet face, dark hair plastered to his head. Blue lips. His beard creeping back in. His legs, treading water, occasionally touching mine, our toes bumping.

"It was awful," I said. "Whatever it was."

268 / *Alexandra Enders*

He looked up at the sky and laughed. His laughter offended me. Then he turned back to me and I could tell he was about to kiss me, my forehead, perhaps, but at the last minute he didn't, he just smiled at me, and I began to laugh too.

"I'm sorry, I didn't mean to laugh at you. It's just you looked so . . ." He didn't finish his sentence. "They're these weird underwater plants. I don't even know the botanical name for them. I call them river growths. They're so creepy. I remember the first time I saw one, I almost jumped out of my skin."

"I did jump out of my skin," I said.

He shook his head like a dog and his hair settled, droplets of water at the end of each curl. "We should get back," he said, resting his hands on my shoulders. "They'll wonder where we are." But he made no move just yet.

"We should," I said. I smiled and he smiled back.

Later, after I'd changed behind a tree, I noticed Dan looking at me. Not in a judgmental way, just in a male-female way, as if he hadn't seen me before. Both men were looking at me, covertly, appreciatively. I smiled to myself then rubbed my hair briskly with a towel and announced I was ready to leave.

That afternoon Dan and Monroe paddled together, Dan in the back. "Do you think we should keep an eye on them?" I asked Owen, but he told me he'd taught Dan not only the J-stroke that morning but the C-stroke as well.

We canoed for a while in silence. I wondered if he was watching the back of my head. Then, "How's your sister doing?" Owen asked.

"Okay," I said. "She's moving next week. She says she likes the new house better than the old one, even if it's smaller. She said it was less cardboard-y."

I didn't expect him to get that, but he chuckled.

"Plus Roger's life insurance is kicking in. It's been really hard, though. She's had to kind of reinvent herself." I thought of my last phone call with her. "It's only pain," she'd said. "I'm still standing. My arms and legs still work."

"I can imagine. How's your brother?"

"Let's see. His house was repossessed. He's getting his third divorce. And he's moved in with my mother."

"Oh dear."

"I doubt he'll stay, though. He's dating a Realtor. I'm sure she'll find him some fabulous guest cottage or other, rent-free. Russ is actually rather enviable. No matter what bad stuff happens, at the end of the day he'll just rewrite it into a more palatable version."

Owen laughed. "Lucky him."

"I know. Owen, I'm sorry about last night."

"Please don't be."

"No, really, I am."

"Okay. Then, I am too."

I turned to smile at him. "You aren't really sorry."

"Nor are you," he said. "Anyway, it's good for me not to always be saintly."

"Saintly?" I said. "Ha. If you're trying for saintly, you're failing."

"You are so full of life, Polly," he said. "You really touch me."

I wanted to downplay his remark, to make an "aw, shucks" reaction, but I resisted. Instead, I said, as lightly as I could, "And you, me." And turning behind me, I reached for the hand he offered. The canoe wobbled a bit but we did not capsize.

Sometime later the river forked. The main body continued rushing on its way, but a small tributary branched to the right. Owen steered us toward that and indicated to Dan that he do the same. The currents were strong and propelled us easily into a miniature version of the larger river. After about a half hour of paddling, the landscape began to change. Instead of fir trees, fields appeared. Now the water was quiet and calm, pondlike. Water lilies dotted one side of the shore, plump green pads set with pink and white flowers. Stiff rushes grew along the other bank. Butterflies chased each other all across the banks and early summer flowers filled the meadows—tiny white stars among the green. It was all so extraordinary and lush, nothing like the coast. I found it hard to believe we weren't that many miles away from the sea, or even that the rest of the river was only a short distance away, the climate seemed so altogether different.

"This is magical," I said, as we paddled along what had become a path of water between the water lilies and the rushes. Moments later a blue heron glided up above us with a soft whoosh. "Do you take everyone here?" I asked and immediately wished I hadn't.

"No. But even if I did, it wouldn't matter. Each time I come, I marvel at it."

We paddled on. Monroe made a *shh!* sign with her lips and pointed. A turtle balanced on a log, blinking. I nodded to show I had seen, and then with a plop it was in the water.

"We'll stay there tonight," Owen said, pointing at a grassy chunk of land in the middle of the river. "We're not that far from the finishing point."

It was a tiny island, hillocky and almost treeless. "The owner used it to graze sheep until recently. He still mows it once a season. Now he lets people camp here."

The island was not much bigger than my lawn in Rockhaven, and was, in truth, more of a promontory than an island—several big rocks connected it to the mainland. It was also extremely buggy. All through dinner we slapped our arms and necks. Still, no one wanted to give up our stargazing, so we put on the most covering clothes we had and slathered any other spots with bug spray and sat together under the stars. It felt to me like we were a little family, only with the roles of mom, dad, baby and uncle merged, redefined.

"Can we see the dog star?" Monroe asked.

"Sirius?" Owen shook his head. "No, you'll have to come back in winter."

"Can we?" Monroe asked softly. Both Dan and I knew the answer, and she did too, but for one minute we smiled and pretended we would think about it.

"There, just off the Big Dipper, is Arcturus, part of Bootes" (Monroe laughed at this) "and the Northern Crown. Remember the story I told you last night, about Ariadne and the Corona Borealis? Well, this constellation is also called the Celestial Sisters. There's another legend about it, a Shawnee one. You'll like this too, Polly." He cleared his throat. "There was once a handsome and bold Indian brave. I've heard different names for him: White Hawk, White Falcon, High Feather."

"High Feather?" I said.

"High Booties," Monroe giggled before Dan shushed her.

"Anyway, as I was saying, one day this young Indian prince comes across a field that has a perfect circle imprinted in the tall grass. He's mystified. The circle has no entrance or exit. He wants to find out who or what could have made the circle, so he hides and waits. He waits and waits, until that night a silver basket descends from the heavens and twelve beautiful maidens jump out. They are the loveliest maidens he has ever seen, in sky blue robes, with long flowing hair. They dance around the circle, beating time on eagle-skin drums. White Hawk falls in love with the youngest star maiden and tries to capture her. Well, instantly they are in their basket and on their way. The next night, he disguises himself as a rabbit, but they still find him. The third night he turns himself into a mouse and this time he is successful. He captures the beautiful star maiden and takes her home as his bride."

"That's abduction," I said. "This is not a very progressive story. Refund, refund."

"The thing is, they are happy together, and even have a child. But still, she misses her sisters and her life in the stars. So one day, when the prince is out hunting, she weaves herself a silver basket, and, singing a magic chant, is carried to the heavens. She stays for a while, visiting her sisters and she's happy. But she misses her family too, so she comes back to be with them. But after that, whenever she was sad or homesick, she would visit her sisters for a while." He paused. "What I like about this story is that it reminds us we're each, some part of us, made from the stars."

Owen seemed slightly embarrassed after he said that and Dan cleared his throat a few times. I was too full, just then, to speak. But Monroe asked for another story.

"Another one? Let me see."

"I'd guess it's bedtime," Dan said. "Time for sleepy girls to be in the tent."

"I've never heard that before," I said to Owen. "What a beautiful story." And I wondered if that was how Bride Island had come to be named. I imagined the dancing maidens, the silver basket coming from the sky, the hunter waiting to capture his bride—of course it wasn't, I knew it wasn't, but still, it was pretty to think so.

The next morning, while Monroe and Owen were packing up the breakfast dishes, I sought out Dan. He was by himself, with a mug of coffee and his cell phone. "I thought I'd call Chloe, but no reception."

"No, I guess not."

"You probably want to talk."

I shrugged and sat beside him.

"I can't let her go now. I just can't do it," he said, almost as if he were talking to himself. "She's settled, she's secure. I would miss her too much."

Dan was a good father—I should have expected this. I nodded. I would learn to be philosophical. In due time.

"But." He looked at me. "You could have her for longer in the summer—six weeks? Maybe seven? And other holidays too—we could work it out." He nodded. "Of course, if you want to come down for weekends sometimes, that would be fine. Later on we can talk about high school."

It was less than I wanted. Far less. But more than I had. We live in a broken world, I thought. We do the best we can. We patch it up and make the best of it we can. I could help her. I could . . . not heal her exactly, but patch together something. More than patch it up. Forge it.

"Yes," I said.

Epilogue

I have a job of it, opening those windows I'd painted shut. I'm not doing that again. Monnie helped, or at least tried to help. At any rate, she got good at ripping into Band-Aids quickly. She's good at other things too: collecting greens for our salad, swishing dead flies out of windowsills, finding whole sea urchin shells and carrying them gently to the house. In fact, she's become someone who finds things: empty birds' nests, a patch of wild blackberries, a sole piece of blue sea glass on a beach of greens and browns.

Most of July we stayed in Rockhaven. During the week, Monnie went to day camp and on weekends we caught a ride out and back with Steven. I still don't have my own boat. It's on the agenda.

We've been on the island almost a week now. Six fat days we've had. Every morning we check the garden to see what's grown. Every evening we read a new book. And in between we do all the important things, like lying on the Bluff, which Monroe calls the mini-isle, and braiding long grasses as we are now. We've been living an utterly contented existence. But still. There is plenty of time to think.

I suggest we take a walk and we head down to the shore. It is a beautiful afternoon in highest summer. I wrap my arm around my daughter's shoulder. I won't have her forever. There have been no magical solutions. I have her more, that is all. She will leave me again and again. The pain will always be there. And in a way, I relish it. I cannot undo what's been done. I can't, like Penelope each night, unthread all the weaving I've already done. But I am lucky to have what I have.

At Colin's cove, a seal bobs its brown, doglike head out of the water and gazes at us calmly. I remember standing here, that wintry day last March. I look down at Monroe. It makes me happy to think she'll keep coming here year after year. In the end, my mother approached my lawyer, who suggested we put the island in trust, with me as executor and island manager. Jenny and I worked out a plan with the nature conservancy so that no one can develop the island. In exchange we pay lower taxes.

Bride Island. The words have a nice shape in my mouth.

When we turn back, up toward the meadow and Indian Cemetery, I think of the story Owen told us, about the group of maidens who came from the stars to dance in the fields. And the brave who stood watching them. At the cemetery I pause to silently greet Colin, to remember Herbert and Roger.

"Elena's coming next week. That'll be fun, won't it? With your cousins?"

"And Grandma?"

"And Grandma. And maybe even Uncle Russ."

We settle down together in the grass. My daughter lies beside me, her beautiful hair splayed over my lap. Both of us have grown our hair this year, hers to the middle of her back, and mine can just about make a short ponytail. I pick daisies and weave them into a crown, which I place on top of her head.

"Mom," she says. "Sometimes I miss people."

I miss people too, I realize suddenly. And I realize that as much as I love this place, it is not the world, that I need the world. I remind her that Owen is paddling over this afternoon in his sea kayak, that if we look carefully we might be able to see him.

"Yay." Monnie likes Owen, and so do I. We've resisted each other so far, but I don't see how we can hold out much longer.

I stroke her hair, then link my fingers through hers. From where we sit we can see a corner of the house and the tiny garden I double-dug myself—the first one we've ever had—which contains five types of lettuce (grown from seed), two tiny cherry-tomato vines (bought as seedlings, more on the way), a striped melon the size of a golf ball, Monroe's own patch of radishes, as well as poppies, cosmos, and tiny blue forget-me-nots. All morning I've been humming a tune by Crosby, Stills, and Nash and now I break into song: "We are stardust, we are golden, and we've got to get ourselves back to the garden."

"Oh Mom," Monnie says. "That sounds terrible."

"Terrible, huh?"

Her little face nods up at me. "Really bad."

We sit here bounded by the cemetery and the sky, the woods and field, and the sea, pocked with other islands, stretching out blue around us. I laugh, and for a moment, looking down, through a trick of the flickering sunlight or optical illusion, I can't tell which of our hands is mine and which is hers. But then she smiles and squirms and we release each other.